NO FURY

MARTIN SHANNON

FREE STORIES

Pixies, Shades, and tribal Magick—having a baby is hard enough, but having a Magician's baby is in a league all of its own...

Sign up at www.martin-shannon.com to get "Danderous Delivery," the Tales of Weird Florida short story only available to newsletter subscribers.

For my readers, who make this all worth doing.

PART I
HELL HATH

1

LOW FUEL

A narrow ribbon of highway stretched out to the infinite horizon beyond the Dad Wagon's faded headlamps. Yellowed bulbs cast a faint and sickly light on wet asphalt, but it was the angry red glow on the dash that really held my attention.

Fuel Low.

Dark branches of vine-covered pines pressed against the edges of the road. The Dad Wagon wasn't happy to be here, and neither was I, but we were on a mission.

Do they have gas in Hell?

This was all part of an existential debate I'd been having with my former roommate for the last few miles. Ed may have lost his hair in the years since college, but he hadn't lost any of his frustratingly positive demeanor. His ex-wife hadn't been able to beat that out of him—and she'd tried hard.

"Okay, let me go over this again. If Hell is a metaphysical construct—"

"Ed."

"No, no. Come on. Go with me on this. If Hell is a metaphysical construct based on the lack of key emotions like love, joy—"

"And that great feeling I get when you shut the hell up," Kaylee, Ed's ex-wife and all around pissed off Swamp Witch said, her reflection frowning in the window.

My old roommate ignored her, a skill he appeared to have mastered many years ago. "—and contentment, then maybe we can use that to our advantage."

My head was already pounding and not very interested in keeping up with my old roommate's fractured logic when the first flickering lights appeared on the road's edge. "Uh, huh."

"So, maybe we just need to *not* want there to be any gas? What about that, Gene? You know, we go all reverse psychology."

"Life is not subjective," Kaylee cried from the back seat where she'd been sitting next to my apprentice and his mother.

For the most part, Adam and Angela had kept quiet. His mother had slept for the last few hours and only began to stir as the Dad Wagon hit the off ramp.

Ed flipped down the sunshade, adjusting the mirror to get a face full of Kaylee's angry green eyes and ginger hair. "Life is very much subjective. It was Hell when we were married, and now it's glorious. Same life, mind you, just infinitely better. That is subjectivism at work."

Deep breath, Gene.

The flickering lights of a derelict gas station rolled into view. Three pumps stood like monoliths in Hell's misty half-light, their dark displays stoic beneath the intermittent flashes of fluorescence.

"Ha! See. I just thought that I didn't want there to be gas, and now we have a gas station." My old roommate pounded his palm against the dash, then tightened a bandana over his bare scalp. "How do you like that?"

The Swamp Witch was not impressed. "There won't be any gas."

"Exactly, and won't it be great?" Ed folded his hands together as if in prayer. "Dear Cosmic Powers of Awesome, I really want there to be no gas. I want this to be dry as the barren well of love that is my ex-wife."

"That's it," the Swamp Witch grabbed her staff off the floor, "I'm going to—"

I threw the Dad Wagon into park and ripped the key out of the ignition. "Stop! Just stop, now."

No one spoke.

"Good. Ed, you get out of the car and check for gas. This is Hell, you see something that doesn't jive you get your butt back in that seat, you hear me?"

My old roommate was a pain, but he was no dummy. In fact, there really wasn't anyone else I would have wanted saddled up and riding with me into the swirling gates of Hell—I just wished he could do it without antagonizing his ex-wife quite so much.

Or maybe I should be wishing for more antagonizing. Damn it, Lovely, now you have me doing it.

"Roger." Ed unlocked the door and slipped out into the mist.

"And you." I turned around to face a very angry Swamp Witch. "You need to—"

Kaylee fingered the wood of her newly restored staff. "You gave my son a Lost Button. Do you really want to do this?"

Yeah, no.

"You need to just sit tight while I figure out the next step."

A thin and clingy mist drifted into the Dad Wagon when Ed opened the door. It stuck to my borrowed flannel like an overzealous lover. My old roommate closed the door behind him and faded into the hazy white, leaving us with only his Demon Hunter outline.

"I so hope there's no gas. You hear me? No gas," my old roommate said, more to himself than anyone else. The problem was Ed didn't possess an indoor voice.

No one else spoke, even the Swamp Witch. Kaylee may have fought with her ex-husband for the last couple hours, but for all her venom, she didn't appear to want him torn apart by whatever lurked in the foggy edges of Gehenna.

I figured she wanted to do that all by herself.

Ed's faded outline vanished.

"Damn it, Lovely," I whispered. "Stay close."

Flickering fluorescent bulbs swayed above the Dad Wagon, their light popping in and out, illuminating the fog and then vanishing again.

"Come on, Ed..."

Bang!

The three of us not sleeping jumped in a loosely concerted fashion.

"Did you *not* want premium or unleaded?" Ed shouted from outside the driver's side window.

I grabbed at my chest and confirmed my heart had not erupted out of it. "Son of a—"

Ed cupped his hands against the glass to surround his face. "Remember, Gene. This is Hell, so you need to not want the—"

"I'm going to murder him." The Swamp Witch white-knuckled her staff.

"I do *not* want unleaded," I said, returning my old roommate's vigorous thumbs up.

Bang!

My old roommate pounded the hood. "You got it. I mean you don't. Shit balls, Hell is confusing."

Ed Lovely vanished into the mist again.

Angela opened her eyes and blinked, awake for the first time in hours. "I'll take a coffee."

Adam shook his head. "No coffee here, Mom. We'll get one at the next stop."

Yeah, no we won't.

Angela sat up. "So, how far to Jacksonville?"

"We're in Hell, Mom."

Mrs. Grayson nodded. "Yep, South Georgia. I wasn't born yesterday."

No one is questioning that.

"No, Mom. This is—"

Angela popped open the door and unhooked her seatbelt.

I spun around and grabbed the back of the passenger seat. "Everybody stays in the car."

Adam's mother shook her head. "I'm just getting some air."

Breathe, Gene.

"This is H—"

"South Georgia," Angela said, fanning her face with her hand. "Sugar, I'm just getting some air. I swear you're as bad as that antique buyer. 'Angela, don't touch that. Angela, please stop rubbing those. Gah! The Tears of Melchor, please don't hold them up as earrings.' He was insufferable, but in a cute way."

Mrs. Grayson was turning out to be a very difficult passenger on the Dad Wagon's Magickal journey to Hell.

Go figure.

"Mom." Adam frowned, showing more spine than I thought he had when it came to dealing with his mother. "Gene means it. We don't know exactly where we are, or what could be waiting just outside the car."

"I didn't say I was getting out. I just needed some air. Besides, her boyfriend gets to get out of the car. Why is that? I mean, if he gets to get out of the car then I should get to get out of the car."

"He is not my—" Kaylee reached over Adam to pull the door shut, but got her arm slapped in the process.

"Oh, sweetheart. You're so hot for him it's warming up the back seat. It's like an estrogen blanket back here. I'm drowning in your mad sex vibes."

"Mom!"

Kaylee opened her mouth and then clamped it back shut again, seemingly unable to speak for the first time in hours.

That was oddly effective.

"Mrs. Grayson," I said with the patience I would have reserved for a five-year-old. "Ed is a Demon Hunter, and he volunteered to see if there was any gas in the pump."

"I don't care if he's the Duke of Earl. It's stuffy in here. Stick-girl's sex-kitten vibes over there are giving me hot flashes, and I need some fresh—"

Bang! Bang!

Everyone froze, that was everyone except for Ed Lovely, our resident gas station attendant in Hell.

Bang!

"Hey, can you guys hear me?" Ed waved and banged on the hood again. "I think this one's empty."

Of course it is. We're in Hell.

The moment I'd plunged the Dad Wagon into that swirling Hellgate I knew we were headed into the deep water without a paddle, but Cathy was here, and that was all that mattered.

"Don't let me go, Dad!" My daughter's words still clawed at my heart, and I couldn't close my eyes without seeing the fear in hers. "Why did you do it? Why did you let me go?"

I had to. The Defiler was coming. I had to close the gate.

"Had to do it, Gene."

"Huh?" I shook away my thoughts of Cathy.

Ed leaned against the driver side door. "We had to check. Pump's empty. I think we need everyone to really want the next pump to be empty." Ed pointed two fingers at his eyes and then directed them at his ex-wife. "Everyone."

The Swamp Witch fumed, but kept her mouth shut.

"What? Yeah, sure." I turned the Dad Wagon's engine over and let the car pull us forward a few feet.

Bang!

"That'll work."

"Would you stop doing that?" Kaylee slammed her fists

down on the seat. "I swear if you bang on the hood one more time I'll—"

Bang!

"Oh, that's it," the Swamp Witch grabbed the door handle, "I'm going to beat you into next Tuesday, Edwin Lovely."

"Huh?" Ed wiped dirt from the glass. "What did I do?"

"Oh, honey." Adam's mother pulled at the edges of her humid blouse. "Just get a room. It'll save the rest of us listening to—"

Angela's voice, along with rest of her, vanished into the mist.

"Mom!"

2

ACROBATICS

*A*dam unbuckled his belt and crawled into the fog behind his vanishing mother.

"What the hell was that?" Ed pressed his face against the glass. "Did she get out of the—"

Black and rubbery claws wrapped the Demon Hunter's mouth, and yanked him away. The pump nozzle clattered to the ground.

"Shit, Kaylee—"

"On it." The Swamp Witch grabbed her staff and pushed open the door. "What're we dealing with?"

A high-pitched shriek answered her.

"Nothing good," I said, pushing up the sleeves of Ed's borrowed flannel.

Kaylee slammed the point of her stick against the hard ground. "Damn it."

"You could say that again. You find Ed, and I'll track down Adam and his—"

"Oh, hell no. You get the bandana wearing pain-in-my-ass. I'll collect the bearded-one and his clinically blind mother." Kaylee's staff lit up red in the hellish mist. I didn't know where it was pulling Magick from, but the ginger's green eyes sparkled a frightful hue in this evil place.

"Got it." I shut the door and stepped out into the nightmarish mist. "Get back to the car as fast as you can."

The Swamp Witch was already gone, her mud-stained jeans fading until all that was left was the bright red halo of devilish light.

Alright, Lovely. You better not be screwing with me.

"Get your Demon hands off of me!"

Well, he's not screwing with me.

"Ed," I cried, reaching for my Magick. "Where are you?"

"Yeah, I know him. The question I have is do you know me?"

I tried to get a bearing on my old roommate, but his voice only echoed.

"Ed!"

"I'm the recipient of the Undeliverable Box. I have stood in the Five Star Toaster's Flames. I am The Stitched Soul. Oh, you think that's funny do you? I bet you and your boys wouldn't last thirty seconds in the—" Ed's boasts vanished in the deepening white.

Think, Gene. Ed may act the fool from time to time, but he's about as smart a Magician as you've ever known, even Morgan's had to defer to his considerable knowledge. That's it!

I turned back to the Dad Wagon and rammed my key into the trunk's lock.

Thunk!

The Five Star Toaster's silvery sides reflected in the misty overhead lights. "Damn it, Lovely. I hope you know what you're doing."

Movement in the devilish appliance's mirror-like finish caught my eye, but whatever it was, it was much faster than I anticipated. Long and wicked black claws hooked under my arms, and I got the distinct impression of being lifted off the ground.

"Oh, no you don't." I reached for the Toaster's trailing cord. My fingers touched that licorice line of black plastic, but couldn't get a grip. The nightmarish appliance fell away along with the rest of the trunk.

No toaster. No problem.

"Ignem alienum!" Magick exploded to life across my fingers, great arcs of flame that drew from the House's reserve. I no longer cared where my Magick came from. I was in Hell already, and my goal was within reach.

Don't let me go, Dad!

"I'm coming, Cathy!" I screamed, grabbing onto the monster's claws. The unholy fire raced across glistening skin like I'd touched a match to kerosene-soaked rags. Deep blues, purples, and finally red, roared. "Suck on that!"

A screeching cry cut short my rapid accent, but I hadn't counted on just how high we'd gotten. The impact was sudden and jarring. I hit the broken pavement like a sack of semi-congealed gelatin. The flames on my hands burned low, just barely staying alight. I pressed myself up only to find more of the black-winged Demons landing on the Dad Wagon.

Fish faces with wide gills that pumped like cheap accordions in the misty air, the Minor Demons nestled like crows along the roof of the car. Their long legs and arms folded up like the gargoyles they resembled, while wide wings jockeyed for position atop the Mazda. I counted at least five, but based on the high-pitched screeches behind me, that was just the tip of the evil-berg.

Always more you can't see.

The largest fish-head leapt down from the Dad Wagon, its claws leaving deep gouges in the metal.

"Oh, you are so going to pay for that," I said, getting to my feet slowly and trying not to let them in on just how bad I was hurting. I let the Magickal flames lick at my fingers like a gas-stove on low.

One by one the Demons climbed on top of each other, at first it was almost comical, but in short order the elaborate act lost all humor. Black flesh and wings assembled like a bad French circus act, their individual faces blending into a single massive head. I'd seen that head before, and the many black tentacles that sprang from it like under-cooked spaghetti.

Asaroth the Defiler.

The Demons moved, their legs and claws forming great lips, while wings opened and closed like wide and unblinking eyes.

Eugene Law.

The Great Demon's words hit my head with the loving caress of a hammer, and I staggered at the sheer ferocity of each syllable. The Magickal flames in my fingers faded to a flicker.

"What do you want?"

I have come to bargain.

The Great Demon's puppeteer lips twisted into a sickly smile.

"I've had enough bargains for ten lifetimes. You know whose standard I carry."

I do, and it is dying.

Winged eyes opened and closed gently in the misty twilight.

"69 Mallory Lane cannot—"

Use its real name, Magician. I do not cower before the Void.

The Defiler's words pounded in my skull. A deep baritone that blurred my vision and frayed my nerves.

"The Void is eternal. It is beyond time. It is—"

Dying, Magician. The Void must die and be reborn. It has happened an infinite number of times, and will happen again, soon.

"I don't believe you," I cried, willing the Magick in my fingers to restore the House's flames. "I will burn your children, and then I will burn you."

The truth cares not for your feelings. I have come to bargain. You will listen to me now, Eugene Law, or my children will destroy them.

The pulsing sound of heavy wings filled the misty air. Adam

and his mother landed on the ground not far from me, their bodies wrapped tightly in black claws. Angry fishlike faces pressed against the sides of their heads, sharp gills drawing blood from unprotected skin.

Kaylee?

The Swamp Witch stumbled into view, her staff in the hands of another flying fish. "Gene!"

"I got this."

Thin streaks of blood dripped down Kaylee's neck and traced painful patterns down her sleeveless arms. "What is it, Gene?"

The macabre acrobatic act shifted, arms and legs moving in a gruesome approximation of laughter.

I am Asaroth, the Defiler of Worlds, the Black Death and the Infinite Pain.

If the Swamp Witch was impressed by its words she didn't show it, in fact, she did the opposite. She spat on the ground. "Do I look like I give a damn? My son is out there," Kaylee kicked at the gravel, "somewhere at the end of a Lost Button and I don't give a damn who you are. I'm going to find him and if that means I go through you, then so be it."

Asaroth paused as if contemplating this unforeseen response.

"Yeah, listen. I've been driving with her for the last few hours, and before that we spent a solid few days together in her swamp shack. You should know she's not kidding."

The sky darkened with scaly bodies of Minor Demons, and the Defiler's circus face opened its mouth wide.

The cycle will be broken, and you will break it for me, and in exchange I will give you the one thing you have always wanted.

"There's nothing you have that I could—"

Small and frail, her hair matted with blood and her eyes rimmed red, my daughter's soul stumbled out of the circus act's mouth.

"Cathy!"

Her spirit flickered like a candle in the wind, one second vibrant and in the next all but invisible. She reached for me, her fingers dirty and crooked. That silly Jiu-Jitsu Gi she'd worn all those months ago was now streaked in the Defiler's inky filth.

I shall return your daughter to you, and in exchange you will stand aside in the final moments and let me take what is mine.

Cathy...

I'd fought my way through Alligator Men, clawed my Magick back from a Darkling, and driven the Dad Wagon straight into Hell to stand here, but even now, seeing her, hurt more than I ever expected.

"Cathy! It's Dad. It's going to be okay. We'll get you out of here. Cathy?"

My daughter vanished like smoke in a strong wind.

"Bring her back! Bring her back right damn now!"

I did nothing.

Ed Lovely, the bandana wearing pain in all of our asses appeared in the mist, his hands clutching the Five Star Toaster, while Jerry's 9D Glasses pressed comically against his face. "He's right, that was me. So, who wants toast?"

3

QUENCHED

"*E*d! It's got my daughter."

The Demon Hunter shook his head and used the Toaster to keep back any winged Fish-heads that got too close. "That wasn't your daughter."

Adam pushed himself up from the damp pavement. "I told you! I've been telling you this since the swamp. Something's not right."

Step aside at the end and I will return your child to you.

The Defiler's words rung in my head, clanging against the sides of my skull like the gong of a great bell.

"How do you guys like your toast? Blackened?" Ed wrapped his fingers around the Toaster's handles.

"Stop!" I shouted, pressing my hands against my head as if I could squeeze the Defiler from it like the juice from an overripe orange.

"Gene, you can't be listening to Asaroth's proxy, trust me." Ed held up his fingers like he were measuring a very small distance. "I've got a bit of Demon experience, and this one is full of it."

Are you willing to take that risk, Magician?

Black wings and tightly packed bodies writhed in unison as if raising an eyebrow on the Defiler's nightmarish face.

Am I?

The tips of flame that danced across my fingers faded to a blanket of blue. "Ed, I…"

"Oh, the hell with this." The Demon Hunter slammed the Five Star Toaster's handles down, taking them to the bottom, then throwing the infernal appliance like an oversized hand grenade. "Get back!"

The shiny metal box bounced across the misty ground before coming to a stop in front of one of the Minor Demons. A fish-faced beast bent down and picked it up, screeching at its own bulbous eyes reflected in the mirror-like surface.

"Uh, Eddie." The Swamp Witch pushed wet hair out of her face. "Shouldn't something be happening now?"

"Yeah, that's odd—"

Whoosh!

The black-clawed Demon burst into flame, much like that time I'd put too much lighter-fluid in the grill.

"There, that's more like it. Must be running a little slow." Ed ducked a set of swiping of claws and raced off for Adam and Angela, Private Petty's silver saber in hand.

My daughter's face flickered in the Defiler's winged eyes, her mouth open in a quiet scream.

"Cathy!"

Make the right choice in the final moment, Eugene Law. Your child's soul depends on it.

Cathy vanished in the explosion of movement that was the Defiler's proxies. Black wings and sharp claws took to the misty air like a flock of malevolent birds.

What have I done?

"Gene!" Kaylee's cry knocked me out of my haze. "A little help here?"

The Swamp Witch's staff was airborne, high above and out

of her reach, while on the ground she'd become surrounded by three Minor Demons.

"Ignem!" The flames on my hands surged, the blanket of blue exploding into a ball of bright yellow and red. Magick roared, my power, and the House's. Together we were a force of nature. I sent a whip crack of fiery death across the back of the closest fish-face, its wings curling in the nascent heat, while behind me the Five Star Toaster roared.

"Your staff?"

Kaylee kicked at another beast and made a run for me. "Think you can hit a moving target?"

Another lancing crack of flame erupted from my fingers, slicing through the misty air like an avenging angel and catching the leg of the staff thief high above.

Screech!

The Old Florida tap root tumbled from its claws, twisting end over end in the Demon filled sky.

"Nice—behind you, Gene!"

Sharp claws dug into the cheap flannel and scored deep gouges in my tender flesh. I spun around to find myself face-to-gills with one of the Defiler's minions.

I grabbed his claws with my fiery hands and squeezed. "This is for my daughter."

White-hot flames raced up the beast's arms. Its skin popped and cracked like crisp bacon, while a thick and toxic smoke filled the air.

"This is for Cathy!"

The flames reached a crescendo, covering the Minor Demon in the fire of unquenchable anger. I let go, kicking its spent husk to the ground.

"Who wants some?"

More black wings and glistening claws filled the space between me and the Five Star Toaster's field of flame. Black shapes against the bright fire of that infernal appliance, they moved in an almost rhythmic fashion.

"Gene, get inside!" Ed held Private Petty's blade, smeared in black blood, while behind him, Adam traced a sigil across the blacktop in chalk as Angela looked on.

The Swamp Witch didn't waste any time. A short swing of her staff shattered the eye socket of a fish-head en route to the makeshift circle.

"It has Cathy!"

"No, it doesn't," Ed cried, the silver saber making short work of yet another Minor Demon. "I'm telling you, that's not your daughter."

They lie.

The Defiler's words boomed in my mind.

The Void is dying, even now you burn through its power. Soon you will be called upon to make a decision, Eugene Law. Remember, the soul of your daughter depends on it.

Asaroth's power pressed against me like a lead blanket. A suffocating will that threatened to pull the air from my lungs.

"Give me my daughter!" I reached deep for my Magick, through the House's sheen and down into a primal reservoir of power—the power of a father who failed once, and who refused to surrender a second time.

"Veni!" I cried, extending my hands to the Five Star Toaster and calling it to me. "Come to me!"

Ed wiped black blood from his face and pressed Jerry's glasses back into place. "Gene, something's wrong with you. What are you doing?"

"Ending it." I caught the Toaster to my chest. Its alien Magick thrummed beneath my fingers and mixed with the powerful flames already engulfing me.

Ed yanked Kaylee into Adam's circle, then stepped out of it himself.

"Eddie!" The Swamp Witch swung around to grab her ex-husband's arm but missed it.

My old roommate shook his head. "Stay in there, no matter what. Use whatever you can get out of that tap root of yours, cause I don't know what's coming. Adam?"

My apprentice bit his lip and continued to trace, never once looking up. "Yeah?"

"Don't let her nag you too much. Oh, and nice job on the seal, kid."

"I had a good teacher."

Boom.

Like a thunderclap, Adam's protective sigil closed, and with it the Magick necessary to keep them safe rained down like an overturned bowl. Kaylee rammed her staff against the asphalt, sending a halo of sparks into the air, and with them more power into Adam's Seal.

Minor Demons filled the sky, their black wings fanning the roaring flames. My old roommate vanished somewhere beyond the distant edge of that fire, but I didn't care.

I had eyes for only one thing.

Cathy.

The Toaster's heat erupted from my fingers. Shock waves of nuclear fire raced over the pavement, striking Adam's shield and exploding in a flash of sparkles. "Give me back my daughter!"

Fish-faced Demons swooped down, only to be caught in the infernal appliance's hellish flames, but still they reached for me, their claws burning up in the unholy fire.

"Gene," Ed shouted from beyond the flame's edge, but I couldn't make out the rest of his words.

"Give me Cathy. Do you hear me, Asaroth? It's my turn now." The flames rose like a great wave of white-hot death. "I am Eugene Law. I am the Banisher, and the Darkling Destroyer. I stand for the Void. My power is eternal. I am Magick!"

Whip cracks of flame snapped forth from my fingers and dragged Minor Demons into the raging inferno.

"Give me my daughter or I will destroy you!"

Somewhere beyond the great fire's edge Ed's bandana appeared again. He waved the 9D Glasses above his head like a signal flare, and in his other hand he held the pump nozzle pointed to the sky like a rodeo clown. There was a sadness in his eyes that I hadn't noticed before. "The Magick, Gene. You are burning it out. There's something wrong, you need to stop!"

My daughter's face appeared in the flames, her body writhing in pain within the twisting column.

"Cathy!"

My little girl's form faded away in the flames, only to be replaced by the inky blackness of the Defiler.

Come and get her, Magician.

"Stop, Gene!" Ed waved his hands in the mist, the 9D Glasses back on his face. "You've got to stop. It's burning you out. The Defiler's playing you like a fiddle."

"No!" I pulled in everything I could, embracing the House and who I'd become. Cathy was there, just beyond my grasp, her face ringed in flames. This time it would be different, this time I would save her and become the father I should have been. This time I wouldn't fail.

"Gene, something's wrong, the House—"

I lost Ed's words in a wave of gut churning pain. Something gave way deep inside me. Like a torn muscle or a broken joint, it popped out of place and I fell forward struggling for air.

"Gene, the Magick is…"

Ed's words faded against the backdrop of my scream.

The Magick sputtered, and in a flickering pop, the roaring fire of unquenchable cosmic power flamed-out and left me crumpled on the wet pavement.

The unstoppable Toaster lay next to me, dormant on the dark asphalt, its fire extinguished.

Without the Toaster or my Magick, nothing stood between me and the Defiler's horde.

4

SACRIFICE

S *plash!*
The sickly sweet smell of stale gasoline splashed over my shoes.

What the...

"Oh, yeah!" Ed shouted from beyond the now extinguished Toaster. "I told you that's how it would work. I bet you *didn't* want me to spray you with gasoline—reverse psychology for the win."

"Ed," I pushed my head up, unable to make out the Demon Hunter through the wall of hungry, black fish-faces. "What are you doing?"

Gasoline sprayed the backs of the Minor Demons.

"We're going old school. Now, get your ass in the car."

My old roommate's head appeared between the confused and screeching faces, a bright silver lighter in his hand. He flipped it open and let the tiny flame flicker.

I tried to push myself up, but I could barely move. Every part of my body ached, from the top of my head to the soles of my feet. It was as if I'd taken a few dozen swings from Kaylee's staff to basically every inch of my tired muscles. "Ugh."

"Come on, Gene."

"I'm trying."

Ed Lovely tossed the lighter into the Defiler's proxies. It bounced off their fuel soaked heads, sending a wave of blue and orange flames racing along their scaly skin.

Whoosh!

Fish-heads scrambled for cover, but Hell's gasoline was faster, and soon the entire lot of them became a confused and burning mass of black smoke and screaming faces.

"Can you try faster?"

I crawled to my knees, but the horizon spun in a decidedly unfriendly manner, and I fell back against the blackened ground.

Adam's surprisingly strong hands hooked under my arms. "Come on, old man. That's our cue."

I stumbled to my feet, my sense of balance strangely missing. "What the—"

"Less talk, more running." Adam dragged me toward the Dad Wagon.

Not far ahead, Angela piled into the back seat, motioning for us to follow. "Run, Adam."

Shriek!

Serrated black gills flashed in front of us, while beneath them sharp claws reached for my apprentice.

"Shit." The bearded one pulled at his Magick. His power shifted around us.

Boom.

Before he could finish whatever he had planned, Kaylee's staff collapsed the Demon's scaly head, and sent it careening into the rest of the melting horde. "Go!"

More strong wing beats filled the sky as their agitated flight broke up the infernal mist.

How many more?

"What's wrong with him?" Kaylee swung her staff like the

wild reaper, splitting Demon skulls and sending black blood and gore flying.

Adam shook his head. "I don't know. Gene, hang in there."

Kaylee's staff smashed a set of unfolding wings. "Tank us up, Eddie."

"Working it." The Demon Hunter had the nozzle back in the Dad Wagon and was pumping it full of whatever octane Hell had to offer.

My Magick...

I reached down into the well of power, but before I could grasp it, the Swamp Witch had the passenger door open. I got an up close view of the seat before a strong set of claws yanked me out of Adam's grasp.

"Gene!"

My head snapped against the pavement, the already confused grey matter inside bumping against the dense walls of my skull. A hazy darkness crept into the edges of my vision, but front and center, were the sharp gills of a fish-head Demon. I reached for my Magick, but the image blurred and shifted until it was Cathy standing above me. Part of my addled brain screamed at me to get up, but the other part was lost in the soft smile on her face. She didn't speak, her eyes too full of sadness for words.

"Cathy... I'm here, just like I promised. I said I would come back for you, and I did. It's me, it's Dad."

Her hand reached out for me, those long and clawed fingers caressing my neck.

"I've missed you, Dad."

My daughter's face exploded in a hailstorm of black blood and gore, Kaylee's staff shattering the fish-head's soft cartilage like a rotten melon.

"No!"

"Get him in the car!" The Swamp Witch's words stretched out like taffy, my head swirling.

Strong hands pulled me across the pavement and into the front seat. Somehow my face ended up pressed into the seatbelt clasp. Kaylee launched herself over me, her staff landing somewhere behind the drivers seat, while the rest of the face-first Swamp Witch collapsed into Angela's ample lap. Adam planted a foot in my gut and a knee across my chest as he too climbed over me and into the backseat.

"Ed!" Kaylee shouted, upside down, her hair covering her face. "Get in the damn car."

Ed pulled the door closed behind him and hit the automatic lock.

Bang! Bang!

Black claws slashed at the windshield and tore deep gouges into the Dad Wagon's dirty hood.

"Punch it, Eddie!" Kaylee shouted.

My old roommate yanked the bandana off his head. "Give me the keys."

"What?!" the backseat shouted in unison.

"Trunk." I put a hand on the door handle. "I left them in the trunk."

"Gene, stop!"

Too late.

I had the door open and pushed myself out into the maelstrom of black wings and sharp claws.

"Gene!"

Hands pressed against the glass, begging me to get back in. The keys were still in the trunk, and no one was going anywhere without them, and if Cathy was here, I wasn't leaving.

Bang! Bang! Bang!

Fish-headed Demons landed on top of the Mazda, their wings spread wide and their claws shining in the eternal twilight of Gehenna.

I ripped the keys out of the lock and twirled them around in my hands. My body was no longer sore, and confusion had left

26

my head far clearer than when I started. "Your fight isn't with them, it's with me, and I'm not leaving unless it's with my daughter."

Shriek!

More black wings filled the sky, and in short order I was surrounded. "You guys know who I am, and exactly what I am capable of. Maybe the word doesn't get around down here, but a lot of people like to say I hit like a dump truck. I'll save you the tread marks if you bring my daughter to me right fucking now."

Demons jumped off the Dad Wagon, the worn shocks bouncing with each leap.

"Gene!" Adam opened the back door. "Come on."

I shook my head. "This is my fight. Go, get out of here. Ed and Kaylee can find a way home. The Defiler has Cathy, and I'm not leaving her again."

"But Gene—"

"Go!"

I threw the keys at Adam. He bobbled them in his hands as Angela reached past him to slam the door shut. "He's not coming—"

Kaylee's face pressed against the glass. "Oh no, you don't get out of this that easily, Eugene Law. You will find my son, or I will bring all of Hell down on your head."

The Dad Wagon rumbled to life, exhaust spitting from its tailpipe. Ed's face filed the side-view mirror, and his eyes told me what his words couldn't.

I'm not leaving you.

I shook my head. "Go!"

Let me be the hero now that I never was back then.

The Dad Wagon sprung forward like a jack-rabbit. Narrow tires tore up broken pavement and sent a hailstorm of grit in my face.

Go...

The Defiler's proxies surrounded me, their jaws quivering in gruesome anticipation. Dark wings beat above, blotting out the flickering lights and leaving me in a blackness of my own creation. I took a deep breath, willing my mind down into the deep reservoir of Magick that sprung like a living well. The House had given me great power, but with it came the taint, the oily sheen that lay like a malignant cancer on the cosmic energy trapped in my soul.

"That's it. Come closer. I want to see the whites of your eyes when I turn them to ash."

The Demons pressed in, their wings beating to a fever pitch. Blank eyes stared while sharp gills squeezed at what remained of the thin mist.

Just a little closer.

I reached for my Magick and let the words of power form on my lips. "Ingitum!" I cried, letting the power trapped in me soar free. There was no bounds, no more controls. I gave into what it was to be joined with the Void. I would do anything if it meant seeing Cathy again, the House be damned.

Nothing happened.

The Demons hesitated, exchanging confused side glances.

"Ingitum!"

Still nothing.

The Magick I'd come to rely on wasn't there—the well was dry.

"Okay, so, there are probably a few things I should have mentioned." A Porter-shaped House stepped out of the shadows, her face calm but doing a lousy job at hiding the fear blossoming beneath it. She sighed and ran a hand through her thinning hair. "Sorry about that."

5

LIFE CYCLED

I backed up toward the wife-shaped House, still trying fruitlessly to bring up whatever Magick lay at the bottom of that empty cistern. "What the—"

"Okay. First, in my defense, you never asked," Porter said, crossing her thin arms.

"Are you kidding?" Black Demons pressed in on us. "I asked hundreds of times, but you never told me."

"Oh, right." My Not-wife tilted her head to one side. "You know something, you did."

Wings flared and claws scratched at the misty air.

"Nigh infinite power. That's what you said. Nigh infinite." I swung my impotent hands in the air. A trickle of Magick left a small dusting of sparks on the wet gravel. "Does that look like infinite to you?"

"Nigh infinite, Gene. That means close to infinite but—"

"I know what nigh means!"

The House and I backed up toward what remained of the Five Star Toaster, the Demons hesitant, but gaining confidence by the second.

Not-Porter gestured toward the appliance's now muted

29

sides. "Damn, you even burned out the Five Star Toaster. That's a feat. How much Magick did you pull?"

"He's got my daughter!"

Not-Porter frowned and stepped over the melted cord. "No, that's not technically true. I returned your daughter to you."

"Technically?" I swung around and grabbed her arm, ignoring the approaching Fish-head's menacing gills. "Technically? Oh, hell no. You're going to tell me now—all of it. No more lies, no more innuendo and half-truths. The Defiler has my daughter, and he wants me to let you die if I'm ever going to see her again, and right this instant I'm more than inclined to do that. So, you need to give me a damn good reason why I shouldn't."

Fish-faces surrounded us, their claws only inches from my loaner flannel.

Not-Porter sighed. "Fine. There's a lot to unpack, but I'd prefer to do it alone." The wife-shaped House directed her eyes at the advancing Demons.

"No Magick, remember?"

Not-Porter placed a hand on my shoulder. "This better?"

A wave of pure Magick bubbled up inside me like a natural spring, the power caressing my tired muscles and stitching my torn skin. "Yes."

"Just don't go over—"

"Mors Aridam," I cried, pulling from that cosmic spring and sending the Magick out into the misty night. The cosmic power rolled over them, and pulled the liquid from their bodies like I was squeezing out a shammy. Fish-head Demons clutched at their gills and collapsed around us, their scales cracked and eyes crystallized in a vacant stare.

"—board." Not-Porter shook her head and kicked at one of the crumpled beasts. "Dried fish? Well, that works."

One of the remaining Fish-heads struggled to stay upright, its gills gasping in the now parched night.

Remember my words, Eugene Law. Stand-aside at the end, or your daughter —

The Defiler's booming voice was cut short by Not-Porter's unnaturally strong fingers. She crushed the Minor Demon's papery throat and tossed it aside. "Now, where were we?"

"You are going to tell me everything, now."

"Fine." The House sighed and flipped up the Five Star Toaster, then proceeded to take a seat on its cooled top. "In the beginning there was the Void…"

* * *

"And then Moab begat Soab and the rest of the—"

"Stop." I clutched at my tired head. "I don't need to know everyone that has ever lived since the beginning of time."

Not-Porter pursed her lips. "You sure? It really helps to add context to the story when you have a sense of the—"

"Just tell me what happened to my daughter."

The House nodded and stretched out her legs. "Oh, that? Why didn't you tell me? You don't need to know about everyone that's ever lived since—"

"Cathy!"

Not-Porter picked up the Toaster's melted cord and twisted it absently in her fingers. "Your daughter's soul shattered on impact."

I'd sucked in enough air to scream at whatever she said, but was completely unprepared for that response. The venomous scream in my lungs escaped like helium from a spent balloon.

The House nodded. "Yeah, pretty amazing, huh?"

Cathy, what happened to you?

I tried to process her words, but like round pegs in square holes they resisted my every attempt. "Shattered? You mean like a Soul-Splitter?" Thoughts of Evil Gene with his perfect popped-collar and black heart came rolling back to me.

Not-Porter shook her head. "Nothing so pedestrian. Soul-Splitters, bah. That's cake compared to a shattering. If only you could be so lucky—"

I struggled to get air into my tightening chest. "Stop! Stop dancing around it, and tell me what happened to my daughter!"

Not-Porter tossed the cord aside. "I just did. Your daughter's soul broke into three shards. It's just how things are. Like when a famous person dies and everyone is like 'hey, they always come in threes.' I wonder if they know by saying that they virtually guarantee it comes true? I bet they do."

"Stop, just stop," I said, my head pounding. "Tell me. Is she okay?"

Not-Porter pushed herself up and wiped the ash from her jeans. "I'm giving you a lot of leeway right now, Gene. I hope you recognize that, because you're going to want to remember this when it's time for you to fulfill your end of the deal."

"What?! My end of the deal? What do you think I've been doing all this time? You've turned me into a one man force of supernatural destruction, equal parts bogeyman and debt-collector, and now you're telling me I haven't fulfilled my end of the deal?"

The House took a few hesitant steps, then stumbled against the empty gas pump. "Yeah, that's exactly what I'm saying. That was all practice."

"Practice?"

Not-Porter nodded. "I needed to know you had the killer instinct to go along with that inhuman reserve of power."

My head spun. "Inhuman?"

"It's a figure of speach. You're just a special monkey—my special monkey—but now I need you to gorilla-up and get ready, because it's not long now, and they're going to do their best to mow you down in the process."

I stepped over the dried husk of a Fish-head Demon. "What's coming?"

"The end, Gene. Asaroth may be a colossal asshole, but he's right. I'm dying."

"But you're—"

"Eternal?" Not-Porter rolled her eyes. "Ha! Everything is cyclical, Gene, *everything*. I've died and been reborn an infinite number of times, and with your help I'll do it again."

"Why do you need my help?"

The House coughed and spit something dark onto the wet pavement.

Blood?

"Because, in the moment of rebirth I'm vulnerable. I become mortal and in that instant infinite Magick is up for grabs."

"And that's what the Defiler wants?"

Not-Porter leaned against the pump. "Bingo."

"But he has my daughter."

"Correction, he has a 'shard' of your daughter, maybe. It's hard to tell. My vision isn't what it used to be."

"So, the girl you brought back, the one that—"

"Plays the lovely violin? Yeah, that's a shard of Cathy too."

It was my turn to stumble and catch my breath. "But it's not all of her?"

Not-Porter shook her head. "No, but it is her. Think of it this way. When you shine light through a prism, it breaks into colors. Well, that's what you have, a one-color version of your daughter. Isn't that better than a no-color version?"

I crossed what remained of the gas station in a rush, grabbing the front of Not-Porter's top and slamming her against the tombstone-like pump. "You promised me my daughter. That was the deal!"

The House smiled and a thin line of blood dripped from the edge of her lip. "And I delivered your daughter to you. Check the fine print, Gene. I did what I said I would do, and I never lied. It's not my fault her soul shattered."

"Give me one good reason why I shouldn't let you die, right here, right now?"

Not-Porter coughed again, this time doubling over and clutching at her stomach. "Well, you already came damn close. "

"Huh?"

"I said 'nigh infinite,' Gene. Could you try not to bleed me dry before the rebirth, okay? Pace yourself, because Asaroth is just one of the things that's out for my head."

"And why shouldn't I just let them have you?"

Not-Porter shifted, her body lengthening and expanding in the lanky shape of Victor Jenkins, my tequila drinking mentor. "Viktor had half of it right. God's Tears was a beautiful place."

"Did you—"

Not-Jenkins pushed his tinted glasses against his eyes. "No, but let's just say it was damn close. I don't want to have that happen again, and I know someone else who doesn't want that to happen..." The House shrunk into the petite shape of my youngest child. Kris's bright eyes stared up at me. "Please, Dad. I don't want to die."

"No, not him."

Kris nodded his tiny head. "Yes, him. You need to know what's on the line here, Gene. You can hate me all you want. In fact, I embrace it, but when the chips are down, you are the only thing standing between me and a lot worse."

Kris placed his hands on mine, his stubby fingers wrapping my callused digits. "There are monsters under the bed, Dad. You won't let them get me, will you?"

6

TINY DANCER

I ripped my fingers out of the House's hand and turned away, unable to look my son in the eye. "But what about Cathy?"

Morgan's hand turned my face back, my ex-girlfriend replacing Kris in the House's macabre game of charades. "What about her? Your apprentice was right. She's safe in Tampa. Playing in a concert soon if my memory serves. She has a talent, that one."

"But that's not all of her."

Morgan threw her hands in the air. "It's enough of her. It's your daughter, you idiot."

"But—"

"No, you don't get to talk now." My old girlfriend pressed her finger against my lips. "Were you not you?"

"Uh…"

Morgan removed her hand. "When your soul was split, were you not you?"

"No. Wait, I mean, I was me, but I—"

"How about when that Illickthid weaved a new soul for the Demon Hunter's disembodied spirit-noggin?"

"That's different."

Morgan shook her head. "No, it's not. It's exactly the same, just like the young woman coaxing beautiful music out of that wooden box is your daughter."

"But the Defiler has my daughter," I cried, grabbing Morgan's arm. "I saw her. She's in pain, so much pain. I can't let him have her."

Morgan grabbed the sides of my head with a ferocity I wasn't expecting. "You need to get your head in the game, Gene. I don't think you understand what's at stake here."

Images flooded my mind. Powerful and painful, a world on fire played out between my ears. The Defiler backed by the power of the Void was a force beyond imagination. Death and chaos reigned supreme in a world where only pain existed. My son bled out in his mother's arms, while her own skin melted away like soft wax.

"No!"

Morgan ripped her hands away from my head. "You like that?"

I only stared, my eyes unable to blink back the images of destruction.

"I didn't think so, and that's just one of the potential futures. Asaroth is circling, but he's not the only one. There's blood in the water, Gene, and I'm low on miracles. You need to put Cathy out of your head. She's not your primary concern now. There are a lot of other monkeys out there that need you. Don't let them down."

"But, can you put the shards back together?"

Morgan flashed a crooked smile. "With 'nigh infinite' Magick, sure, except the tank for amazing is almost dry, Gene." She pressed a soft hand against my chest, her fingers caressing the tired muscles beneath that loaner flannel. "And more importantly, right now I need you to be a lot more judicious with those Magickal allocations going forward, cause when I'm out…" The House let its voice fade away.

"How much time do I have?"

Morgan shook her bright green hair and adjusted the low-cut top of her leather corset. "Got me."

"So I am just supposed to just sit here and wait for you to die?"

"Hardly." Morgan coughed, spitting more blood on the ground. "Be careful what you wish for, Gene. If the end came now, you'd be toast. You need the rest of the stupid squad. I may not like Ed Lovely, but he and Swampwater Suzy are a powerful duo to have on our side."

"Kaylee."

"Yeah, her. That redheaded monkey and her bang-stick are nothing to sneeze at. She's managed to draw Magick from the tap root of old Florida. I'd almost forgotten you could do that."

"And Adam?"

"The bearded one has value. This newer generation is creative and has finally gotten over the whole Latin fad. Sure, he's a pain, but he's a pain you need if you want to see me through a successful rebirth."

"And Angela?"

Morgan shrugged. "Every team needs a sacrificial lamb, or in your case, a sacrificial walrus."

"But they're gone. I sent them home."

Morgan took a deep breath. "You of all people should know better. Peanut man and the cashew crew aren't going anywhere without their head nut." My old girlfriend laughed and sent herself into a violent and wracking cough.

She fell to her knees and against my better judgement I grabbed her hand. Like a summer breeze, Morgan shifted back into the woman I loved. The newly restored Not-Porter fought through a few wheezing breaths. "Damn, I hate this part."

"You aren't lying, are you?"

"No, I'm not, Gene. I haven't always been upfront, but I've never outright lied."

I brushed a hair out of Not-Porter's face and she smiled.

"I haven't always understood monkeys, but that's not to say I don't appreciate your intricacies."

Don't fall for it, Gene. This is not your wife, this is 69 Mallory Lane, this is the Void. Stop!

"I know it's hard to believe, Gene, but I've had a lot of protectors, but I've never had one like you. Let's just say I've been going for the soulless-killer-type for far too long. With you I have something I've never had before."

"What's that?"

"An attack dog with a heart."

Damn it, Gene. This is the House. It's not your wife. This is Magick beyond limits.

Not-Porter grabbed my hand. "Magick was made for monkeys, and I am Magick, so I guess you could say, I was made for you."

"Touching."

"Yeah, whatever," Not-Porter pulled herself up and leaned against me to catch her breath. "You aren't going to abandon me, are you, Gene?"

I knew it wasn't Porter, but her gentle breath against my neck was almost too much to take. I'd missed her so much. Every rational part of my mind screamed out to leave the House to die, but I couldn't lose the woman I loved in the process.

"No."

"Good—" Not-Porter hadn't finished her words before she dropped like a stone, her knees striking the pavement and her head knocking against the withered corpse of one of the Defiler's proxies.

"Porter!"

"The Demon Steed Obelleron rides again! She's done it. That damn girl's done it."

I slipped a hand beneath the House's head. "What?"

"She's torn open a brand new front in her personal war for control of Hell. Typically I wouldn't give a damn, but she's using too much Magick, and way too fast." Not-Porter's eyes darted back and forth as if watching a movie only she could see.

"Who?"

The House grabbed my head, its fingers like honed steel. "I'm not ready. You need to put a stop to this—now. Time to go be the hero, but save the last dance for me, Gene." Not-Porter placed her lips upon mine, Magick flooded my body, and every cell screamed out in pain as they tore themselves apart.

Save the last dance for me.

7

RUN, RABBIT, RUN

I opened my eyes to warm denim, my lips pressed against a pair of mud-splatted jeans.

"Gene?!"

Kaylee?

I turned my head to find myself face to button-fly with a very displeased Swamp Witch. "Get your head out of my lap."

"Uh…"

"Now."

I pushed my head up to find the rest of me spread across the back seat and draped over a rather flushed Angela.

"Your hands are on my thighs. So help me, Eugene Law. If they slide one inch, I'm going to ram this staff where the sun doesn't shine." The ginger-haired Swamp Witch's eyes indicated she wasn't kidding.

"On it," I said, trying to disentangle myself from Ed's ex-wife's lap when the Dad Wagon swerved hard to the side, putting my face directly into that button-fly.

Shit.

Kaylee pushed me off, then screamed at her ex-husband. "Can you keep it on the road?"

"Is that Gene?" a very surprised Demon Hunter asked from the driver's seat.

"Yeah, it's me."

"How the—"

"The House. It's a long story. How about you pull over and I tell you all about it?" I pulled myself up only to find Adam's concerned beard inches from my face. "Are you okay?"

"No, but that's pretty much par for the course as of late."

"Hold on!" Ed cried.

The Dad Wagon cut across three lanes, sending Team Backseat into a crushing pileup on a staff-squeezing Kaylee. "I can't do a damn thing if you keep swinging us back and forth," she cried, pushing back on my borrowed flannel.

"You tell that to the stampede." Ed tapped the brakes and forced me to leave an impression of my skull on the seat back, then punched it again and sent me right back into Kaylee's lap.

"Ed!" the Swamp Witch shouted.

The Dad Wagon's engine whined in protest, its tires scrambling to keep a grip on whatever it was we were flying down.

I rubbed at my sore head. "Stampede?"

Dark and fiery horses thundered alongside the old Mazda. Like one of those beer commercials, but with more evil. The equine herd had us boxed in. Tips of flame flickered from their manes, while thick puffs of smoke poured from their wide nostrils.

"Ed..."

My old roommate clutched the wheel and swung it hard again. "Demon Steeds, Gene. This is my first time seeing them in their natural habitat. Remember that time in Ocala? Oh, right, you were out of the hero business back then. Hold on!"

This time Ed's warning was enough to keep me from landing on top of Angela, but only just barely. I'm pretty certain my butt ended up way too close for Mrs. Grayson's comfort, however her personal space wasn't high on my list of concerns at the moment, and it was a rather handsome butt.

The Demon Steed Obelleron.

"You got anything, Kay? I mean this would be a great time for some Magick." Ed tapped the brakes again and pulled back to avoid clipping one of the flaming stallions.

The Swamp Witch white-knuckled her staff. "Not unless you stop moving. I can't get purchase."

I scooted off Angela's hip. "Ed, just stop the car and let the horses go."

My apprentice shook his bearded head. "No can do, boss. Turn around."

A six-legged war horse pounded the pavement not far behind our impromptu clown car. Massive and jet-black with thundering hooves, it carried a rider decked out in makeshift armor cobbled together from old street signs, electrical cables, and anything else you could scrape together from this ruined wasteland. His face was covered by the hood of a railroad crossing light, while beyond the edges of that black metal, long strands of multi-colored rags whipped like malevolent streamers in the wind.

The rider wasn't alone. A wave of similarly dressed soldiers roared behind him, mounted on the same fiery Demon steeds that ran free alongside us. Their faces weren't covered, and it was easy to see why. The Damned didn't need protection. Blackened eyes and ashen skin, the burned mouths of New Dead soldiers screamed with the thrill of the chase.

"New Dead."

"What?!" Kaylee swung around, the confidence in her voice not nearly what it had been just moments earlier.

The lead rider raised his spear, a shiny Mazda emblem swinging from his neck.

"So, they want my car?"

Ed swerved again, a sharpened spear clattering to the

ground not far from where we'd been. "It certainly appears that way."

"Oh, hell no—it's paid off."

Ed pumped the gas and pulled us between a pair of wild Demon horses, their fiery bodies so close you could touch them. "What's the Dad Wagon got in the way of countermeasures?"

"Countermeasures? Ed, it's a family car."

My old roommate nodded. "Yeah, yeah. But what about your defenses?"

"Did you have defenses on the peanut truck?"

"No."

"Then what makes you think I would have—"

"Lookout, Eddie!" Kaylee pointed at a pile of mangled metal in the road.

"Hang on!"

The Dad Wagon cut back across multiple lanes, its tires squealing in protest. Wild horses shifted around us. They jockeyed for position and to stay ahead of the New Dead Thunderdome steadily gaining ground.

"I didn't have them on the peanut truck because I had them on the trailer. If you'd asked I would have explained it to you."

"Would that have been before or after you told the little wooden boy to pour vinegar into the Prussian curse bucket and stop my heart?"

"Hey, that was the tar and I—"

Angela grabbed the seat back. "Car!"

Another pile of broken metal filled the windshield and my old roommate pulled the wheel hard back the other way, narrowly avoiding flipping and putting to test the airbags I wasn't sure we had.

"There's more of them." Adam pointed to the minefield of partially demolished cars littering the highway in front of us. "We're being herded."

"Hell yeah we are—could one of the lovely Magick wielders

in the car whip us up a little awesome?" Ed slalomed between a pack of fiery stallions. "Like, now."

Kaylee held her hands up. "You're moving too fast. I can't get a grip on anything."

"Adam?"

My apprentice bit his lip. "I've got an idea, but I'm not sure if you're going to like—"

Shatter!

A piece of sharpened rebar exploded through the rear windshield and impaled itself in the center console.

"Eddie!" the Swamp Witch screamed.

What happened next could be best described as being caught in the washer on spin cycle. Arms and legs flailed wildly with each gut-churning flip of what had been my favorite car ever. I slammed into the headliner and hovered briefly in that nauseating feeling of weightlessness, only to be thrown back into the console. Somehow I missed the rebar, which I was really happy about, right up until my head hit the gear shift and everything went dark.

8

IN HER EYES

"Gene?"

Everything hurt—my arms, my legs, my head, and all the unnamed parts in between.

"Alive…" I said, not exactly sure that was true anymore, but I went with it. "That you, Ed?"

"Yeah. How d'you end up in the front seat?"

"No seat belt."

The balding top of my old roommate's head hung above me, the rest of his body still strapped into the driver's seat. "That's crazy dangerous. Frankly, I would have though better of a guy with two kids."

"Ed."

"Yeah."

"Shut—"

The Demon Hunter detached his seatbelt, his head hitting my chest and ejecting the air from my lungs.

"Adam, are you okay?" Angela pressed her bulk over me in an attempt to reach her son. "Adam!"

"I'm okay, Mom." My apprentice's head, along with the rest

of his body, was pressed against a broken windshield and what remained of the sun visor.

"Oh, thank God."

Somewhere in the backseat Kaylee's staff rattled against the broken glass. "I've got a few cuts, but I'll live, in case anyone was wondering."

I pushed aside someone's foot. "Did we lose the murder posse?"

My old roommate shook out of his bandana, then tied in on his head. "It would appear not."

Black and fiery hooves, exactly three pairs worth, filled what remained of my broken windshield. More Demon Steeds milled about beyond them, and alongside the armored legs of the New Dead welcome wagon.

Shit.

"Adam, Eldero's Eighth. Now."

My apprentice fumbled a grease pen out of his hoodie and set to work tracing the sigil on the headliner.

Angela grabbed her son's shoulder. "What are you doing? They're right outside the car. We've got to run."

I detached Mrs. Grayson from her son with possibly a little more force than I should have. "He's saving your life. Now, sit down, and shut the hell up."

Magick trickled into the sigil.

"Come on, Adam. You got this."

"A little help here…" My apprentice squeezed his eyes shut and pressed a hand against the seal.

I reached for Adam, but Ed Lovely's fingers caught mine before I could help the bearded wonder.

"Don't do it, Gene. He can do it, or Kaylee can help him. You need to conserve your strength for what's coming." Ed's lips may have been moving, but it was the House's voice.

What exactly have I signed up for?

Angela's scream shook me out of my introspection.

The blackened eyes and ashen skin of New Dead filled the broken glass. "They live." A long and eel-like tongue raced over peeling lips "But not for long."

A pale arm clawed for my apprentice.

"Close the seal, Adam," I cried.

"I'm trying."

Boom.

Like a thunderclap, Eldero's Eighth Seal closed up tight as a drum, and severed a New Dead arm in the process. The ashen limb, wrapped in what looked like highway reflectors and old tar-paper, flopped around on the headliner before Ed tossed it into the back seat.

"Hey!" The Swamp Witch wasn't pleased with his gift.

A newly armless member of the Damned pulled back its cauterized stump to rage at Adam's seal. All around it, more New Dead pounded against the Dad Wagon, rocking it back and forth, and screaming like wild banshees.

"How long will this hold?" Angela asked, her hand once again on her son's shoulder.

Adam continued to squeeze his eyes shut while tiny beads of sweat formed along his brow. "Have to concentrate, Mom."

"Gene, look!" Ed pointed to the New Dead we'd recently de-armed. His shout earning him a withering look from Adam's Mom. "What's he doing?"

The New Dead shuffled up to the lead rider. Now off his monstrous horse, he wasn't nearly as physically imposing as I'd previously thought. Narrow and toned, the scrap metal and tar-paper had gone a long way to bulk up what appeared to be a much lighter individual. My mind immediately went to Tristan. It had been a year, but I could still close my eyes and see his gaunt face. If that was the Shelldeck boy, he was as good as dead, the House be damned.

The New Dead held its stump up to the rider like a child showing off an undeserved wound.

"Does anyone else feel that?" The Swamp Witch pressed her staff against the back of the seat.

Magick!

It was different, but at the same time almost familiar. There was a subtly to it, like steel wrapped in velvet. It had its wild edge, but there was a quiet confidence in the way it moved.

"Gene…"

Ed directed my attention back to the rider and his soldier. The armored man pressed a gauntlet covered hand against the New Dead's stump and pulled. Licorice-like strands of ashen flesh unraveled like home-made spaghetti from the broken hole.

Magick, a dark and haunting Magick, flowed like fine wine. Even with the rocking Dad Wagon I held my breath. In that instant, I remembered where I'd felt that Magick before. It was only once, in a fleeting moment that had come far too soon, and brought with it the unholy attention of Old Dead.

"Cathy…"

"What?!" Adam lost his concentration and with it his hold on the Seal. Eldero's Magick crumpled like cheap paper and set the New Dead free to tear their way into the broken Dad Wagon.

"Adam!" Angela's voice vanished through the shattered remains of the passenger window, New Dead arms pulling her out of the ruined car.

"Mom!"

Ashen fingers hooked the pouch of Adam's hoodie and before I could stop them, dragged him out the open wind shield.

"Kaylee!" My old roommate lunged for his ex-wife, but the New Dead were faster, they had the Swamp Witch out of the car and separated from her staff in seconds.

Ashen hands grabbed my arms, but I shook them off. Together Ed and I fought off the Damned, our knuckles bloodied with the black gore of New Dead, but still they came.

"Gene, look out—" Ed's words were cut off by more hands than he could stop. They slammed him against the driver door, bouncing his head on the jagged metal before dragging him onto the waiting pavement.

New Dead hands vanished from the Dad Wagon entirely. Armored legs stopped at the windshield and the rider crouched down until we were face to face.

It can't be...

Gloved hands pulled up on the metal shroud, showing me a face I knew but at the same time didn't.

Catherine...

It was Cathy, but not the daughter I remembered. When I'd lost her to the gates of Hell, she'd been barely old enough to drive. The woman who stared at me with my daughter's eyes now had to have been in her mid-twenties, if not older. Fine wrinkles and tiny scars pockmarked a face that should have been young and carefree.

I opened my mouth to speak, but the words wouldn't come. They couldn't. All the things I'd planned to say had become moot, the pointless muttering of a broken man.

All that mattered was just a few feet away.

Tears streamed down my cheeks. They'd been held back for a moment that deep down I didn't believe would ever come, and there was no stopping them now.

The young woman ran a hand through her tangled mane, hair that looked so much like her mother's, and yet so different. She extended a single gloved hand, cold steel swimming with Magick, and shining in Demon Steed's flickering light.

"Dad?"

9

THE CALAMITY

"Cathy?" I extended my hand, but her gauntlet-covered fingers pushed it away.

With a surprising strength, my daughter grabbed the threadbare edges of my shirt, and pulled me from the car, only to deposit my tired body on the highway's gravel beside the rest of the team.

"Gene, is that—" Ed didn't get to finish his words before a New Dead soldier's armored foot cracked across his jaw.

"Eddie!" The Swamp Witch didn't fare much better. A sharp rap of rebar against her back sent Kaylee's face into the pavement.

"Calamity, what would you have us do with them?" The New Dead's voice rattled against my ears like distortion from a poorly placed mic.

Calamity?

My daughter held Kaylee's staff in her hands and examined the smooth wood, while high above her the thick clouds of Hell seethed, rolling over each other in a horizon-stretching battle for supremacy. Bright flashes of lightning cut lines through the boiling darkness and cast their light on the crowded pavement.

A large contingent of New Dead soldiers surrounded my daughter, their ashen bodies and black tarry eyes hungry against the perpetual twilight.

Cathy split the staff across her knee and tossed the remains to one of her soldiers. "Get him up."

"No!" Kaylee screamed before being pushed back into the asphalt.

Ashen hands dragged me to my feet.

"Cathy? It's me. It's Dad. I promised you, I'd—"

Crack!

My daughter's gloved fist slammed into my face. Folded rings of rusty metal left angry grooves and sent my head reeling.

"You promised? You promised me Hell."

Blood trickled from my cheek, while all around me New Dead hollered.

"Cathy, I didn't—"

My daughter's hands swung again, but I did nothing to stop them. Tight fists rammed into my gut and ejected what air still resided there, doubling me over with little effort.

"No! You don't get to use that name. Your deceitful mouth doesn't get to speak it."

Cathy's arms didn't stop, even after I hit the ground her tight fists kept coming, each blow plowing my soul to make room for more painful words.

"You let me go!" Cathy screamed, tears marring the dirt on her face.

"Stop—"

"You sacrificed your only daughter to the fires of Gehenna, and for what?"

I struggled to get air back into my lungs but still her hailstorm of anger showed no sign of relenting. "The... Defiler..."

Cathy pounced on top of me, her knees tight to my sides and her fists continuing their unceasing rain. "No excuses. You don't get excuses." Tears mixed with the fire in her eyes. "You let me go!"

"I'm sorr—"

"Oh, no." Cathy's balled-up hands pounded on my chest. "You don't get to say you're sorry. You let me go. You're no father—you don't get my forgiveness."

"I didn't—"

"Do you know what it's like to look into your father's eyes and see only the Hell that awaits you?"

My words caught in my throat.

"Look! Look at my eyes now. What do you see?" Cathy's red-rimmed eyes sucked out my breath far worse than any fist.

A frail and broken Eugene Law floated in the dark pupils of my daughter's eyes.

Failure. I see a failure.

"Do you see fear?"

"Y—"

My daughter's fists rained down again, each punch another brick in the fortress of my guilt.

"I can't hear you! Do you see fear?"

"Yes," I said, my voice weak and broken.

Cathy stopped swinging long enough to pull wild hair away from her face. "Yes, you do. You see your own fear. Do you know why that is?"

"I..."

"Do you know why I am alive today? Do you know how I survived this? Do you even care?"

I couldn't look away.

"It's not because of you, it's in *spite* of you. I live because everything that was your daughter is *dead*."

"Cath—"

My daughter's hand struck my face. "I told you. You don't get to use that name."

A wild cheer erupted from my daughter's soldiers.

Cathy pressed her face up to mine—angry eyes telling me more than her words ever could. "Catherine Law is dead and buried. I am the Calamity."

New Dead soldiers roared in response, their voices unified in an unholy refrain. "All hail the Wild Reaving! The Calamity has come!"

What have I done?

"He had to stop the Defiler," Adam said, his words meek in the face of Cathy and her horde.

"Adam." My daughter turned away from me, her face feral in lightning's flashes. "The apprentice. How I envied you, did you know that?"

Don't say anything, Adam.

"No…" My apprentice's soft voice sputtered.

"It's true" Cathy practically purred.

Shit.

"He taught you things. So many things. He spent more time with you than he did his own daughter. Did he condemn you to hell?"

"No…"

"I can't hear you?"

"No, but he had—"

My daughter pushed herself off and tore into Adam. "He had to? Is that what you were going to say? He had to let his own daughter die to save what? The world? The city? His pride? Take your pick, Adam. Which one was it?"

Stop talking, Adam.

My apprentice shook before the Calamity. "Your dad never gave up hope. He took a deal with the House to bring you back."

"Am I back? Did he save me? Oh, please, tell me, Adam. Did Eugene Law the great and powerful save his only daughter?"

"He brought you back. I saw it with my own eyes. I've heard you play the violin."

Stop. Talking. Now!

The Calamity shook out her wild hair. "More lies. He failed. He left me here to rot. He left his only daughter to burn in the fires of Hell. Do you see any fires here?"

"No…"

"You will."

The New Dead laughed, their voices echoing in the infernal twilight.

"But he gave up everything he had to find you. He believed you were still here, against all odds he believed it. Your father lost everything, and he's here now. Do you know what I would do to see my father again?"

"Adam." Angela reached out for her son, only to be pulled back by the howling dead.

"You are wrong." Cathy ripped off her gauntlet and threw it at my feet. In the blink of an eye she had my neck in her fingers like a pit viper's jaws. "He hasn't lost the one thing he cares about."

Cathy's bare skin hit me like cold rebar. My daughter's power had grown, but in doing so it had become dark and twisted. When I knew her, Cathy was just learning the latent talent she'd possessed for communing with the Dead—the Calamity had taken that to a whole new level.

"He has his Magick, that's all he's ever cared about. But… I have mine too."

A lone tear slid down Adam's face. "There was nothing he could do. I was with him. The Defiler was coming. He had to close the gate. I told him as much. Fault me, not him. It's because of me you are here. All of this is on me."

The Calamity laughed. It wasn't the kind-hearted sound I remembered, it was hollow, cold, and unforgiving.

"He is Eugene Law, hero of the people, and savior of the lost. You expect me to believe there was nothing he could do to stop Asaroth? You of all people should know better."

Cathy's bare hand burned against my skin, the Magick inside it squirming like a malevolent eel.

"What… have they done… to you?" I squeezed out words through her crushing grip.

"This? This is how I survived." Cathy's nails bit into my neck. "The Defiler's caress. Do you like it?"

"No."

"And neither did I. So I let her die. Cathy is no more, I am the Calamity. This is *my* Hell."

Wild cheers erupted from the New Dead that surrounded my daughter. My head swam, trying to process everything I'd heard.

"Cath—Calamity, I'm sorry," I said, finally getting enough wind to get a full sentence out.

"You will be. You will see me in my moment of triumph." My daughter motioned to the monstrous Demon Steed, its six black legs striking the pavement like hammer blows. "This is Obelleron," Cathy wrapped her gloved fingers around the massive beast's bridle, "and he is mine, as is the rest of my family." My daughter turned her hand to sweep across the assembled soldiers behind her. "Together we will bring an end to the Defiler. Atop the Demon Steeds, we will ride like a cleansing fire over the whole of this place." My daughter pressed her cheek against the beast's long and powerful snout, her hands gently caressing a black and tangled mane. "And in that moment, you will know fear, Eugene Law, because this will be *my* Hell."

A cheer erupted from my daughter's soldiers. The blackened tongues and ashen eyes alight with excitement. "Long live the Wild Reaving! Long live the Winnowing Fan! Long live the Calamity!"

Cathy… What have I done?

My daughter, the young girl who'd once bounced on her father's knee, now stood tall in the chants of New Dead adoration. She mounted Obelleron, her face defiant against the distant storm.

"What do we do with them?" An ashen foot soldier asked.

"Take them to the tower."

"And the car?"

"Leave it for the mechanics."

Strong hands grabbed my slumped shoulders. "You heard her, boys. The Tower of Unceasing Torment awaits!"

PART II
PARTS OF THE WHOLE

CHAIN GANG

D *rip, drip, drip...*

The Tower of Unceasing Torment lived up to its name. Infernal drops of water grated on my already frayed nerves, while thick cuffs of heavy iron kept me tied to a wall.

I tried to reach for my Magick again, for what had to have been the fiftieth time, and again a sharp pain burned on my head.

Kilpsee's Burning Bind—Son of a bitch.

The fiery sensation on my forehead brought with it memories of the past. I'd been screwed back then too, but this time at least I didn't have the Five Star Toaster lighting up the kitchen.

The Magickal lockdown gave me very little to do beyond count the stones in the distant wall, and with them, the number of ways I'd failed my daughter.

It wasn't bad enough that the young woman who'd called me dad had been lost to the gates of Hell. Now she'd been split into pieces and each one of them had more than enough reasons to hate me.

The Calamity.

Images of Cathy's violent shard cut a path through my head, sowing seeds of guilt with each swing of her jagged sword.

You failed me!

I sighed and pressed my back against the damp rocks. I'd failed a lot of people. Cathy, Porter, and even Kris, each one of them deserved a better man that I could ever hope to be. Maybe I should have taken Jenkins' advice way back when.

'Don't be the hero, be the husband.'

That thought was only the lead off slugger in a rotation of depressing memories, and it wasn't long before I'd batted the cycle thinking about Adam, Ed, Kaylee, and even Angela.

I pulled at the chains on the wall and traced their thick loops of iron up into the darkness above. Beyond the incessant dripping water that was sure to drive me insane, my cell was largely empty. It was just me, my thoughts, thick chains, and Kilpsee's Burning Bind—such a fun way to go out.

I closed my eyes and tried desperately not to think about the dripping water, or the sudden urge to pee it brought on, and instead focused on trying to think up a way out of this cell.

No Magick.

The Burning Bind was there to make sure I didn't do anything remotely Magickal, lest I set myself on fire, which would do little to improve my general position, but would remove a lot of other issues.

Focus, Gene.

I banged my head against the wall, letting the damp stone wet the back of my scalp and the sound echo through the empty cell.

"Would you please stop? Some of us are trying to sleep here."

I froze.

I'd heard that voice before. Thin and nasally, with a hint of arrogance stretched taunt over a rubbery palette of general disdain.

"Stewart?"

Somewhere in the dark above me a tiny gasp escaped diminutive lips. "Boss?"

"Stewart the Annoying, is that really you?"

The scuffling of feet and tiny wings answered me. "Maybe… How do I know it's you and not one of her tricks?"

"Damn it, Stewart. It's me, Gene. You know, the guy with all the expressive women?"

"Gene?!" The little Imp's voice jumped an octave. "It really is you."

"Yeah, it sure is."

"Oh, you've come to save me. I knew you would."

"Stewart."

"I knew that eventually you'd brave the gates of Hell and come here to release me from your daughter's prison."

"Stewart."

"Hold on, Boss, I'm soaking in this joy thing for a few seconds. We Imps don't get joy very often, it's kind of a new experience for me. You know, the Tower of Unceasing Torment really lives up to its name and all."

"Stew—"

"Oh, will you look at that? My skin is changing color. Wow, so that's what happiness looks like? Who would have thought it would have an iridescent hue? I mean, not this Imp."

"Stewart the Annoying, shut up now!" Only the faint creak of old wood and the clink of chains echoed in the distant dark. "That's better. Now, listen. I'm chained up down here and some idiot placed Kilpsee's Burning Bind on my forehead. I'm basically as useful as man-nipples. So, I'm going to need you to come down here and free me."

Silence.

"Stewart the Annoying, you may speak."

The tiny Imp's voice switched on, and in an instant, I was treated to a crazy broken stream of Demonic and English.

"Whoa, slow down."

Stewart barely caught his breath before he unloaded again. "She captured you?"

"Cathy—"

"Oh, snap. You didn't call her that did you?"

"Yes."

"And now I know why you're in here. Don't get me wrong, she hates you, but honestly, I think she hates that name more."

This much I know.

"How did this happen?"

The tiny Imp's wings beat against what sounded like metal bars. "Okay, first, I need you to know I did exactly what I said I would do. I kept your daughter safe."

"Her soul is shattered."

"Right, and you've never dropped a plate once in your life? Come on, do you have any idea how hard it is to keep an innocent soul together down here?"

"No, but—"

"Exactly. It's a damn miracle that I was able to keep her from breaking into more pieces. Not that I expect a medal, but a few goat sacrifices under a brindle moon would be a great show of appreciation and would go a long way in—"

"Stewart?"

"Yeah, Boss?"

"Are you caged?"

"Yep."

Shit.

"Why?"

The diminutive Minor Demon sighed. "I tried to get the Cathys back together. Let's just say 'The Calamity' isn't much for rejoining her sisters."

My hope soared. "You can put them back together?"

"Hell no, but I'm thinking someone might be able to. I mean, it's a pretty big universe, and I've got plenty of time."

"Actually, you don't. What do you know about the Void and rebirth?"

The sound of Stewart slapping his rubbery forehead was unmistakable in the damp, dark of the prison cell. "Really? Now?"

Images of a weak and tired Not-Porter came to mind. "Yes."

"Well, then it's time to strap in for a wild ride. Are you still the House's errand boy?"

"I—"

"I'm going to take that as a yes. Well then, things just got a lot more interesting, and fast."

"What do you mean?" I asked, straining to make out the Imp or his cage in the blackness above me.

"I can think of at least two challengers that'll want to take a crack at it, and you, in the process."

"The Defiler has already offered me Cathy in exchange for throwing the fight."

"Well, that beats being torn-apart by a thousand hungry mouths for all eternity."

"Huh?"

"The last guy to cross Asaroth—nasty way to go."

Shit.

"But I have the House's power."

"Well, you do, right up until you don't. When the Void goes dark, there is a time before the rebirth when there's nothing."

"Nothing?"

"Nothing." Stewart's wings beat against metal bars. "But, the bigger problem is the Calamity. If she figures out that's what's going down she won't settle for her Hell, she'll want the whole thing."

"Cathy would become—"

"The Calamity would become the infinite source of all Magick, or you'd have to kill her first."

My heart sank. "I... I can't do that."

"Then you better hope the Defiler does it for you, because either way once she gets wind that the House is going on the market, your daughter's not going to pass on an opportunity to move uptown."

Kill my own daughter?

Even though darkness had settled on the Calamity's shoulders, they were still the shoulders I'd held close in a summer storm when she was a child, and they were still connected to the same forehead I'd kissed before bed countless times.

But a Cathy with infinite Magick...

The thought dried my mouth and tightened down on what little remained in my gut.

"But honestly, I wouldn't worry about any of that," Stewart said, the sounds of his cage settling.

"Why?"

"Because, she rarely keeps prisoners for long. I expect you'll be New Dead in a few hours."

"What?!"

The Imp twisted in its cage. "How do you think she built such a massive army?"

"I didn't—"

"Yeah, well you should have. You think she just happened on them? The Calamity is a hell of a recruiter, but she also lives up to her name. You may not approve of who she is now, but she's a lot like her father. Cathy doesn't mess around."

"I..."

"Oh, sorry, I meant 'The Calamity.' She really hates that name."

What have I done?

11

TILT AND SPIN

I clung to the chains and dangled half-way up the stone wall. My muscles burned, while my fingers reached for Stewart's cage.

"So close." The Imp shook his head. "Just a little further."

"Can't you swing or something?"

"I'll get dizzy."

"Damn it, do I look like I care if you—" My fingers slipped and the rest of me joined them in sliding back down the sharp metal a few feet. "Gah!"

"I bet that hurt."

I squeezed the sweaty chain in my hands. It sure did hurt, along with just about everything else, but if I could get Stewart's cage open, then there was a good chance he could unlock mine. "It did—tell me again why you can't use your Magick?"

The Imp's wings unfolded in frustration and smacked against the edges of his tiny prison.

"Rules of the game here. In your world, I'm Magickal as the day is long, but in here," he shrugged his diminutive shoulders, "I'm about as exciting as pre-chewed gum."

"That's... just... great," I said, pulling on the rusty metal again, my arms throbbing.

"Really? I think it's rather annoying."

I reached the top of the chain, and this time looped my fingers through an over-sized iron eye-bolt at the top. "Okay, now, I need you to swing toward me while I reach out."

The tiny Minor Demon crossed his rubbery arms. "I'll get dizzy."

"Stewart the Annoying, I command—"

"Fine!" The iridescent Imp's color slowly shifted to a decidedly irritated shade of pink. "But if I throw up I'm doing it on you."

"Whatever. Now, swing."

Stewart plopped down on his butt and extended two tiny legs out the side of the cage. "Like this?"

"Yes, but kick your feet."

"But then I'll start swinging."

"Stewar—"

"Ugh." The tiny Imp kicked out with his knees haphazardly. First, he'd send one foot up into the air, then the other. The net effect was that his cage just bobbled around on its chain and remained just out of reach.

"Damn it, together."

"Huh?"

"You have to swing your legs together."

The Imp tilted his rubbery head to one side. "Really?"

"Yes!"

"Oh, well why didn't you say so."

Deep breath, Gene.

I tightened my grip on the eye bolt and leaned further out, the heavy chains on my opposite hand making it all the more difficult to reach. "I did—just kick your damn feet together and swing toward me."

Stewart swung his knees roughly in unison, and lo-and-behold the Imp's birdcage-like prison began to swing. "Hey, this is fun," the Minor Demon said, starting to get a handle on the process not unlike a toddler. "Whee!"

"Great, I really don't care. Just keeping kicking." My outstretched fingers nicked the tips of his rubbery toes and sent the tiny Demon spinning.

"Whoa—I'm getting dizzy."

I dropped my hand again and tried to get a bead on the spinning ball of caged pink. "Just keep kicking."

"The room is spinning!"

"Damn it, just keep kicking."

The Imp's cage twirled like a top, and the Minor Demon inside was now pressed uncomfortably up against the bars. "I'm gonna hurl."

"No you're not." I nicked the metal bars and sent the cage into a more violent tailspin.

"Ugh." Stewart the Annoying's spinning face took on a decidedly green tint. "Make… it…. stop…"

I pulled in my knees and tucked them against the stone wall.

Miss this and it's a long way down.

I shook the thought out of my head, falling to my death in the Tower of Unceasing Torment didn't sound like a wholly bad way to go given the recent alternatives.

"Hold on," I cried, launching myself off the wall and hoping I had enough strength to overcome both gravity and the chains weighing me down.

Bang!

I hit Stewart's cage and sent the already twirling wood and iron on overdrive. My hands fought for purchase on the oversized prison, catching the edge of the bars and tilting the entire apparatus at a hard angle toward the ground. The tiny Imp's bulbous nose and now green cheeks pressed against the bars above me.

"I don't feel so good." Stewart's lips curled into a nauseating frown.

"Don't you dare vomit on me."

"Ugh."

The cage continued to spin, my body weight, and the chains pulling at it. "Just give me a second and let me think. There's got to be a way to get to the lock."

The Imp's tongue hung out.

"Wait. Where's the lock?"

Stewart burped and swallowed back something that sounded positively vile. "There isn't one."

"What?! You wait until I'm hanging from your cage, suspended above a bone-breaking stone floor to tell me there isn't a lock on your cage. If there isn't a lock then how do you get out?"

"I don't know. You're the one that thought this was," Stewart paused to take a deep breath, "such a good idea to do this. I never told you to—"

Belch!

Stewart burped up a nauseating wad of blue-green bile. It hit my hand and instantly stung. "Argh! What the hell is that?"

"I told you not to make me dizzy."

I tried to shake the caustic saliva off my hand, but that left me with only one set of fingers holding onto the cage. The sudden shift sent Stewart banging against the bars on the opposite side, his newly green tint darkening by a few more shades.

"How do I get the cage open if there isn't a lock?" The muscles in my arms screamed at me to let go, but the thought of hitting the floor was still very much unappealing.

The clearly disoriented Imp tilted like a drunken sailor. "How the hell am I supposed to know? This whole stupid thing was your idea. Not that it isn't great to see you and all, Gene, but I'd prefer to not be in the spin cycle."

"There's got to be a way to open this cage."

Burp.

The Minor Demon stumbled toward my side of the twisting cage. "Incoming!"

"Don't you dare vomit on me."

Too late.

Stewart the Annoying let out a projectile spray of algae-like vomit that somehow missed the bars, and my hands, but instead landed smack on my face. "Sonofabitch!"

Crack!

The wooden bottom of Stewart's cage gave way. The dinner plate of wood snapped open like an upside down trap door and pinched my fingers against the bars. "Son of a—"

A pink and dizzy Minor Demon dropped out of the cage like a gelatinous stone, his wings barely unfolding before he disappeared into the dark.

Hold on Gene!

My finger ached and my face burned, but still I clung to the twisting cage.

"Well, I feel a lot better."

"Stewart?"

The tiny pink Demon flapped into view, his rubbery skin no longer tinted green.

"That's great," I said, still twisting. "Mind giving me a hand here?"

"Sure thing, Boss."

Stewart landed on my shoulder, his weight pulling down on my already overtaxed fingers, then placed his claws on my head and turned my face.

"What are you doing?"

"Just hold still."

My fingers slipped just a little more, the combined twirling and the extra house-cat worth of Imp not helping my grip in the slightest.

"Stewart, I command—"

69

The pink Demon wiped a sticky hand down my cheek, coating it in burning vomit. "I got you, just hold still."

Creak!

My right hand dropped off the cage and Stewart jumped back into the air, his wings keeping him aloft long enough to guide him to my other shoulder.

"What are—"

Smack!

I received a palmful of Imp vomit to the forehead.

Pop!

Kilpsee's Burning Bind snapped, and at roughly the same instant, my fingers slipped off the lilting cage and put me on a collision course with the distant floor.

The tiny Demon waved a clawed hand. "You're welcome."

"Stewart!"

* * *

"Well, it worked didn't it?" The Imp perched on my chest, cleaning vomit-covered claws with his tongue.

"Technically, yes," I said, rubbing at the bump on my back-side. "My Magick returned the moment you burned off Kilpsee's tramp stamp."

"Yup, just like I planned."

"You planned?" I sat up and pushed the tiny Demon off my chest in the process. "If I recall correctly, you weren't too keen on the entire plan from the start."

The Imp leapt into the air and hovered above me before returning to his preferred spot on my shoulder. Stewart wasn't much larger than a slightly overweight feline, but unlike any cat I'd ever seen, the Imp was rubbery, demonic, and one hell of a talker.

"It grew on me." Satisfied his claws no longer held any vomit stains, Stewart spread his wings and stretched. "So, what's next?"

I tossed the now unlocked manacles aside and pointed to the door. "Next, we find the rest of them and get the hell out of here."

"Rest of who?"

"My friends."

The tiny Demon's claws grabbed my head and twisted it enough to make eye contact. "Friends? Who are you, and what have you done with Eugene Law?"

12

PLAGUE OF HOPE

"*J* don't get it," I whispered, leaning around a narrow stone corridor and peering into the dimly lit darkness.

Stewart cuddled up to my ear, his wings folded back. "The Tower of Unceasing Torment? Oh man, this thing has been here for an eternity. It's kind of got that old dark ages vibe. I think the architecture is rather impressive honestly."

In the distance, a pair of New Dead soldiers rounded the corner, their mis-matched armor reflecting in the broken light before they vanished again down yet another hall in the maze-like Tower.

"No, the New Dead. Of all the things my daughter could have ended up with."

"It's brilliant, actually." Stewart's claws tickled at the edge of my ear. "In fact, it's why the Calamity is even alive today."

"How do you figure?"

The Imp sighed. "She's so much like you it's dizzying."

"Keep it in your belly, buddy," I said, slipping down yet another open hallway.

"Yeah, yeah. Don't make me swing."

I ducked back into an alcove to avoid the black-eyed gaze of distant New Dead. "Deal."

"Where was I? Oh right, why New Dead? Well, I'll tell you. Cath—The Calamity, took pity on them."

I stepped out, then pulled back. "Pity? On the Damned? They are evil to the core. Those black eyes and burned skin are a mark of—"

The Imp rapped me on the head. "Gene, I'm from Hell, you don't have to explain New Dead to me. Do I go around explaining tacos to you?"

"No."

"Exactly."

Satisfied the hallway was clear I slipped back out, and together with Stewart, we shot around the next turn. "So what did she do?"

"She cared."

I stopped cold. "What?"

Stewart's claws pinched my shoulder after the sudden stop. "Whoa, you don't exactly come with seatbelts. Try to give a Demon some warning would ya?"

"What did you say?"

"I said she cared, and she did. Your daughter has a flare for the dead, but you knew that. She showed you as much at that cop's place, remember?"

I did, but I wasn't thinking about that. I was thinking about Cathy's words in the heart of the Green Swamp, when all was lost in Sturkey.

So much pain, Dad. There's so much pain.

Was the Calamity really lost? Or was a real part of Cathy still in there?

"Gene, New Dead, move!" Stewart's claws on my earlobe directed me into a tiny alcove while ashen face soldiers crossed the hall not feet from where we'd been standing.

"She took pity on them."

73

Stewart nodded. "She sure did, and I got to be honest with you, that's just not an emotion we get a lot of down here. Really took root, flourished if you will."

I pressed my back against the stone wall, trying to both process Stewart's words, and keep from drawing attention to myself.

The Imp crouched down with me, nestling his body against my head. "So anyway, she cared. Your daughter's whole compassion thing rolled over Hell like a plague of hope."

"I don't think that's the right—"

"Plague of hope. Yeah, I'm sticking with that. As you no doubt know, The Defiler's been hoarding New Dead like a Dragon hordes trinkets. So, it should come as no surprise when I tell you what happened next."

"My daughter took on the Defiler and won?"

The Imp chuckled, then immediately clamped a claw down on his mouth. New Dead passed not far from us, pausing only once to sniff the air like fox hounds before continuing undeterred, their makeshift armor scraping on the hard stone.

"Oh no, your daughter got her ass handed to her."

"Then how—"

"How is she still here?"

I jogged down to the next junction and tucked into another corner. "Yes, how?"

"The New Dead."

"What about them?"

The Imp tightened down his wings and blended into the darkness with me. "They came to her aid. It was a full on revolt, the likes of which we haven't seen down here ever. I mean, New Dead are the whipping boys of Hell, Gene. We all took turns pushing them around. You know, they are the Damned and all—good times."

"But…"

"But your daughter gave them hope. It was unheard of.

New Dead? Hope? These sorts of things just didn't happen. Yet there they were, organized, fighting for each other, doing things the Damned just didn't do, and who did they do that for?"

"The Calamity?"

Stewart peered around the corner then signaled the all clear. "Damn straight they did, and Hell went sideways not long after. You see any lakes of fire? Hell Fleas?"

"No."

The Imp shook his head. "Yep, all that disappeared, even that great crevasse I'd had back when you opened that first gate here and I got sucked out? You remember that, Gene?"

"I do. You were a lot smaller back then."

The Imp waved me off. "Yeah, I may have gotten bigger, but you certainly haven't gotten any smarter. That's the hallway." Stewart pointed at a narrow arch about a hundred yards ahead in the hazy dark.

"That's where my friends should be?"

Stewart giggled. "Yeah, sorry, still feels so strange to hear you and friends in the same breath. The Tower of Unceasing Torment's been around a long time. It's not my first time here, except typically I was on the doling out side of the equation and not the receiving end."

"New Dead?"

"I beat em like a drum. It's just what we did."

"How's that sitting with you now?"

The tiny Demon shook his head. "Hell's a strange place anymore. I honestly don't know what happens if the Calamity wins."

"Do you think she can beat Asaroth?"

"Well, I doubt it—no offense—but she'd need to up her game. I mean, she's got the army, but she needs more firepower. Heck, I'd say she'd need to enlist the help of the Demon Steed Obelleron, but there's no way she pulls that off. The Hell Horse hasn't been ridden in a hundred years. There's no way she gets his help."

"Obelleron?" I ducked under the archway into a narrow room with a single heavy iron door. Cold rivets in reflected the dim light. "Six-legged horse about yea big," I held up my hand, "jet-black mane, flaming hooves, digs bareback riding?"

Stewart leapt off my shoulder, his wings unfolding in the air. "No! Are you serious?"

I nodded, pressing my head against the damp and rusty metal. "She rode down the Dad Wagon on top of him."

Stewart's wings folded back up, and he dropped to the ground with an overly dramatic flop. "Well, this whole place has really gone to Hell. The Demon Steed Obelleron has sided with Cath—the Calamity? That's one of those things I never thought I'd see in my eternal life. You sure it's him?"

"Are there other six-legged devil horses down here?"

Stewart shook his head. "No."

"Then yeah, I'd say I am sure."

"Well, I'll be damned. I take it back. The Calamity may do the unthinkable. This may *really* become her Hell."

"Gene?" A faint voice barely made it through the heavy iron. "Is that you?"

Kaylee.

"Yeah, it's me. Give me a minute and Stewart and I will get you guys out of here."

"Gene, they took him!"

"Who?"

Kaylee's words broke into sobs. "They took Ed. They took him because of his stupid stitched soul."

My stomach churned, and I pushed my ear against the door. "Where, Kaylee? Where did they take him?"

"I don't know!"

Stewart's wings unfolded and he leapt into the air. "I do."

"Where?"

"The Soul Ripper."

"What the hell is that?"

The tiny Demon beat his wings harder and fluttered toward the archway. "Not all Soul Weavers end up moving on to better places, Gene."

"What are you talking about?"

"We have Illickthids down here, and they aren't the soft and cuddly things you find in your world. The ones that end up here are decidedly terrifying."

"Hold on," I cupped my fingers against the iron door. "Kaylee, we're going to find him, I promise."

"Gene, I know I say some terrible things, but if I lost both of them... I..."

"I know, that's not going to happen. I promise."

Stewart's claws pulled on my borrowed flannel. "Boss."

"Just a second," I said, shrugging him off. "Is everyone else there with you?"

"Yes." Adam's faint voice said. "Mom is here too."

"Good. As soon as I find—"

"Gene!" The Minor Demon's claws dug into my skin.

"Damn it, what is it?" I swung around to find myself face to tip with a pair of hammered-rebar blades wielded by two heavily armored New Dead. Eyes of liquid black leaked tar down angry ashen cheeks.

"That!"

I put my hands up. "Hey, guys! Did you know the Calamity and me are related?"

"Nice one, Gene," Stewart said, before beating his wings and vanishing into the dark above me.

Ah, Hell.

13

FIGHT IN THE DOG

I reached for my Magick, letting my mental fingers dig deep for the well of power that rolled deep beneath the skin. It was there, but for the first time in a long time it felt gossamer, almost faded.

The House is dying...

The sudden press of hammered rebar against my neck jolted me back to the here and now.

"Should we kill him?" The New Dead's black tongue licked at forever dry and flaking lips.

"The Calamity says no," his partner in malevolence said, pushing away the blade with ashen and burnt fingers. "She has a plan for him."

"Do you think he needs his legs for her plan?" The rusted edge pressed against my thigh.

New Dead lips broke into a wide grin. "Nah."

Shit.

"Listen, guys," I said, doing my best to back slowly toward the cell door. "If you cut off my legs, it would be a total pain to carry me around everywhere. I'd be all 'off balance' and easily toppled over. Then you'd have to construct some sort of mechanism to prop me up so I could see the Calamity's final battle—that sounds like carpentry to me. Are either of you carpenters?"

The New Dead hesitated.

"Yeah, I didn't think so. Carpentry is a skill, I bet you don't know the first thing about joinery. What's the most complex wood joint you've ever done?"

The rusted blade dipped slightly, and the New Dead holding it tilted his head. "Uh…"

"Now, Stewart!"

Nothing happened.

"Stewart!"

Still nothing.

The New Dead soldiers brought their blades back up, this time pressing them against my chest just enough to draw blood. "Unlock the door. We'll put him with the others."

Guided by the rusted metal, the soldiers pushed me aside and set to work unlocking the heavy iron cell door. Flattened rebar bit into my skin but I remained silent.

Clunk!

The lock's tumbler dropped into place and the first New Dead pulled on the simple iron ring, the door swinging slowly against the hard stone floor.

Come on, Stewart!

The second soldier kept his sword pressed tight to my skin. "Do we have enough chains?"

"Eh, yeah, I think so. Let me see." A burnt and ash-covered face pushed its way into the darkened cell. "Yeah, there's at least one, but they are a little on the small side."

"We could always shave his wrists down."

The first guard shrugged his shoulders. "Works for me."

I pulled my hands into my sleeves. "Uh, guys. Are you sure the Calamity would be okay with shaved wrists?"

"We'll keep most of them." The soldier chuckled, flecks of lip flaking off with each rumbling laugh.

"Let's not get hasty guys," I said, trying to slide down the wall away from the cell. "I mean, maybe my wrists fit already? I don't remember the last time I ate."

The pink and glossy form of Stewart the Annoying crawled out of the darkness above us. He paused briefly to press a finger to his face in the universal symbol for don't talk about this, then grabbed the door frame and flipped into the cell like a circus performer.

Gets dizzy my ass.

Hammered-rebar blades once again brought me back to the present.

Clang!

Sparks showered the ground from where the New Dead had scored the wall, cutting short my painfully slow retreat. "Where do you think you're going?"

I held up my hands, letting the undersized sleeves of Ed's borrowed flannel fall away from my wide wrists. "Just limbering up."

"I say we kill him and tell her he died during the escape."

The second soldier shrugged and raised his rusted blade. "Sounds like a lot less work."

"Wait, are you sure you—"

Clang!

The tetanus-on-a-stick blade never reached me. Thick chains wielded by a surprisingly grown-up Adam stopped it cold. My apprentice twisted the heavy iron like he were wringing out a towel and caught the makeshift weapon, then yanked it away and bought me another chance at life.

"Nice work, Grayson."

The genuine look of appreciation on his bearded face was short-lived as the other New Dead turned his sword on my savior.

Shit.

I lunged at the Damned, throwing my shoulder into his midsection and hoping I wouldn't find some way to impale myself on his cobbled-together armor.

Bang!

We hit the ground like a half-empty tuna can, the soldier's bent-street-sign plate mail clattering on the dense stone.

So much for staying quiet.

The New Dead's wicked sword skidded into the dark, out of reach but not out of mind.

I scrambled for control, once again really wishing I'd spent more time learning something from my daughter's jiujitsu days. A swift kick to the man-parts proved I hadn't. "Ugh!"

The New Dead shifted his legs like a pro, twisting his hips out from under me and then yanking my arm forward. The combined effect of this maneuver meant my overextended body fell right into his trap.

What the hell?!

I tried to fight it, but the Damned was faster. He had my wrist pulled into his chest and his metal covered legs wrapped around my neck.

Twinkling darkness tugged at the edges of my vision and ringed the tar-filled eyes of angry New Dead, but there was something different. Normally the Damned were a wild and unruly bunch, but this soldier's face showed no signs of the unbridled aggression of his burning brethren.

Had the Calamity really done the undoable? Had my daughter built an army?

Boom!

The Swamp Witch's tiny boot smashed into my assailant's head, releasing his blood-stopping grip on my neck in the process. "Ugh."

Kaylee had the rebar blade in hand and it took her only seconds to press it against the New Dead's neck. "You okay, Gene?"

"Yeah, I think," I said, pushing myself up and trying to shake off the latent effects of the monster's chokehold. "What about the other one?"

I should have known better than to ask. Adam had him tied up in the chains, while Angela did her best to hold up the heavy hammered-steel blade. "Wow. Nice work you two."

My apprentice smiled, his lips vanishing beneath a beard that desperately needed a trim. "Thanks. Gene, you look like hell. Did they burn your face?"

Stewart the Annoying flapped into view, his pink body jarring against the dark stone. "That's just the vomit, he'll be fine."

Angela gasped and heaved the flattened rebar blade at the Minor Demon, just missing him, and me in the process.

"Mom, stop! That's Stewart!"

The elderly Grayson covered her mouth, but the damage had been done. The heavy rebar sword clanged against the ground, the rusted metal's noise bouncing down the stone hallways and sure to draw far more attention than we wanted.

"I'm sorry, Adam. I thought it was more of those things."

"New Dead!" Stewart landed on my shoulder in a huff. "You thought I was New Dead? Me? I mean, are you color blind?"

"Holy crap, it talks!" The senior Grayson took a step behind her son.

"It's an Imp, Mom. He won't hurt you."

"He might," Stewart said, his tail twisting uncomfortably against my neck.

I frowned. "No, you won't. Don't worry, Angela, Imps are relatively harmless here and I'm sure Stewart won't—"

The pink Minor Demon leapt off my shoulder and folded his wings like a torpedo before landing on the fallen solider at my feet. If I hadn't seen it I wasn't sure I'd have believed it. The tiny monster dug his claws into the New Dead's ashen neck, effort-lessly shredding tissue and tearing apart ligaments. In seconds, Stewart had its head removed. The tiny Demon kicked it across the floor like a soccer ball. It rolled to a stop against the far wall —vacant black and soulless eyes stared back at us in shock.

The defiant Demon returned to the air and shook the gore from his claws. "You were saying?"

No one moved, even the other New Dead soldier wrapped in Adam's chains was speechless.

"What?" Stewart said, landing on my shoulder and drawing more than a few surprised looks from the rest of the team. "He would have alerted the others."

The sound of metal on stone echoed in the distant halls.

"It might not matter. Adam, keep the rebar blade. Kaylee—"

The Swamp Witch was already at the archway. "I'm not losing him. I'm not losing Ed."

"Neither am I."

The Minor Demon launched himself back into the air, causing both Angela and the Swamp Witch to pull back like they were afraid of getting their heads torn off. I was pretty sure Stewart reveled in it. "This way," the tiny monster said, giving me a wink before flying out the archway and down a side hall.

"Are you sure he's safe?" Adam asked, closing the cell door behind him.

"Totally."

I hope.

14

UNBOUND

*T*wists of black thread, too many to count, draped the wide room in great bundles of unholy darkness. The dense lines hung in billowing bolts of uniform fabric, shimmering gently with a faded light all their own. While it wasn't a spider's web, it brought back memories of the vile spidery creatures that prowled the shadowy corners of the Gloom.

Umbralings.

The threads filled the room like the cords of a piano, stretched taut in spots, and loosened into great loops in others. At the center of the swirling pattern, they vanished into the crustaceous back of a monster-sized Illickthid.

Black mantis arms extended out in great hooks from a massive carapace, their razor sharp tips gently twitching against a still form laid out on the stone table before them. An angular and insect-like face focused intently on the task at hand, while whisker feelers drifted gently in the damp air.

"Eddie…" Kaylee whispered in hushed tones.

The Demon Hunter lay before the black and purple beast, his stitched soul clearly visible above a battered body.

The Swamp Witch grabbed my arm. "You've got to do something."

Together we huddled at the open archway, still out of sight of the pre-occupied monster.

"Adam, Angela," I whispered directing my apprentice and his mother to the hallway outside. "Keep an eye out for New Dead."

My apprentice nodded. "What are you going to do?"

"We're going to save Ed."

Adam scrunched up his face. "How?"

"No idea, but since when has that stopped me?"

* * *

THE MANTIS DUG a sharp hook into Ed's stitched soul, catching the edge of a tender thread and pulling it tight.

Snap!

The glowing strand broke. Ed's translucent soul screamed out in pain, while beneath it, his body twitched against the stone table.

"There, there, my darling. Soon, I'll have these threads unraveled, then the twisted knots inside you will be free and unbound."

My old roommate took a deep and stuttering breath. "What if I like... my soul threads... right where they are?"

The Soul Ripper gently teased out a long, silvery line and let it billow gently in the dark. "No, no, you only say that because you haven't seen the other side. Did you ask to be woven? Did you ask to have these knots?"

"I kind of like these knots. See, I wasn't much more than a head before." Ed tried to pull back the long soul string but found his hands bound. "I didn't want to die then, and I don't want to now."

The mantis looped the thread around one of her claws, the

bright silver fading to black. "But there is no death here." She swung the opposite claw and gestured to the thick bundles of black fiber. "Here you will be a part of me. You will exist forever."

"That's not really what I had in mind."

"No?" The Illickthid slid Ed's now black thread into a dense bundle behind her.

The Demon Hunter pushed his head up. "No. You see, there's this girl, and while she can be a real pain in the ass, she's the only woman that's ever understood me—heck, I think she's the only one that ever will."

From our perch behind a large bundle of spent soul threads, Kaylee's hand squeezed mine. "Ed..."

"Uh huh." the Illickthid nodded, stabbing her hooked claws back into Ed's glowing body.

"Argh!"

"Do go on." the Soul Ripper hooks picked at one of Ed's seams. "I find it helps me locate the tightest stitches."

"I... I... screwed things up. We couldn't have a child, and I refused to accept the son she—"

Snap!

Ed's scream cut me to the core, and I had to grab Kaylee to keep her from launching herself at the beast's hooked claws and certain death in the process.

"Ah, that was a tough one. You had a skilled weaver. These knots are nice and tight, just the way I like them. Now, what were you saying about that girl?"

Ed fought to catch his breath, his chest heaving against the stone, while silvery threads unwound and drifted on an unseen current. "I... I don't know. What girl are you talking about? I've known a few over the years. You've got to give me some more details. Blonde or brunette?"

"Excellent." The Soul Ripper wrapped the thin thread

around her claw with an almost child-like giddiness. "I'd love to hear about all of them, sweetheart. But for now, perhaps you could tell me about your child?"

The delirious Demon Hunter nodded. "What would you like to know?"

"Eddie, no." The Swamp Witch tried to pull away from me, her red-rimmed eyes shining in the light of her ex-husband's fading threads. "Gene, please. We have to stop her. I'm losing him. I cannot lose them both."

Stewart pressed his claws against my skin, his small head and oversized nose peering over my shoulder like a frightened child. "Are you crazy? Do you *want* to get your soul unraveled? Because that's how you get your soul unraveled."

The Illickthid drove her claws back into Ed's spirit and teased at what appeared to be a difficult knot. "I'd like to know all about your child. Was it strong?"

Ed's feverish head lolled to one side, his eyes unfocused and drifting. "Strong as an oak. Which is because that's what he was —the little wooden boy."

"I see." The mantis pushed aside a loose strand and let it dangle in the air. That silvery line fluttered like Ariadne's Thread in the dark and gave me an idea.

"Is this sadness I'm seeing?" The great Illickthid said, her soothing words jarring against the backdrop of Ed's pain.

"No."

The Soul Ripper pulled at the stitch but her hook slipped free. "You're lying to me young man."

The Demon Hunter's chest shuddered. "I am."

Mantis claws resumed their probing. "I cannot help you undo these threads if you don't talk to me. Tell me about your wooden boy?"

"I never told her why."

"You never told who, dear?"

The Demon Hunter's head twisted back and forth. Tears appeared at the edges of his already red eyes. "Kay... I never told her why I left."

The Illickthid's hook tugged at a stitch. "And why was that?"

"Because I'm no father."

Kaylee crumpled against the ground. "Oh, Eddie..."

"Ah ha," the mantis said, its hook finally catching on the tight stitch. "Tell me all about him. Let's start with his name. What was his name?"

"Edwin Lovely Junior."

The Soul Ripper's claws dug into the Demon Hunter's soul. "Excellent, let's see if we can't get that untangled, shall we?"

"Gene, we've got to do something," Kaylee said, pulling hard to break my grip.

"Right, we need to get the heck out of here." Stewart's eyes were the only thing visible above my shoulder. "This whole thing puts off a decidedly Gloom-like vibe."

"That's it!"

Ed grunted in pain as the Illickthid dug her claws deeper.

"Gene, what do we do?" Tears streamed down Kaylee's red-rimmed eyes.

I took a deep breath and squeezed the Swamp Witch's arm. "We ring the dinner bell."

"The dinner bell for what?"

"Umbralings."

"Oh, hell no." Stewart leapt into the air, but I grabbed his leg and yanked him back.

On the stone table, a confused and broken Ed Lovely cried out in pain again.

"Such a nice tight stitch..."

Kaylee wiped a hand across her eyes. "I'm in. I'll do whatever it takes."

"Good." I handed her Stewart's writhing leg. "But I need you to lose that optimism."

"Huh?" Kaylee tilted her head.

"Nothing but sadness, disappointment, and confusion until I say otherwise. You got it?"

The Swamp Witch frowned. "No?"

"Perfect."

15

STITCHES

"*D*o you have any lipstick?"

Kaylee furrowed her eyebrows. "Do I look like the sort of woman who carries lipstick around?"

"Let me go, you harpy." Stewart yanked at his trapped leg.

"No, in hindsight, you don't." I shrugged. "I just need something to draw the sigil with, something to focus the Magick and open a portal to the Gloom."

Now it was Kaylee's turn to go white. "The Gloom?"

"I told you he was certifiable." Stewart flapped his wings erratically. "Now you have all the proof you need. He's going to open a gate to the Gloom and pull in Umbralings by the dozens."

"Gene, but Ed..."

The Demon hunter cried out in pain again, while the Soul Ripper continued to tug at the persistent strands.

"It's the best distraction I've got. We flood the room with hungry Umbralings and grab your ex-husband in the process, but it all comes down to something to draw the sigil with."

"Here." Kaylee shoved the petulant Imp's clawed-leg back in my hand and made a break for the entryway.

"See," Stewart said, watching her slip out into the hall. "That's the look of someone who has seen your plans before."

Just beyond our thread-blind, the Soul Ripper let out a gleeful squeal. "Ah ha, there she is, just the spot I was looking for. So, young man, tell me about your son again."

"I…"

Damn it, Kaylee, what are you doing?

"I need more to go on." The Illickthid's voice echoed in the wide room. "What was life like for him growing up?"

"He was…"

"She's abandoned him, Boss," Stewart said, pointing me toward the exit. "If she's not staying for this guy, neither should we."

"I'm not going to—"

"I got it." Kaylee appeared in the archway with something metal in her fingers.

"An army?" The Imp asked.

"No, lipstick."

I caught the silvery tube of makeup. "But how…"

"Angela."

"Works for me." I handed Stewart's leg back to the Swamp Witch, then popped the top off and twisted up the stem, dull red lipstick greeted me on the other side. "Perfection. Okay, back up, and get ready. The moment this gate's open I need you ring the pain and sadness bell for any Umbralings nearby."

"How do I do that?" She asked, keeping one eye on Stewart and another on the distant Illickthid.

"See those hooks?" I said, pointing to the Soul Ripper's black and hairy mantis claws.

"You can't mean—"

"Yes, you need to stab him with them. Ed's been chumming the water with pain, but we need a full on feeding frenzy."

"Gene, I can't—"

"Just think of it as couples therapy."

Kaylee dragged the Imp like an aggressive parade balloon to the side of our makeshift hideout, her eyes darting back and forth between me and the Soul Ripper. "Whatever, just hurry, Gene. She's digging deeper."

I set to work on the Seal and couldn't focus on the Illickthid, or even my old Demon hunting roommate. I had to pour everything I had into making sure Ten Spins' Bent Key was right. I'd entered the Gloom before, but that was with a Sojourner's Jacket and a boatload of naivety. A goodly bit had changed since that evening in the Plaza of the Americas, and while I was an older man now, I wasn't necessarily smarter.

"There," I said, stepping out of the Bent Key. "I've made a few modifications that should keep the gate open longer."

"Just do whatever you are going to do, Gene. She's tearing out another stitch!"

The Soul Ripper scraped her claws across the edges of Ed's soul. "It was so nice of the Calamity to bring you to me. I haven't had stitches this tight to pull apart in ages. Now, lets dig in a littler deeper, shall we?"

Ed shuddered, his body and soul appearing to tire from the constant barrage of tearing. "Ugh."

"Excellent."

Kaylee grabbed my arm. "Do it, Gene, before I lose him!"

I knelt down in Ten Spins' violent and cryptic design and closed my eyes. My Magick was so thoroughly mixed with the House's, that there was no telling where one ended and the other began. The dark and oily sheen was no longer a break between its power and mine, they were now inseparable. I dug into the combined Magick and reveled in the joy of its power, but something was off, missing. The Void was dying, and with it went its Magick, and it would seem mine as well.

Snap!

Ed's scream rocked me back to the present. I pushed all I could into the Bent Key and willed the Gloom gate to open. The

Magick swirled inside the confines of the sigil, its twisting design acting like a magnifying glass and focusing every ounce of power I dared muster.

"Gene!" Kaylee's voice strained against the roaring Magick.

Boom.

With a shuddering thunderclap the Gloom opened, and in doing so flung me out of the Seal entirely. I skipped across the hard stone before coming to rest at the foot of Ed's table. "Ugh."

The swirling power of the gate peeled apart like the rind of an overripe fruit and spilled out across the stone floor of Hell. The two worlds mixed, disparate and deadly, and like oil and water they pushed back against each other violently.

Shit.

Pulling apart the seams of reality to open a black and freezing tunnel to the Gloom certainly appeared to be more than enough to get the Soul Ripper's attention, but I wasn't counting on doing that and being launched out of the sigil like a rodeo clown. "Kaylee…"

The Swamp Witch didn't waste any time dashing between the billowing threads and vaulting on to the stone table. The Soul Ripper raised her claws like a jammed sewing machine, but Kaylee was faster. She hugged one of them to her chest and dropped her whole body onto the hard table next to the Demon Hunter.

"Argh!"

Ed's scream shook the drifting strands and reverberated in the cavernous room. The Soul Ripper's claw plunged deep into his spirit and sent shock waves of pain rolling over me and directly into the Gloom.

Come on…

Stewart's pink face appeared next to mine, his tiny claws slapping my cheek. "You idiot, did you forget to factor in the Infernal Constant?"

"I… maybe?"

The tiny Demon smacked his forehead. "That's an unstable gate."

"What does that mean?"

As if in answer to my question, dark blue flames erupted along the threads closest to the yawning portal. The strange fire raced into the larger mass of dense fibers.

Stewart pulled at my arm. "It means we are gonna get cooked or crushed to tiny bits in the implosion."

"Implosion?"

Jet-black and glistening feelers yanked the tiny Imp away from me.

Stewart!

Umbralings poured though the wavering portal like ants from the mound. Hundreds of black and bulbous creatures clamored over each other in a brainless hunt for dinner, with our flesh and pain being foremost on the menu.

I kicked away a set of sharp feelers and the spidery beast attached to them, while even more surrounded me. "Kaylee, get Ed. I've got to save Stewart."

The Swamp Witch didn't respond.

Ed's ex-wife had more than enough problems of her own. The Soul Ripper had pinched her tight between its two razor-sharp chitinous hooks.

"My threads! What have you done to them?" The Illickthid squeezed the ginger's flesh, drawing blood.

"Gene!"

Ed wasn't doing much better. The black wave of Umbralings swarmed past me and onto the table, their glistening bodies and sharp fangs hungry for the Demon Hunter's semi-lucid soul.

Somewhere surfing along the tops of that horde was the pink and rubbery body of Stewart the Annoying, his bat-like wings flapping in and out in a futile attempt to get airborne. "Get off of me!"

Blue flames popped in and out along the burning threads.

The cold fire sent the already famished Umbralings into a frenzy. Strands fell from the ceiling only to vanish in thin wisps of smoke, while behind them the portal rippled, its seams struggling to hold back the pressing power of Hell itself.

Ed's stitched soul turned its head to the side, two translucent and unfocused eyes met mine. "Oh. Hey, Gene. What are you doing here?"

"Trying to save you." I kicked away more hungry Umbralings.

The Demon Hunter smacked his ghostly lips, his spirit turning over gently, like he were just waking up from a long rest. "Save me from what?"

"From the Soul Ripper, these Umbralings, and the implosion from a Gloom gate I created without applying the Infernal Constant."

Ed's spirit continued to roll over, while behind him his ex-wife struggled to free herself from the Soul Ripper's grasp. "Gene?"

"What?!"

"Did you know there's a mass of giant spiders on my—" My old roommate's ghostly eyes shot open. "Gene, there's a mass of giant spiders on my body? Why am I not in my body? Gene!"

Aw, hell.

16

VIKING BLOOD

"Ed, get back in your body." I pushed away the hungry fangs of yet another Umbraling only to watch the worn and drifting spirit of my old roommate launch himself at the Soul Ripper. "Damn it, Lovely!"

Bits of the Demon Hunter's soul flapped like the threadbare flag of some derelict ship, but that didn't stop his all out assault on the Illickthid. I'd forgotten how fast Ed could go from barely functional to possessed lunatic. When I'd lived with him it had been a curse, but right now it was a blessing.

Rip!

Umbraling fangs tore through the denim of yet another pair of borrowed pants. They caught my leg in the process, and injected enough venom to send a wave a bone-chilling cold over my tired muscles.

"Oh, hell no." I kicked the hungry beast away, my leg quickly going numb beneath me.

Shit.

I ignored the pain and pulled myself onto the stone table with far fewer acrobatics than Kaylee, then set to work undoing the Demon Hunter's restraints. "Ed, get back in your body!"

"I ever tell you about my rodeo days?" My old roommate scrambled over the chitinous claws of the Soul Ripper and looped the torn edges of his stitched soul around its neck.

Is that even going to work?

The Illickthid dropped Kaylee and turned its attention to the ghostly spirit of Ed Lovely. The Demon Hunter clung to the beast's neck like a bull rider, his threads the only thing keeping his soul from being bucked off and tossed into the hungry mass of Umbralings. "Yippee Kai—"

The Soul Ripper twisted violently, her claws knocking aside the bulbous spiders climbing her many legs, while my old roommate pulled on his glowing reigns.

Huh, well I'll be damned. It's working

The Swamp Witch stumbled to her feet, narrowly avoiding a wild mantis claw in the process. Blood dripped from long scrapes on her chest.

"Kaylee." I pointed at the blackened soul-thread straps holding Ed's body down. "Help me, we've got to get him free."

The Swamp Witch nodded and knocked aside a few smaller Umbralings enroute to the table. "I got him—Gene, behind you!"

The piercing stab of Umbraling fangs lanced my back. They were followed by a wave of soul-crushing cold that coursed down already tired muscles. "Argh!" I pulled the creature off and tossed it aside, but the damage had been done.

Kaylee yanked at the soul-strands holding Ed's arms down. "Gene, are you okay?"

I couldn't feel my fingers. "I'm fine."

The Swamp Witch vaulted back onto the table and sunk her teeth into the blackened threads, tearing them like a mom opening a troublesome popsicle wrapper.

Why didn't I think of that?

"Go," Kaylee cried, wrenching her ex-husband's arm free,

and narrowly avoiding the fangs of a hungry Umbraling in the process. "Get the damn Imp. I've got Ed."

Stewart!

The tiny pink Demon's wings surfaced briefly only to drop back beneath a bulbous and chittering tide.

Shit.

The plan was to jump off the table and make a run for the spider-surfing monster, but, my mind had not filled my legs in on that. I hit the floor and my lower body immediately dropped out from under me, the Umbraling venom rendering my legs all but useless.

"Gene—" The Swamp Witch shouted something, but I lost it in the mass of fangs and milky blind eyes. I swung my arms a few times, trying desperately to club back at the advancing beasts, then slipped beneath the folds of the black soul strands like a tangled-up cat.

"Gene!"

Adam.

A hammered-rebar blade shattered the bulbous heads of a score of Umbralings before cutting me free. Adam's chubby hand pulled me up, only to have my numb legs fold underneath me again. "Gene, what the hell—"

"Umbraling venom, I'll survive. You've got to get Stewart."

My apprentice kicked away an advancing pair of Gloom beast fangs. He sent them tumbling into the burning strands, while behind him the gate rippled. "There's no time, Gene. They're coming."

"Who?"

"Them!"

New Dead soldiers appeared in the distant archway, their cobbled-together armor shining in the blue flames.

That's a problem.

Stewart's pink body surfaced in the mass of herding spiders, his wings folded unnaturally against his back.

"There." I pointed to the distant Demon before he vanished again. "Get Stewart. I'll be fine."

Adam shook his head and yanked me up again, this time depositing me in Angela's matronly arms. "No, you won't. Mom, here."

Angela's surprising strength caught me off guard. "What are you—"

"Mom, get Gene to the Gloom."

"Huh?" Angela and I said in unison.

"The crazy, freezing hole of terrifying death." Adam pointed to the Gloom gate. "Right there. You two go through that gate. I'm going to save Stewart."

My legs may not have been working, but my hands did, so I swung them like crazy. "Adam, we can't survive in the Gloom without protection. It would be suicide!"

My apprentice glared. "I've got an idea. Mom, get him in there."

"Sweetheart, don't you think we should listen to Gene?"

I nodded vigorously. "Yes, you should!"

Adam hefted the rebar blade like a Viking of old, his unkempt beard no longer scraggly, but almost regal in the flickering blue flames. Umbraling blood marred a hoodie that could do little to hide the young man growing up before our eyes. "No, Mom. I know what I'm doing."

You do?

My apprentice swung the sword and cast aside another wave of Umbralings, sending them crashing into the burning strands. "Get him to the gate. We're going into the Gloom."

Gah!

I struggled in Angela's grasp. "Wait, we don't have protection. No one can survive in the Gloom without a Sojourner's Jacket. The cold will kill us."

Blue flames raced up the walls as New Dead fought their way into the burning room.

"And so will they." Adam smashed another Umbraling. "Mom, remember winters with Aunt Sue and Uncle Charlie? The sheep?"

"I do."

"Then go!" My apprentice pointed to the rippling gate, its edges pulling in faster than I remembered.

"Sheep? What the hell are you talking about? Sheep?"

"What about you?" Mrs. Grayson hefted me like a shield maiden of old.

"I'm going to save my friends." Adam put on his most heroic face and flipped his hood up. I was pretty sure it was meant to inspire confidence, but it completely cut off his peripheral vision—an Umbraling slammed into his side and knocked him to his knees.

"Adam!" Angela shouted, almost dropping me.

My apprentice pulled the spidery beast off and tossed it aside, then flipped the hood back with a sheepish grin before disappearing into the chitinous horde.

"Let me go, Angela, this is nuts. Your son doesn't know what he's talking about. We can't survive in the Gloom without protection. It's too cold."

The elder Grayson shifted hands and scooped up a thick bundle of black soul-strands. She slapped them against my lap a few times until she was confident they were no longer burning, then dragged me and the strands toward the Gloom.

"What are you doing?"

"I used to live in Minnesota."

"Damn it, woman. It's not the same."

Angela kicked at a twitching pair of decapitated Umbraling fangs and the head they were attached to. "Oh yeah? You been to Minnesota in the winter?"

"No, but—"

"Then shut it, Florida boy."

Ed Lovely, Illickthid rider extraordinaire, swung in and out of view beyond us. His broken soul-strands did a decent job of keeping him connected to the Ripper, but it was starting to look like he didn't have a plan for what came next.

Kaylee pulled her ex-husband's body off the table. "Eddie, come on!"

Umbralings surged over the Soul Ripper's carapace. Hooked claws swung wildly but still the Demon Hunter held on tight and guided the beast into the chittering masses.

"Go! I'll hold her back," my old roommate cried, his translucent hands clinging to the glowing threads.

"Oh, hell no." Red blood matted the Blood Witch's torn shirt. "No heroics, Lovely. Get your ass off that giant bug now."

The Soul Ripper twisted violently, sending Ed spinning around in front of the massive mantis and her claws.

"On second thought... I'm coming." The Stitched-Soul of Ed Lovely dropped off the Illickthid and beat a path for his ex-wife and his body, while behind him, his bare soul threads snapped like the tail of a box kite.

The Swamp Witch dragged Ed's body toward the gate. "What are we doing, Gene?"

"We're—"

Angela tilted her head toward the rumbling gate, now half its prior size. "We're going into the freezer-hole thing!"

"Going back to the Gloom, eh Gene?" Ed's soul clamored over the bodies of crushed Umbralings.

I shook my head. "No! This is a terrible idea."

Angela dragged me toward the pulsing portal. Great gusts of freezing wind rolled over us. "Ignore him, he's a cold weather wimp."

Crash!

The Soul Ripper's claws split the stone table in two and she surged forward.

"Kaylee!" I cried, reaching for the young ginger.

The Swamp Witch turned, but not in time. Mantis claws

plunged deep into her back, their bright red and bloody tips erupting from the front of an already torn shirt.

Blood sputtered from her lips. "Gene?"

Ed's Stitched Soul leapt for his ex-wife, but the Soul Ripper was faster. She pulled the Swamp Witch up like a worm at the end of a hook, dragging the young woman, body and soul, out of Ed's grasp.

"No!"

17

DOOM AND GLOOM

With a flick of its claws, the Soul Ripper tossed Kaylee's bloody body aside. She hit the ground hard, a lifeless lump, her flesh bruised and torn. Behind us the Gloom gate rippled and belched out a fresh wave of cold blue flame, while the clanking sounds of armored New Dead filled the distant edge of the wide room.

Back in his body, my old roommate grabbed the torn limb of an Umbraling and ran for his ex-wife.

The Soul Ripper's claws cut at the air, hungry for Ed and his stitched soul.

"Ed, stop," I cried, but the Demon Hunter ignored me. "I've got to do something. Angela, sit me down."

"What about the—"

"I'm not letting my friends die. Put me down so I can focus."

Adam's mom released her grasp, and I collapsed onto the hard ground. She immediately set to work getting me up right. "What can I do?"

"Get me two black soul-strands."

Adam's mom scooped up the thick, yarn-like strands and placed them in my clumsy hands. "Now what?"

I tugged at the edges of my Magick. "Don't let me fall over."

Angela knelt behind me and used her size to keep me upright, then did what she could to push away any Umbralings that got too close.

"Ed!" I leaned against the matronly woman. "Telgrin's Knots!"

My old roommate pushed the bandana off his bald head and choked up on the broken Umbraling leg like a baseball bat. "Do it, Gene."

"What are you doing?" Angela's strong arms pressed against my shoulders, while behind her the Gloom gate continued to ripple and send out great blasts of cold fire.

"What I do best—improvising."

I dug deep for my Magick, pulling it up like a trawler scrapes at the sea bed. The House's power was there, hopelessly inter-mixed with my own, but they were both fading. Like an ebbing tide they weren't what they'd been only days earlier, and for the first time I got a good idea what the nigh in nigh infinite meant.

My old roommate faced down the great Illickthid, the broken leg in his hands the only thing between him and certain death for both them. The Soul Ripper raised her bloody claws for the killing blow.

Ed tightened his grip. "Now, Gene."

"Anima nodum!" I shouted, letting the Magick course down my hands and into the soul-strands. The lost lives of countless spirits screamed out for justice from those twisted fibers. Their moaning voices pushed back on the roar of the Gloom Gate and gave the Soul Ripper pause.

"Go." I let my fingers release the vengeful threads. "Bind with guilt. Bind with pain. Bind with suffering, and bind with blame."

The black strands shot out of my hands like they'd been fired from a cannon. They twisted in the air, shooting past the Demon hunter and slamming into the Soul Ripper's claws.

"What's this?" she cried, surprise in her alien voice.

The thick black strands of Telgrin's Knots stretched and pulled, dancing between those hooked claws like a spider's web, tying off the Soul Ripper's strongest weapon.

I squeezed my hands and pulled back against the Magick's ebbing tide. "Ed, get to Kaylee. I'll hold the Illickthid."

Ed tossed aside the Umbraling leg and scrambled for his ex-wife, while above him the Soul Ripper fought against the knotted strands.

The Gloom gate rippled and let out another burst of cold blue flame, but this time it was accompanied by a deep rumble.

The gate is closing...

Ed pressed his hands against Kaylee's bloody body. "She's breathing."

"Can you move her? I can't hold the Ripper for long."

Adam's mother dug in to keep me upright. "Honey, you're feverish."

"It's the Magick. It's running out." I gritted my teeth against the cold fire surrounding us. "How are we doing on company?"

The sound of rebar blades slicing through Umbralings echoed off the distant walls. They were coming, and Adam was right, we really didn't want to be here when they arrived.

"Never mind them." Angela wrapped a motherly arm around my chest. "You do what you have to do. I won't let go."

Angela's words, a mother's words, put wind in my sails and I pushed as much Magick as I could into Telgrin's Knots.

Come on!

The Soul Ripper raged against the twisted spirals of soul strand that bound her claws, and with each swing of her great arms she made a little more headway. It was quickly becoming apparent that I would run out long before the Illickthid did.

"Ed, get your wife and come on!"

The Demon Hunter pulled a bloody and broken Kaylee to his chest, then scooped up her feet. "Just hold it a little longer."

Crash!

The Soul Ripper slammed her tied together claws like a pick-axe into the hard stone.

"How about you move faster!" Angela shouted, her lips way too close to my ears for comfort. "He's doing everything he can."

I took a deep breath and pushed more Magick into the strands. "Just run, Ed!"

My old roommate made it just a few steps before he was surrounded by hungry Umbralings.

Shit.

The Gloom gate wavered and sent out a great burst of blue flame. Cold fire washed over Angela and me and disrupted my concentration. "Argh!"

Rip!

The Magick shattered, and the Soul Ripper had no problem tearing apart the feeble soul strands.

Ed kicked aside a hungry Umbraling then turned to take on the full dark majesty of the Soul Ripper. Her raised claws shined in the terrifying glow of the cold fire's flames. "I would have preferred to remove your stitches one at a time, but I'll settle for shredding your body and soul."

My old roommate hugged Kaylee to his chest and bowed his head.

Ed, no!

The Soul Ripper's claws cut the air fast, but something else cut it faster, the sharp metal of hammer-rebar blade wielded by the surprisingly strong hands of the best apprentice a Magician could have. "Nobody's getting shredded today!"

"Adam!" Angela cried, getting to her feet and helping me up.

Crack!

The bearded Magician's rebar blade cut through the thin spots in the Soul Ripper's chitinous armor and separated a leg from her body. Oozing stumps of broken exoskeleton sprayed dark blood and gore on the three of them, and with it garnered the attention of the Umbralings.

The Gloom gate rumbled, the cold wind vanishing in the sudden change of direction.

Implosion!

Adam's mother must have felt it too, as she grabbed my arm and pulled me toward the inhospitable Gloom. "It's closing!"

Umbralings surged like a black and glistening horde, their hungry fangs rushing past the broken claws and swarming up the thrashing Soul Ripper.

The bright pink and bloodied body of Stewart the Annoying flapped into view. He struggled against the pull of the Gloom. "You can't survive on the other side without protection."

"I know, but would you rather take your chances with them?"

Dozens of New Dead soldiers filled the entrance to the wide room, their swords bloodied with the gore of an untold number of Umbralings.

"You have a knack at terrible choices, boss."

"Just lucky, I guess."

Boom!

A fresh burst of cold flame signaled what appeared to be the gate's final collapse.

I pointed to the dark, ash-filled world beyond the narrow edges of the swirling portal. "Go."

Stewart closed his wings in and vanished like a dust ball on the wrong side of the vacuum nozzle, his body sucked up into the freezing dark of the Gloom.

"Ed, Adam, come on!"

"Stop them!" The Calamity appeared at the front of her New Dead militia, Private Petty's silver saber shining in her hand.

The ground shook with the wild cry of New Dead.

"Go!" Adam put himself and the battered edge of a rebar blade between the New Dead and the Lovelys.

"Adam." Angela let me go and reached for her son.

I grabbed her foot as the first few streaming threads of

blackened soul threads whipped past us and into the hungry dark of the Gloom.

What the hell am I doing?

"No, Angela—"

"Let go of me. I'm not giving up my son."

Her words hit me like a sledgehammer. In that instant, I was back at the Hellgate, my hands desperately trying to cling to Cathy's thread.

'I'm not giving up my daughter!'

The hate-filled and tarry eyes of New Dead consumed the space between us, and all I could do was hang onto Angela's leg.

"Come on, Boss."

Bright pink claws looped around my shoulder just as the portal imploded and sent a chain of unlikely travelers hurtling into the cold dark of the Gloom.

What have I done?

FLORIDA BOY

*T*iny motes of spent ash settled on my bare skin like snow.

The Gloom.

A cold and dark reflection of the world around it, in Hell the Gloom lived up to its name. Here the Tower of Unceasing Torment had become a fractured remnant of its demonic glory. Broken walls and collapsed stone afforded me a wind-swept view of the ash-laden hills the spread out beyond the Tower's missing walls.

The Calamity has come.

Bitter cold stung my face and squeezed the blood from my fingers.

The Gloom beyond the walls of the tower was a desolate place. It cast a stark light on just how far my daughter had taken her personal mission. The Calamity had built an army, and in doing so she'd transformed Hell in her image. The Gloom was a dead reflection of the change she'd wrought.

'There's pain here, Dad. So much pain.'

Try as I might, I couldn't shake those words. They remained

stained on my heart like Sturkey's mud on these borrowed jeans.

Is there any of my daughter left in the Calamity?

The unnatural chill of the Gloom forced the air from my lungs like a bellows and along with it, any thoughts of Cathy. I pulled my hands against my chest, using them to trap what little body-heat I had inside the confines of Ed's old flannel, but without a Sojourner's Jacket my chances of survival in the Gloom plummeted by the second.

Where is everyone? The gate!

The final moments came rolling back in exquisite detail. Adam, Ed, and an all but lifeless Kaylee, must still be trapped on the other side. They were alone against an army of New Dead with my daughter at the lead, and Private Petty's blade in her hand.

Angela!

I found Adam's mother a few feet away, her body already half-coated in a layer of ash and soot.

"Angela!" My voice stung in the sharp cold. "Wake up."

The still form of Adam's mother didn't budge.

Shit, shit, shit.

I dug my tired legs into the stoney ground and shuffled off toward Adam's quiet mother. "Angela!"

The distant woman remained unmoving in the silence of the Gloom.

Minnesota my ass...

The chilling stone stung through the thick flannel of my borrowed shirt, but still I crawled. My hands were numb, and the tingling in my toes signaled they would be next.

You don't have much time.

She laid covered in small piles of feathered ash. It was impossible to tell if Adam's mother was alive, but I refused to believe otherwise.

"Damn it, Angela," I said, speaking not so much for her, but to keep my lips moving in the cold of the Gloom. "What about all that talk of Minnesota, eh? Thought you were tougher than this."

I brushed flakes of soot away from her blue-tinged face.

Shit, shit, shit.

I pressed a hand to her nose, overjoyed to feel the slightest bit of air escape frosted nostrils. "Oh, no," I said, brushing the rest of the ash from her bruised cheeks. "You don't get to freeze to death. You're from the great white north, remember?"

Her body was cold, too cold. She wasn't going to survive much longer without something to protect her from the elements, and neither was I.

"Damn it, Adam. Sheep? What the hell was that supposed to mean? You couldn't have taken a few seconds to let me in on the details of your monstrously stupid—"

The soul-strands.

A dense bundle of the yarn-like soul fibers lay not far from us, rapidly vanishing beneath a soft layer of ash and soot.

Wool.

"Of all the crazy things." My fingers shook in the Gloom's unceasing chill. "You guys were going to cover yourselves in soul-strands."

Adam's mom didn't move, but she didn't stop breathing either.

"So, you're going to leave it to the Florida boy to save your butt, eh? That's fine."

The soul-strands are too far away.

"Think you can hold on for me?"

Angela didn't budge.

I'm going to take that as a no.

I pressed my body against the woman's cold form and reached for my Magick, closing my eyes and digging deep for the cosmic power trapped in my body, and possibly the only thing keeping me alive.

Come on...

Thin wisps of power drifted in and out like a trapped bird, no sooner would I get a handle on one, then it would slip out of my grasp again.

Focus.

I squeezed my eyes tighter and tried to block out the cold, the pain, and the fear. "No one is freezing to death in the Gloom on my watch damn it."

Come on...

The Magick retreated deeper, but still I dug for it. The House was dying, and with it the nigh infinite power it had granted me was coming to a terrifying end.

Gotcha!

The Magick twisted like a truculent worm dangling precariously on the end of my hook. There wasn't much, but I wasn't about to let it go unused.

I pressed my hands against Angela's frozen cheeks. "Ignis Calorem,"

The blue tinge faded ever so slightly, and as it did, her breathing improved.

I tried to pour more Magick into her, but my power flickered and then vanished like ash in the wind.

"Damn it!" I shouted, but my only response was the cold wind and ash that drifted on it like snow. I pressed myself against Angela's rapidly cooling body and closed my eyes, pulling my arms and legs as tight as I could to my chest. My teeth chattered and my hands throbbed.

You can't just lay here and wait for death. You've got to do something.

My eyes drifted to a dense bundle of blackened soul-strands that lay in the distant ash. I had no idea how useful they'd be—the Gloom wasn't Minnesota—but soul-strands had to be better than nothing. The thick bundle of threads wasn't far from Adam's mother, but they might as well have been on the moon for all the effort it would take to reach them.

Damn it. You had to land there?

"Okay," I said, willing words over freezing lips. "I'm going to go get your soul-strand blanket. You just need to stay alive until I get back. You hear me?"

Angela breathed softly, ash tumbling aside with each exhale.

"I'm going to take that as a yes. If you die on me, so help me I will track down your soul and totally kick its matronly ass."

I pushed with my knees, inching across the grey and uneven stone away from Angela and toward the blackened fibers. Like a drunken worm, I crawled over the soot-strewn ground, my body barely functional in the painful cold.

Come on, Gene. Don't give up.

The rat nest of fibers lay just out of reach, their promise of warmth tantalizingly frustrating in the dark of the Gloom.

Take a break...

I collapsed against the ground, my tired legs unwilling to push further—everything ached. If I could just pause a bit here and catch my breath I'd be fine.

No, you stop and you die.

I brushed that thought away and let the cold wash over my numb legs. The Umbraling's venom might be waning, but the Gloom was more than happy to take its place.

Just rest...

My eyes drifted in the bone-chilling cold and I let my head droop against the hard stone. I'd come a long way, but still the black bundle, and the hope it represented, remained just beyond my grasp.

Gather your strength.

Something moved in the edges of my dimming vision. It wasn't Adam's mother, and it wasn't the bobbing click of Umbralings, with their spindly legs and hungry fangs. This was gossamer and light, like a worn and tattered bedsheet left out on the line far too long. I knew what it was, but for some reason my freezing brain couldn't get the thoughts out fast enough. The best they could muster was a single-syllable mental shout.

Move!

I willed my legs forward, pushing them through the ash. Inch by inch I drove them on and fought against the stubborn muscles that refused to open. More shapes slipped in and out of my dimming vision. Black wings snapped in the chilling wind, while long dark claws reached for me.

The bundle was only feet away, but might as well have been a mile. Every muscle cried out in pain, until my legs cramped up solidly beneath me, no longer willing to move and now pressed tight to the ground.

Go!

My brain demanded action, but the rest of my body gave in. I let my shoulders drop and tucked my chin against my chest, nuzzling for warmth I didn't have on the cold and desolate ground.

You have to move or you both die.

Soft ash tickled at my eyes and I blinked it away, fighting to keep those heavy lids from closing completely. My mind drifted in and out in time with the gentle sound of rippling cloth and leathery wings.

Somewhere in the recesses of my mind panic tried to get a foothold, but it was lost to the soul-numbing cold of the Gloom.

I'm sorry, Angela.

Those were my final thoughts as I tumbled into a dreamless sleep.

19

PAST MISTAKES

*T*he thick leather of the Sojourner's Jacket lay heavy against my shoulders, its zipper between the fingers of a young and vibrant Morgan Crowley. Her crooked smile and bright green hair brought with them a reminder of darker days from my past.

"Gene..." My old girlfriend yanked the zipper all the way down, exposing me to the bone-chilling elements. "Whoops! You've got to keep this on. Without it you won't survive in the Gloom."

"Morgan, stop!"

I grabbed at the sides, trying to hold the coat together, but it flapped in the wind like a rogue flag.

"Oh, Gene." Morgan pried my fingers away, her sharp nails digging into my flesh. "Don't you like this?"

"No!"

"Stop fighting it. You're only going to make it worse. Let me put the damn shroud on you."

Morgan's fingers grew longer, expanding until they became the black and insect-like arms of Deacon.

"Gene!" His hairless face unfolded like a filleted fish, while a serrated stinger flashed in the recesses of his vile jaws. "Stop fighting me and put the shroud on."

Shroud... Death Shrouds!

Empty hoods pushed forward out of the shadows, their long and fingerless hands reaching for me.

"Stop!"

Worn cloth touched my face, and I pushed it away.

"You want to freeze to death? If not, I'd suggest you put the damn shroud on now."

Angela?

I shook my head, casting aside the terrifying visions of the past, only to find a fresh set of terrors awaiting me in the here and now.

"You're as bad as Adam when he was little," the matronly woman said, her own body covered in the thick and tattered remains of a Death Shroud. She draped a similar robe over me, its dark fibers trapping what little warmth I had against my skin. "There. Now, isn't that better?"

Black and winged shapes moved about behind the senior Grayson.

"Angela." I yanked her toward me with uncoordinated hands. "We're surrounded."

"I know dear. They're the ones that gave us these robes."

Cold blue flame flickered from a narrow fire and cast the black figures in a dim and twisted glow. Bat-like wings pulled in tight beneath stone walls and pressed uncomfortably against thin and gangly bodies. Distended bellies and sagging faces frowned in the fire's dim light.

"Inncubi..." I pulled Angela against me, her shroud warm in the cold fire. "Don't talk to them and whatever you do, don't let them touch you."

"Oh, honey. It's fine. Your little pink monster said as much."

"Stewart?"

As if on command, the tiny Demon drifted down on bent

wings, then landed awkwardly on my shoulder. "Yeah, I did, and we'll stay fine provided you do what I said you'd do."

"What's that?" I asked, keeping my back against the wall and my eyes affixed on the grotesque shapes in front of me.

"You're going to help them escape the Gloom."

"I'm what?!"

* * *

THE TINY PINK Demon bobbed his head. "You're going to use your Magick to open a portal out of the Gloom so this nice family of Succubi can leave."

"Stewart, I—"

The Imp grabbed my ear with his sharp claws. "Yes, you are going to use your power as a servant of the Void to open a portal."

"But I—"

"Can't go back to Hell right now? They understand. In fact, they have no interest in returning there. None of them do. The Calamity holds court there, and no one here wants to see her again, right?"

A loose chorus of nods from the bat-winged Demons said as much.

"Stewart, may I talk to you for a minute?"

The Imp shook his tiny head. "Not a good time for that, no. I told them you need a break to commune with the Void and prepare the appropriate sigil, then it's off to the real world for all of us."

"Stewart, I'm not a ride-sharing service!"

Black wings opened and closed around us, frustration apparent on their horned faces.

"I think what you *meant* to say, is that you are very pleased with the gift of the Shrouds they have left for you and the blind woman."

"I'm not blind—"

Stewart waved Angela away with a pink clawed hand. "And that you will use this tribute to prepare the necessary Magick."

"Stewart…"

The diminutive Hellspawn leapt into the air, his damaged wings beating badly in the cold of the Gloom. "We must prepare the Magick. Leave us to our work."

"No." The largest Demon shook his gaunt and horned head. "We are staying right here."

"I would advise against it." I took a deep breath and closed my eyes. I pushed aside the dark cold of the Gloom and reached for my Magick. I let what little power I could scrape up rattle my words like a megaphone. "The Void is eternal and without end. It is Magick, and Magick is me!"

A little melodramatic, but when dealing with Demons over the top is acceptable.

I opened my eyes to find the Demons filing out a broken door, their long tails dragging on the ash-covered ground.

Stewart flashed me a wink.

This is great and all, but I have no idea how I'm supposed to—

"Eugene Law?" a thin and shrill voice said from the retreating masses.

"Uh…"

A twisted and broken nose greeted me from the crowd. Her claws bent and wings torn, the weak half-succubus shuffled out of the pack. "Eugene Law, the father of Cathy Law?"

Stewart flapped frantically, trying to block the young demon and her words, but it was too little, too late. The retreating monsters had returned.

"Do I know—"

The half-demon's wings flared open as she pointed a withered finger at me. "I am Lucina Crowley."

Oh, shit.

20

WITHOUT END

"$\mathcal{G}$ene…" Angela pressed against me, backing away as the angry mob returned.

"Lucina, it's good to see you."

The Demon girl's wings shuddered. "This is the Calamity's father. You want to bring her to her knees? You start by ending her father."

Stewart flapped in front of the young woman and waved his hands erratically. "He speaks for the Void—I would be very careful what you say."

"And you." Lucina held up her black and withered arm. "You did this to me. You sided with a Magician over one of your own."

The room took a decidedly sharp turn away from potentially helpful and straight into the rough road to ruin.

"I did what my master asked of me—"

Strong black claws ripped Stewart from the air. The host of monsters pressed in on us.

"He was only trying to protect me from you," I said, keeping Angela behind me. "If I recall correctly, you were the one that tried to suck my life force out through a straw."

"Your daughter didn't stop!" Lucina cried, her human half showing through the tears that rimmed those dark eyes. "She followed me here, then destroyed the only other world I've ever known."

"She's confused—"

"The Calamity knows exactly what she is doing, and she's not going to stop with Hell."

"What do you mean?"

Lucina swung her withered arm in a wide arc. "The Gloom is next, and from there, other worlds. Her army grows bigger by the day, as do her plans for it. She has broken Obelleron and set in motion the end of all of us."

"And what if she has?"

"Gene…" Angela tightened her grip on my shoulder.

"So what? Last I checked, Hell was full of the darkest evil and vile things ever created. So what if she destroys them?"

"This isn't exactly helping," Angela whispered, her surprisingly strong fingers clamping down on my shoulder.

"You're right." Lucina unfurled her diminutive wings to their full size, the broken bones beneath painful to watch. "It doesn't matter what happens to us, the monsters under your bed. To you we can all die, and your world would be a better place."

Demonic faces shared concerned glances.

What is she getting at?

Lucina paced the narrow gap in front of us, her tail sweeping the ash-covered stone. "But then, what fills that void? I mean, you should know, shouldn't you? You are the Void's proxy. You are the defender of Magick eternal."

"Well—"

The young Demon clutched her withered hand to her sagging chest. "When there's blood in the water, the sharks come."

I shook my head. "I'm getting a lesson in life from an apex

predator, now? You wouldn't have stopped. You would have consumed all of me."

"I eat to survive, to stay alive, and take my place in the great plan. You think this place happened by accident? The Damned aren't just some play thing. They had their chance and have been judged. Their burning skin and tar-black eyes are an eternal reminder. It is our job to keep them contained."

"So, you failed. Listen, as a guy without his wife, his daughter, and his son, and whose car was just torn apart by an army of those very same Damned, I know failure. You could say it's my thing, but I don't go around pointing fingers. I get up, dust myself off, and keep going."

"What happens when we're gone, Magician? Have you ever stopped to ask yourself that?"

"I—"

"Where the New Dead go, Hell will follow." Lucina pointed to the thick scars on the body of a nearby Succubus. "Do you think it stops here?"

"Cathy is—"

"The Calamity isn't satisfied with this Hell, and she won't be until we have all been destroyed."

"And what happens then?" I asked. "What happens when you are all gone?"

Lucina grabbed the edge of my Death Shroud coat and pulled me to an opening in the broken stone wall. She showed me the distant dark and swirling ash of the Gloom. "We are the gatekeepers, the jailers, and the tormentors. You want to know what will happen without us in Hell? Look."

Lucina pointed a withered finger at the horizon where the Gloom had taken on a reddish glow. It wasn't often, but I'd seen the Gloom burn before, the Library's doors, and the worst showing of Demon High to name a few.

"I've seen the Gloom burn before. It's not new—"

"That's not the Gloom burning, Gene." Lucina shoved my face toward the horizon's edge. "Look closer."

I squinted in the chilling breeze. She was right, it wasn't the Gloom burning, it was something else, something bigger. It moved like a fire and consumed everything in its path.

Cavalry!

"What do you see, Magician?"

"I see—"

"You see the Calamity. She has come, and with her Hell follows."

Thundering and fiery hooves rumbled over the distant hills like a rolling wave of death, and with them came the blood-chilling cries of an uncountable number of New Dead, their rusty blades held high.

"Did she stop with Hell?" Lucina asked, her words sharp and biting.

"She's come to the Gloom…"

The Half-Succubus nodded. "She has, and from here she will come to your world. The dead do not suffer the living. Your daughter has done the unthinkable. She has challenged the Defiler and rides Obelleron into battle, and in doing so upset the balance on an infinite scale."

Cathy… What have you done?

"I…"

Crash!

A Demonic face filled the open door to our narrow room. "The Damned!"

The sounds of battle echoed down the hall. Rusty blades and claws rang out in the cold air of the Gloom. Lucina grabbed my arm and pointed to Angela. "Get them both. We will bargain for our lives by giving the Calamity what she wants."

"Lucina, I know you have no reason to trust me, but if you give me up to her, she won't stop. I know my daughter, she won't let you—any of you—live."

Horned and hesitant faces turned to me, and the young Half-Succubus.

"He's lying—"

"Look at what she is capable of." I pointed to the distant horde. "She is the Calamity, the Wild Reaving. Do you think her army stops for any of us?" I shook my head. "We're an ink stain in the annals of her new history. They'll mow us down right along with the rest of you. If we have any chance of stopping what my daughter has become, we have to do it together."

"Ignore him, he's trying to confuse—"

"Behind you!" Angela cried.

A long and wicked blade erupted from a large Demon's chest, dark blood spilled on the stone ground.

New Dead!

Wild ashen faces swarmed the narrow room, their hammered-rebar blades cutting a bloody path of destruction. Demon wings unfurled and claws slashed, and in an instant, it became impossible to see past the melee.

"Angela, where's Stewart?"

The pink Demon stumbled into view, his already crooked wings twisted painfully behind him. "I'm here, Boss."

Adam's mother scooped him up and tucked him to her ample bosom like a practiced pro. "I got you."

Lucina's long claws clutched at my Shroud, while tears glistened in the red-rims of her eyes. "This is the Calamity! This is what you brought us. It will come for you. It will come for all of you."

"Gene, look out!" Angela's shrouded hand pointed behind me.

A New Dead rebar blade cut the air in a perfect arc designed to detach my head from my shoulders.

Clang!

The Half-Succubus caught the sword's edge with her good hand and lost a finger in the process. "Argh!" The young Demon immediately went on the offensive, her long legs tearing into New Dead like the claws her withered hand lacked. "Do you mean it?"

"Do I mean what?"

"Will you stop her?" Lucina asked, her body slowly being surrounded by ashen faces of burning Damned.

"The Wild Reaving cannot be stopped!" the Damned shouted, their blades leaving deep gashes in the young Demon's skin. "The Calamity has come!"

Our eyes locked, and in that instant Lucina's human half shone through. She wasn't a monster. She was a young girl who'd made a lot of mistakes, and somewhere along the way had lost sight of who she was. The Calamity had taken that from her, and wouldn't stop there. My daughter would rain Hell down upon more worlds than this.

The dead do not suffer the living.

Rusty blades tore through Lucina's flesh and cut away at the broken and dying girl. Wings ripped, and a withered arm faded beneath the hailstorm of tarry eyed anger.

The Calamity had come, and there was only one thing I could do about it.

21

STANDARDIZED TESTING

"Gene," Angela shook me out of my haze. "We need to go, now!"

Clang!

Rusted blades clashed against stone-hard claws, and while the Demons had fought hard, they'd been no match for the Calamity's soldiers.

New Dead cut them down like saplings.

"Right, come on," I said, pulling up the hood to cover my face. "Tuck Stewart under your shroud and stay close."

Angela nodded, appearing to be brave, but the fear in her eyes told me otherwise. She might be pretty comfortable around the Magickal world, but we were in the deep water now.

Adam's mother and I slipped out the open archway, our shrouds decent cover in the shadowy darkness of the Gloom. We turned down one hallway after another, our tired legs driven like plow-horses by frantic minds. While I was sure she wanted to, we didn't dare speak. New Dead and other less-savory creatures of the eternal twilight paid us little attention as we passed, in some cases giving us a wide berth given the terrifying nature of our disguise.

After what had felt like hours, a cold and quiet hand tugged on my shroud. Angela's worn face appeared beneath the folds of the Death Shroud's hood, her skin sagging and her eyes tired. "Rest…"

I lead her into a small stone room, and pushed out the lone Umbraling nesting in the corner, then made sure there were no more lurking in the dark waiting for a nice snack.

Angela flopped down in the now empty room and gently retrieved the tiny pink Demon from her arms. Stewart was in rough shape. I'd seen him beat up before, but never like this.

The dead do not suffer the living.

"Will he… survive?" a worried mother asked.

I nodded. "It takes a lot more than that to kill an Imp."

"How do you know?" Angela laid the diminutive Demon on the Umbraling's discarded nest.

"Because I've killed one before."

Adam's mother looked at me with sad eyes. "Why?"

Bile swirled in my clenched gut. "I—"

"Because I told you to."

The House!

Angela's voice twisted into the unmistakable and alien timbre of the shifting Void. "What happened to listening to me?"

"I'm not abandoning my friends."

Adam's mother shook her head and laid a gentle hand on the sleeping Imp. "I didn't ask you to do that. I told you that you would need the whole bag of mixed nuts if you were going to stop what's coming."

"The Defiler? I can—"

Angela chuckled and flipped the Death Shroud's hood back. "Asaroth? He's the least of your problems now."

"What do you mean?"

Angela pointed to the cuts on Stewart's pink and rubbery skin. "The Calamity has grown powerful, too powerful. She's not satisfied with Hell, Gene."

"I'm not going to kill my daughter."

Angela sighed. "You might not have a choice. What will you do when the Wild Reaving comes to take me? Will you let the Calamity hold infinity?"

A vision of my daughter, Private Petty's saber in hand, and leading a charge against the House, thundered through my mind. Wild hair streamed out like unholy fire from her helmet as she cut down everyone I'd ever loved, Petty's silver blade stained red with the blood of my friends.

I shook the vision away. "But what can I do?"

"There's only one thing you can do, Gene. You cannot let any of them destroy me in my moment of rebirth."

"Them?"

Angela pulled stray hairs away from her matronly face. "Yes, them. It would appear more than Morgan escaped the library's prison."

"Prison?"

"Yes, prison. Do you think you're the first Magician since the dawn of time to have to deal with this? I've been reborn before, and sometimes, when there's chum in the water, it brings some pretty big sharks."

"So, you built the library?"

"Of course." Angela tucked the sleeping Imp in the Umbraling's downy webbing. "And you made sure Morgan ended up inside. While I wasn't convinced she'd pose a threat when it came down to it, it wasn't worth risking either."

My stomach dropped. "You knew. You knew all along that I would—"

"I knew you would do what it took to be the hero. You always have, even when you weren't sure you wanted to."

"I carried that guilt for years."

Angela nodded. "How do they make steel, Gene?"

"I don't—"

Adam's mom pushed herself up and stretched her tired body.

"They beat the hell out of it. That's what they do. They shove it in the flames, hammer the heck out of it, then into the water and start all over again. That's what you and I have been doing all this time. We are hammering you into a razor's edge."

"Why me?"

"Because, Gene." Angela placed a shrouded hand on my shoulder. "You care."

"But you could have had anyone, Viktor, Morgan, even one of the Magicians of old."

Adam's mom shook her head, her short hair tangled in soot and ash. "I've tried trained killers, Gene. I've tried attack dogs and murders—never works."

"But why me?"

"Because you have a heart. It took me a few rebirths to figure it out, but I didn't need power—I can provide that right up until the end—what I did need is someone that cares. I needed a father, and not just any father. I needed a monkey that was willing to do whatever it took for the greater good. I needed someone so willing to sacrifice that they would give up their own child."

The vision came fast, crashing through my skull like a tidal wave. I held Cathy's Thread in my bloody hands, while my daughter twisted like a box-kite above the infernal pull of Hell itself.

"Dad! Don't let me go!"

My hands shook and I blinked back the tears but the memory kept coming.

"He's coming, Gene! The Defiler is coming! You have to close the gate!" my apprentice shouted, his hand on my shoulder.

"I can save her!"

"No, you can't. You have to let her go."

Cathy's red-rimmed eyes pleaded with me. "Dad, don't! Dad!"

"Close the gate." Adam's words echoed in my ears.

"Finis!"

The burning flare cut through my skin like a hot knife, my blood mixing with the sulfurous flame and sealing the sacrifice that stopped the Defiler, and in doing so, created the Calamity.

My shoulders dropped. "It was all a test…"

"Of course it was." Angela smiled. "It's been a test since the very beginning, but like I said before, you are a special monkey. You have so much power. Magick loves you, did you know that?"

I didn't answer. My mind was lost, trapped in the eyes of my daughter.

Angela didn't bother waiting for me to respond. "It always has. You have a way with it that few do. Sure, Viktor was an amazing Magician, but the Magick didn't love him. Even Ten Spins, for all his soul-crushing strength, he never understood what Magick truly is."

"What is it?"

"It's the lifeblood of the universe, Gene. It's what makes this whole stupid thing worth doing. It's the smile in Porter's eyes, and the giggle from your son's mouth. It's the rain on a perfect day, and the sadness of a daughter lost. You can't paint a picture with one color, you need them all. Magick is the music of life, Gene, in all of its joy and pain." Angela winked. "And life likes complicated people."

I closed my eyes, blotting out the House, its words, and everything else until all I could see was my daughter. Not the Calamity, with her wild hair and devil steed, but the Cathy whose smile reminded me exactly what made life worth living.

What do I do?

My imaginary daughter placed a hand on mine and spoke no words, her soft fingers cold against my skin.

I can't do it to you again.

Cathy broke apart before my eyes, her face blowing away

like dust in the wind until all that remained was the black and charred remains of a spent flare.

"You've said your goodbyes, Gene."

"Goodbyes? What do you mean? I'm not killing my daughter."

Angela sighed and returned to her seat next to Stewart. "In the end you may not have that luxury, but for now, you are doing no one any good in the Gloom."

"I don't have the Magick to get back to Hell."

Adam's mother coughed. "I am well aware of just how much Magick you have and don't have available. We need some help, and I have a bead on exactly what sort of help that will be." Angela gently scooped up Stewart and pressed the tiny Demon into my hands. "You'll need him, and others."

"Others?"

Angela nodded and placed both hands on my shoulders. "Yeah, they are irritating, but sometimes irritating is what the day calls for."

"I don't understand."

"You will."

Angela's smile vanished in a wash of white.

22

REUNION

*B*eep.

Tiny lights, like cheap Christmas bulbs, winked in and out in the dark. First, red, and then green, the diodes flashed in a rhythmic pattern, while above them a computer display rattled off a series of numbers.

"Angela," I whispered, groping in the darkness for the familiar shrouded form.

"Gene, what happened? Where are we?"

The subtle sound of movement caught my heart in my chest. "I'm not sure, I think it's a—"

Yip! Yip! Yip!

The dog's piercing bark set my hairs on end, but that was nothing compared to the dull thump of a cane against my head.

Smack!

"I'm not dead yet!" a voice cried out in the dark. That shout was immediately followed up by another polished metal rap against my temple. The room spun, and I stumbled into Angela, knocking her and Stewart's sleeping form to the floor.

I raised my hands to stop my unseen assailant. "Stop, I'm not—"

Smack!

"Death Shrouds?! Oh no, wasn't enough to send one of you, they had to send two, huh? Well, it doesn't matter, because I'm not done yet."

Smack!

The metal cane cracked across my fingers. "Ouch! Stop, I'm not a—"

Sharp teeth bit into the folds of my makeshift disguise, yanking on the heavy fabric.

Grrr!

I tried to pull the tattered shroud back but only received another cane strike for my effort.

Smack!

"I'm not dead yet!"

Click.

Bright fluorescent bulbs illuminated the thin form of a balding man. A cane tight in his whitened knuckles, he stood tethered to a nearby hospital bed, his gossamer gown doing little to hide withering skin. He raised the polished metal for yet another smack, when Angela threw back her hood and stopped him cold.

"Huh? You aren't Death Shrouds?" He tilted his head.

There was something oddly familiar about that guy.

Grrr.

A tiny ball of fur tugged on my sleeve. The dog wasn't much bigger than a shoebox, but appeared ready to match the old man's aggression pound for pound.

I pushed my hood back. "No, we're not Death Shrouds."

"You're not?"

"Do they normally do this much talking?" I asked, undoing the loose threads that held the robe together.

"Well, no…"

"Right." I nodded. "That's because we aren't Death Shrouds. Listen, I'm sorry we scared you and your dog, but we aren't here to hurt you."

The old man shook his head. "Ha! I'd have liked to see you try. Seriously, anything to shake up the boredom."

There was something about that voice, something I couldn't place. I'd heard it before. I was sure of that, but where?

Leaning on his cane and with his tiny dog in tow, the old man returned to his bed. He gathered up his long wires and tubes with a practiced precision and gently laid them aside. "You better not be here to ask me to knit you anything."

Knit?

"No, I don't think we are," I said, sharing an equally confused look with Angela.

"Good, cause I'm busy with another project."

Adam's mother removed her shroud and deposited it on a nearby chair, her arms still cradling the resting Stewart.

"Imp," the old man hissed.

Yip! Yip! Yip!

The orange ball of rabid fur bounced to attention, while his master reached for the cane again. "Magicians..."

Harold!

The memory came back like the rushing wind. I'd met that feisty Illickthid in a hospital room much like this one so many years ago that the details were hazy. Back then he hadn't been the patient, that had been Ed Lovely, or what had remained of him. Harold and his wife were Soul Weavers, and they did the unimaginable—they knitted Ed's soul.

"Get out of my room, now!"

"Harold?"

The Illickthid's second eyelid blinked. "Do I know you?"

"It's me, Eugene Law."

"Doesn't ring any bells."

I placed my hands on the foot of the bed, then yanked them back lest they get nipped off by the dog's tiny teeth. "It was a long time ago. You and your wife saved my friend, Ed Lovely.

She knit his soul back together, or what was left of it. We were in a hospital much like this one."

Harold scrunched his patchy eyebrows together. "Gainesville?"

"Yes!"

Yip! Yip!

The dog bounced around at the foot of the bed, ready to pounce should I get a single step closer.

"Bobbin, down." Harold snapped his fingers and the tiny dog dropped to its stomach, but didn't take an eye off me.

"I think I remember you. Didn't you try to sell us life insurance?"

"No, we went into the Gloom to—"

Harold waved me off. "Well, I could use some life insurance now, even if it's just for Bobbin. I have no idea if she'll take care of him after I'm gone. I mean, she talks a big game, but you have to be wary of anyone with—"

"Harold, we need your help."

The old man crossed his arms. "I already told you. I'm not knitting anything."

"No one said anything about knitting. I need the Harold that cut down Reavers like a champ."

"Those were the good old days."

"Can you do it? Can you change back into him?" I asked, keeping a wary eye on the tiny dog and his impossibly sharp teeth.

Harold sighed. "Only one more time. The change takes a heavy toll, kid. I promised Dorothy I wouldn't."

Dorothy? His wife.

"What about her?" I asked, checking the rest of the room. "Would she be willing to help?"

Harold sighed and pulled the tiny orange monster into his lap. "She would if she were here." He turned his attention to a small photo on the nightstand. It held the younger and smiling face of Harold's wife, the Illickthid who'd single-handedly restored Ed Lovely in the hour of our greatest need. "She was the real talent. I was just the guy who held the threads."

"Your wife?" Angela asked.

Harold nodded. "She passed two years ago. At least, I think's been two years."

Shit.

I joined Angela at the bedside and started to say something, but she gently cut me off. "I'm sorry. My Charlie has been gone for a long time, too."

"Does it get any easier?"

Adam's mother shook her head. "No, I'm sorry, it doesn't. But," Angela extended her cupped hand and the undersized puffball climbed out of Harold's lap to inspect them. "I can tell you this. I wouldn't want it to. He's with me all the time." Angela ran a hand down the dog's fur. "You know he built a coffee table?"

"That's nice."

Adam's mother nodded. "It's terrible."

Harold snorted out a light-hearted chuckle. "Yeah?"

Angela smiled and let Bobbin lick her fingers. "Oh yeah, it wobbles so bad I'd swear that was by design. He put a drawer on it and then proceeded to glue it shut."

Harold laughed, coughing a bit in the process. "Oh, no."

"Oh, yes." Angela opened her arms and the orange puffball jumped into them. "It's a complete eyesore, but every single time I stop myself from putting a cup on it, I remember Charlie."

"He was just trying to be useful," Harold said, his old fingers drifting to Dorothy's picture. "I wish I could be useful now, Eugene Law, but I'm afraid my days of fighting Reavers are behind me."

Adam's mom placed the dog back in the elderly Illickthid's lap. "You're a sweet man, and he's a sweet dog."

Click.

The room plunged into darkness.

"Angela!"

Adam's mother screamed, while sharp thorn-like spikes dug into my skin and pushed me back against the wall. I'd felt claws like that before, a long time ago. "Deacon!"

The thin gasp of a woman's voice caught me off guard. "Gene?"

Click.

Light returned to the tiny room, and I'd almost wished it hadn't. It had been over a decade since I'd seen Sofia, and things weren't looking good for the Wild Magick wielding Skeeter. She'd taken to shaving her head, the hair too thin to keep. The rest of her body held a mosaic of tattoos, each one more complex than the last, and each a sigil in its own right. Her torn leather vest afforded easy access to the six insect-like arms that retracted against her rib cage.

"Sofia—"

Colored a deep and angry purple, Stewart hovered poorly on damaged wings next to the door. "Let him go, or I swear I'll use every ounce of my newly restored power to introduce you to a bug zapper."

Wild Magick swelled like you'd sucked the air out of the room with a hose. The pressure drop told me exactly what I hadn't wanted to know—Sofia had been practicing.

The Skeeter's tattoos lit up in a bright and angry red.

Crap.

2 3

KNITTED POTENTIAL

*I*nsect arms pressed me against the cold and sterile wall of Harold's hospital room. They were much longer and sharper than I remembered them.

"Everybody calm down," I said, trying desperately to keep an already crowded room from going nova.

The bright and sparkling aura of Magick crackled around Stewart's tiny fingers. "Are you okay, boss?"

"Boss?" Sofia wrinkled her face. "You're cavorting with Imps now?"

What little Wild Magick there was in that science-laden hospital room washed over me.

"Imps?!" Stewart's bent wing barely produced enough power to keep him aloft. "Gene and I are exclusive, thank you very much. Right, Gene?"

"Stewart," I said, my voice strained from the Skeeter's pressing rib arms. "This is Sofia. I haven't seen her since forever. She's not going to hurt me… I hope."

"That depends." Insect arms twisted deeper into my skin. "I need that net, and if you even think of taking it from me…"

"Net?"

Harold opened the tiny drawer of his hospital-issue night-stand. "She's trying to catch a Duplickity." He retrieved a tightly wrapped bundle of dark and light fibers.

"With that?"

The old Illickthid nodded and gently unwrapped the complex knitting in his lap. "Yes."

"You don't need a net to catch a Duplickity," I said, shaking my own head in the process. "You just need to be willing to join the Flock."

Sofia frowned. "They kicked me out."

"What?" I'd never heard of someone getting kicked out before, because they typically didn't survive the aftermath. "How'd that—"

"They refused to give me an egg." The glow in Sofia's tattoos subsided, and she retracted her insect arms, returning them to the hidden gaps between her ribs. "And I need one, Gene. I have to have it."

"Your dad..."

The Skeeter closed her eyes and turned away. "He's worse now, much, much worse. I've traveled the length of the state and consulted with anyone I could find. There is no cure left, nothing short of a Duplickity egg can undo the transformation now."

Miguel...

My mind drifted back to the early days of my marriage to Porter. That first job, first real apartment, and as luck would have it, our first real run-in with terrifying evil as a couple. In the waning moments of the Blood Queen's reign, my wife had been transformed, much like Sofia's father, except I'd had an ace up my sleeve—a pregnant Duplickity. The tiny Invisible Yard Art gave away its life to grant me that egg. Brimming with potential, the crystalline gift brought with it the one thing I needed—a chance for Porter.

But not Miguel.

It was my fault. I shattered the egg and at the same time doomed her father to a hellish existence as the Magick of Delia's twisted Viburna ate away his humanity.

"Yeah. So I made her a net in exchange for setting me up in this nice place," Harold said, his voice interrupting a rather somber moment.

"Will that even work?"

The Skeeter turned back to me with red in her eyes. "It's the only option I have left. I joined the Flock, but they refused me an egg, just like they refused Delia, but unlike her, I have friends."

The old Illickthid bobbed his tired head. "Sofia was my dear wife's nurse in her final days. She came to our house and brought her food. In those last weeks, this young woman gave so much of herself for someone else that my wife felt a duty to help her in return. You remember how she was…"

"I do," I said, thinking back to the Soul Weaver's work on Ed's stitched soul.

"So that brings us to this." Harold unfolded the shimmering net in his lap, letting the edges tumble down the sides of the bed.

"Is that really a Duplickity net?"

Harold pursed his lips. "Well, yes and no. Those tiny pink birds are such confusing creatures, but I think they have enough spirit to be wrapped up in a Soul Net."

"Soul Net?" Angela asked, leaning over to run her fingers along the narrow threads. "You can capture Souls with this?"

"Only lost ones, but yes, that's what you'll be able to do with it when it's done. The problem is, I'm not the artisan my wife was, and she hadn't finished it before she died. So—"

Sofia placed her tattooed hands on the bed, letting them trace the net's intricate weave. "So, I called in a bunch of favors and got Harold a spot here, at the Hospice."

"Hospice?" Stewart asked, landing on my shoulder.

Harold nodded. "It's where you go when you are going to kick the bucket."

"Oh."

The old Illickthid sighed and tugged at the edges with his fingers. "I have no idea if I'll be done in time, but I'm going to try."

"Sofia," I said, placing a hand on the unnaturally warm Skeeter. "There's a much bigger problem, and I'm afraid if we don't resolve it first, there won't be a Miguel to save."

"What are you talking about?"

"Do you remember the House? Do you remember when I asked you to think about it, to imagine the peeling paint and tall weeds?"

Sofia furrowed her eyebrows. "Yes."

"I let it out."

Yip! Yip!

Mosquito arms erupted back out of Sofia's sides like a trap-door spider's surprise attack. She had both Stewart and I pinned to the wall again, except this time there was a much more murderous look in her eyes. "Why? Why would you do something like that? Do you work for it now? Do you work for 69 Mallory Lane?"

"Yes."

Sofia's eyes took on a decidedly angry hue. "So, you are here to take my Duplickity, is that it? You want the Soul Net so you can find yourself an egg and undo all the mistakes you've made."

"No."

"I don't believe you. You're the one screwing with my Magick. You and your Imp."

I shook my head and let my shoulders drop. "No, that's not me. That's the reset."

"Reset?"

Stewart's tiny claws swung at the Skeeter but were too far away to make contact. "The reset, the rebirth, whatever you want to call it. The Void resets every so many years, and it's about to happen again. In that moment, Magick will stop, just long enough for it to collapse and then be born again."

"That's crazy. You expect me to believe that?"

"It's the truth," I said, no longer fighting against the mosquito arms.

"If that's so, then why are you in this, Gene? What's your angle?"

"I lost my daughter to the gates of Hell, and when I couldn't get her back, I did unthinkable…"

Sofia's sharp claw-like arms relaxed slightly. "You unlocked the door."

"I did. I let the House back into the world, and since then I've been trying to make it right. My daughter's soul shattered into three pieces, one of them is here in the real world, one is trapped in the Defiler's black tentacles, but it is the last that has turned Hell upside down. My daughter has become—"

"The Calamity," Stewart said, still fighting against Sofia's claws.

"The who?"

"The leader of a New Dead rebellion."

Harold sat up in his bed. "New Dead?"

Stewart nodded. "Yes, you know, black tar-filled eyes, ashen skin? The whipping boys and girls of Hell? Yeah, she's built an army and it would appear she's decided that Hell is not enough."

"I don't understand how this affects me?" Sofia said, tightening her grip on the rubbery Demon.

Harold shook his head. "It affects all of us."

"How?"

"In the moment of rebirth the Void is defenseless," I said, pointing to the bed-ridden Illickthid. "As you can imagine, that's when it's going to be open season on the power of infinite Magick."

"Infinite Magick..." The words tumbled off Sofia's lips in a decidedly scary fashion.

"Yes, well, that's the theory. It's my job to make sure that doesn't happen."

"Watch it, boss," Stewart whispered.

The elaborate tattoos on Sofia's skin shifted, colors popping in and out along the complex lines. "So, without you the House is defenseless."

"Wait, Sofia, you don't understand—"

The Skeeter let go of her Soul Net. "No, Gene, you don't understand. I'm done waiting. I'm done watching my father's brain rot like a gut-fish in the sun. If I can't get a Duplickity egg, then I'll get something far better."

Magick crackled around Stewart's tail. "Boss..."

"Sofia, don't do it. This is an Imp. You know what Imps are, and what they are capable of. This Minor Demon can screw with your Magick something fierce, you don't want to make—"

"Boss?"

"Stewart, I'm trying to make a point here—"

"Boss? We have a bigger problem."

"Damn it, Stewart. What is the problem?"

The tiny Imp pointed to the door where a woman I didn't expect to see again in my life leaned against the frame.

"Hey, Gene."

Morgan!

24

FRESH BATTERIES

"*W*ho the heck are you?" Harold asked, his inner eyelid snapping in and out like a high-speed camera.

"An Illickthid? My goodness, Gene. You keep really interesting company anymore."

"Boss, that's the—"

"I know who it is, Stewart." My fingers tightened into fists and I had to fight to keep my boiling emotions in check.

Sofia had no such compunctions.

The Skeeter's unused insect arms unfolded like a switchblade, snapping out of the open side of her chest and reaching for Morgan. Sharp tips quivered in the air and stopped cold only inches from my ex.

Apparently unimpressed, Morgan titled her head. "What are you? Some sort of hideous mantis love-child?"

Sofia growled and pushed harder, her segmented legs vibrating with frustration.

Stewart pressed his body against my head. "Boss…"

Morgan's Magick ticked away with practiced precision, the clockwork nature of it so unique and also so deadly. My ex rarely left anything to chance, and it certainly appeared that was still the case now.

Wait, something's different...

Morgan's Magick was still rigidly precise and organized, much like the woman behind it, but something didn't line up. There was a twisted tint to her power, something I'd never directly felt before. It was not unlike the House's oily sheen, but more violent and erratic.

Her Magick is not entirely her own!

My ex sauntered into the over-crowded hospital room with an air of superiority, her power easily keeping Sofia's insect arms at bay. "Gene, you're a tough person to find."

"Funny. After you ran scared from that Old Dead, I thought I wouldn't see you again."

Stewart pressed his lips up to my ear. "Boss, you want me to disrupt her Magick?"

"Not until I know what she's here for."

"Smart."

Hardly.

The Magician's heels clacked on the polished floor. She made it about half way into the room then stopped. She tilted her head as if to taste the air. "It is true! I almost didn't believe it when he told me. You took the deal with 69 Mallory Lane, didn't you?"

I didn't respond. I didn't have to.

"You did! Oh, Gene Law, the infallible, the holy, the faithful, you took the House's deal—"

"Yes, I did. I did it because my daughter's soul was sucked up into a Hellgate. A Hellgate that was created—"

"That was created by your apprentice, not me." Morgan's icy voice echoed in the tiny room. "I didn't doom your daughter. You did the moment you brought her into this world. She was weak, and whose fault was that?"

"Who is this, Gene?" Sofia's claws dug into my flesh, and I

really wanted to know what Magick Morgan was using to keep the same thing from happening to her.

"This is—"

"Morgan Crowley." My ex gently pushed aside the Skeeter's hungry arms. "I'm the woman who taught Gene Magick, and I'm the same one whose Thread he snapped after I taught him how."

Sofia turned back to me. "Is this true?"

"There's a lot missing, but yeah."

The Skeeter wiped a hand across her bald head. "I don't care. Neither of you are getting my Duplickity Net."

Morgan furrowed her brow. "What's that?"

"Don't play the fool with me. You're here for the Duplickity Net, but I'm not going to let you have it."

"Sweetheart, why settle for fish sticks when you can get the whole tuna?"

Now it was Sofia's turn to look confused.

"I don't need a little plastic bird's egg, as interesting as they are, because I'm here for the Void's protector. I'm here to stop the one person standing between me and infinite Magick."

Given the look on her face, this Sofia understood. "Get in line. He's mine. If infinite Magick is up for grabs, I can use it to undo my father's curse."

Morgan smiled, the same sort of expression apex predators flash right before they devour their prey. "Father? Trust me, sweetheart, you don't need him. As one woman to—well, whatever you are—you can let the old man there die. He's not worth it."

Harold looked up from his net, his face set like flint. "I wasn't sure at first, but now that you've stood in my room and breathed my air, I am. You are the same young woman who summoned Reavers from the Gloom in my hometown. You are the same woman that let my good friend die at the hands of the same. I never forgot your scent."

The rarely flustered Morgan took a scant step back, apparently unsure what to make of the bed-ridden old Illickthid. "That was a long time ago."

"We don't forget," Harold said, pulling the sheets off his bed.

Yip! Yip!

"Now, Boss?" Stewart's lips tickled at my ear.

I shook my head.

"When?"

I settled on a side-eyed glare and hoped the tiny Demon would get the hint. I wasn't sure if it worked, but he did stop talking.

Morgan held her palms up. "You don't want to do this, old one. Trust me. Just get back in bed and stay there. You want nothing to do with the power I run with now."

There it is! I knew there was something different about her. She's not alone, but who is she working with? Knowing Morgan it could be anyone. Had she sucked up some poor soul? Or was it something worse?

Harold placed his pale and wrinkled feet on the polished ground. The hospital gown swished gently in the cool air. "I'm not afraid of you."

"You should be." Morgan's Magick prickled the air, its deadly precision circling like a boa constrictor, but there was something more violent in the constricting coils.

Harold yanked the tubes from his arm and tossed the bleeding stubs on the bed.

Blood!

It wasn't much, but the Skeeter folds of Sofia's jaws rippled just a bit.

Shit. Can this get any worse?

The piercing wail of a Reaver shattered the relative quiet of the hospice.

"What the hell was that?" Angela asked, scooping up the tiny dog and hugging it to her chest.

Harold's frail hand wrapped around the collar of his frail gown and with a yank he tore it from his withered body. "Reaver!"

"Now, Boss?"

"No."

The old Illickthid's skin split, his flesh giving way to the chitinous exoskeleton hidden underneath. The knotted head of an iridescent mantis erupted from the withered flesh of Harold's face and shined in the harsh light.

Sofia's insect arms ripped out of my body, her attention now fixated on the budding Illickthid. "Stop, you can't survive another transformation. You know that!"

Harold's gruff voice twisted into the screeching and high-pitched tone of an angry Illickthid. "I don't care. If I die, it will be in battle, not wasting away in this bed."

"But the net?"

Mantis claws unfolded from the remains of Harold's pale and sickly arms. "Our deal is done, little one. I have given you all I could."

"No!" Sofia blocked the rapidly expanding monster's path, her jaw unfolding like fleshy origami. "That's not the deal."

The screeching wail of a Reaver cut through the walls and was quickly followed by the screams of something else.

Innocent people... Crap.

Morgan's Magick flooded the tiny room.

"Now, Stewart."

The tiny Imp nodded. "You got it, boss. Let's see how she likes this." Stewart snapped his tail like the crack of a whip.

Nothing happened.

"Stewart…"

The Illickthid's razor-like claws scissored the air in front of Sofia, their long hooks wicked in the bright hospital light, while behind the angry Skeeter, Morgan was busy preparing something. The room practically crackled with my ex-girlfriend's newly violent Magick.

Where is she getting this from?

The Void was dying, which meant Magick was at a premium, but somehow Morgan seemed to not be affected by this recent turn of events.

"Give me a second." Stewart snapped his tail a few more times. "I don't get it. This always works…"

Morgan's sly smile gave us our answer. "Something not working over there? Is someone having performance issues?"

"Stewart, what's going—"

The tiny Imp bounced around on my shoulder like a frustrated Pixie. "I don't know."

"I've learned a few things since the last time we met, Gene."

A Reaver's wild yell shook the door.

Morgan squeezed her hands into her chest, the Magick erupting from them was strong enough to force me to cover my eyes.

Morgan's never held that much power before.

The black metal of a Dead Man's Tongue ring reflected from its perch on her finger. Morgan had herself a new battery, and it appeared she'd stepped up the voltage.

Illickthid claws clashed with Sofia's insect arms. The Skeeter's jaws hissed, and the serrated stinger inside quivered in anticipation.

Stewart's tiny Demon body clung to the sides of my head. "What do we do now?"

Morgan answered for me. "Die."

25

REAVER FEVER

"*A*ngela!" I swung around to tell Adam's mother basically anywhere was better than here, but Angela and the dog she'd been holding were gone.

Whump!

Stewart's wings flared open, their pink and rubbery skin making it impossible to see.

"Stewart, get out of my—"

Crash!

The hospice door shattered, and a Reaver filled the newly opened space. The beast resembled a nightmarish Picasso painting, twisted and bent, with arms and legs protruding in an almost haphazard manner. The rest of its body was peppered with faces that screamed out in unchecked malice. A creature of Magick and chaos, Reavers were as terrifying as they were powerful, and their summoning was a specialty of my ex.

If Morgan had brought one, there were sure to be more.

"Reaver!" Harold's claws cast aside Sofia like a clingy nuisance, sending her into the wall where Adam's mother had been standing not moments before.

Harold had tussled with Reavers before. In those days, I'd

149

had a first row seat to his slashing fury, but this Illickthid wasn't the same one I'd fought beside in the heart of the Gloom. Harold was dying, and even in his insect form that was plain to see.

Bright red light poured from the Magick that surrounded the Reaver. It filled the room with an angry glow that sparkled along the Illickthid's exoskeleton. Morgan shouted something to the chaotic beast, but I lost it in the creature's wild yell. Dozens of mouths screamed in discord.

I knew who they were here for—me.

Stewart leapt into the air and I pushed up my sleeves, reaching for the Magick I knew was hidden somewhere deep inside. Furtive and frustrating, the power I'd come to rely on in situations exactly like this slipped away from me like the falling tide.

The House was dying and with it went the power.

That's just great.

Stewart dodged a muscular arm. His tiny body twirled in the air like a winged acrobat. Harold wasn't remotely that dexterous. The Illickthid took the bulk of that same fleshy meat hook across a lightly armored and iridescent head.

Crash!

The mantis slammed into one of the visitor's chairs. His claws caught on the cheap metal, while his many legs scrambled to get the rest of him upright.

Power roared from Morgan. It funneled into the Reaver and pulsed through the room with a bright and angry red glow.

"It wasn't my choice." Morgan's hair whipped in the waves of Magick. "I would have preferred to let you live, but he had other ideas."

I ducked another wild haymaker and slipped behind Harold's wheeled bed. "Oh yeah? That's great. How about you give me that ring and then we'll see who the real power is?"

"Nice try, Gene."

Strong Reaver arms grabbed the narrow bed and yanked it to the side, but the wires connecting it to the wall snapped it back like a tetherball's elastic band.

"Ha! Bet you didn't expect—"

The creature's fist caught my head and sent the room spinning.

Premature celebration is going to get you every time.

"Gene!" A bright pink blob of rubbery flesh popped into view, his body wrapped around a mutilated and clawing hand. Stewart's broken wings beat like mad and did just enough to keep me from taking another blast to the face from the chaotic Reaver.

"Stewart, be careful!"

"Boss, get out of the—"

A second arm slammed against the first. The beast clapped its strong hands together and crushed the Minor Demon between great folds of twisted flesh.

"Stewart!"

The pink monster hit the bed with a thud, his eyes closed and his wings no longer moving.

"No!"

I ducked another wild swing, then grabbed the edge of the bed and launched myself under it. Like my son on a slide, I popped up on the other side, only to be forced to scamper out of the way of yet another haymaker.

"It's useless, Gene." Morgan's voice echoed with the sickening power of the Dead Man's Tongue. "Even if you defeat one, you won't stop them all." More Reaver screams echoed down the hall, except these were followed by the blood-chilling cries of children.

What have you done?

I hesitated, and in that moment of hesitation, the Reaver had its opening. A muscular and oversized arm set off on a decapitating collision course with my confused head.

Slice!

Harold's mantis claw cut the trunk-thick limb in two, sending the fleshy and broken appendage tumbling to the ground.

Hell yeah! Oh no, blood, that's going to—

Sofia's jaws flared wide, their twin wings unfolding like a bird taking flight.

Morgan was not expecting that. "What the—" Her Magick faltered, not much, but enough for the Skeeter's insect arms to pierce her defenses.

"Argh!" Morgan screamed. Insect claws dug into the sides of her thin frame and forced the Magician to drop her arms and with them her hold on the Reaver. Harold saw his advantage and took it. His claws tore deep gouges of Reaver flesh and sent those chunks flying.

Sofia pulled Morgan toward her, my ex-girlfriend doing very little to stop the Skeeter's crushing grasp.

I used the distraction to my advantage and beat a path back to the bed. Stewart's limp body lay on the rumpled sheets.

Damn it.

I tucked the tiny Demon up in Harold's Soul Net, his body uncomfortably weak in the soul-strands' embrace, but no sooner did I have him in my arms then I was forced to duck another wild swing from the Reaver. Harold's claws had made a dent, but the chaos beast was clearly stronger. The older Illick-thid's pace slowed. Dark splotches bloomed along his hard exterior.

Harold was bleeding.

Crack!

A Reaver arm connected with the Illickthid's angular head, crushing a multi-faceted eye like jelly. Harold stumbled and flailed out with a wild hook, that claw narrowly missing me, before taking another chunk out of the Reavers boil-covered flesh.

I ducked a return jab from the grotesque monster's many arms. "What can I do?"

The glittering remains of the Illickthid's eye oozed down his face. "Stop the Magician," he growled, his mandibles clicking erratically.

"Right. On it."

And how are you going to do that?

Sofia pulled Morgan in, the Skeeter's bare arms and chest now exposed, and her tattoos soaking up whatever Wild Magick they could get like a shammy. My ex dropped her own arms and dug at something in the tight confines of her pants.

"Sofia, look out!"

Too late.

No sooner had the Skeeter brought Morgan close enough to get the fleshy folds of her jaws within striking distance than my ex slammed something small and multi-colored against her chest.

The Cube.

Morgan's twisted Rubik's Cube, the tiny puzzle piece imbued with a frenetic chaos all its own.

"No!"

Sofia had no idea what hit her and neither did the sigils tattooed on her body. Ink lines bled into each other as the Skeeter's body twisted like modern art. The young woman's cries quickly descended into a bubbling mess of fleshy discord. Insect arms twitched helplessly, their sharp edges bent in impossible directions while the flapping jaws lay like limp noodles. Whatever Wild Magick the Skeeter had been channeling erupted in an uncontrollable burst of narrow-beam destruction. That bolt of violent energy slammed into the Reaver, peeling apart flesh and raining gore on the already bloody floor.

"Harold." I dove out of the way of Sophia's impromptu death lasers. "Now's your chance."

The Illickthid didn't need to be told twice. Razor-sharp mantis claws dug deep into the confused monster, but the Reaver reared up and pulled Harold off the ground.

The mantis struggled in an armor-crushing embrace.

Morgan ducked away from another wild burst of Magick erupting from Sofia's twisted body and pulled her hands together. Cosmic power roared from the Dead Man's Tongue and from there into the Reaver.

Harold's body twitched, his claws digging deeper, but still the Reaver squeezed. Illickthid legs tore out great chunks of flesh, but the monster only tightened its grip.

Zap!

Another shot of Wild Magick ionized the air and I hit the deck. I squeezed my body under the bed while the bloody melee continued unabated on the other side.

Is this what it's come to? How the hell are you going to save your daughter if you're huddled under some bed like a moron?

The Reaver screamed, and somewhere outside a second one joined it.

The kids...

I held Stewart's still form and closed my eyes while visions of a Cathy I'd never see whole again rolled past. I wondered when the final blow would come, and when it did, if it would even matter.

MEMBERS ONLY

*T*he Reaver's triumphant scream echoed in my ears. It wouldn't be long before it crushed Harold and turned its attention on me.

Click. Click. Click.

Somehow the faint sounds of tiny metal legs made it past the Wild Magick's destruction and the Reaver's roar.

What's this?

I opened my eyes to find myself face to beak with the bright orange snout of an under-sized plastic flamingo. Sofia hadn't been lying, there was a Duplickity nearby. The little bird took a few hesitant steps toward me, her metal legs wobbly on the polished floor.

Zap!

Another bright beam of Wild Magick lanced across the room, tearing at the walls and sending distant cabinet contents tumbling down. The tiny bird shivered.

I wrapped Stewart and the net around me like a baby carrier. The Minor Demon now safely cocooned to my chest, I reached out a cupped hand for the tiny bird. "Hey there, little one."

The flamingo's neck tilted as if trying to get a bead on me. She sniffed at my shaking fingers.

"I know, smells like Hell."

The Duplickity's metal leg raised up, but before she could puncture my hand, a burst of Wild Magick toppled the bed we were hiding under.

The tiny bird vanished.

Damn it!

Morgan crossed her arms and borrowed Magick filled the room, pressing down on me like a lead blanket, while next to her, the Reaver had almost completed crushing Harold like a bug on its radiator grill.

"Let go of the damn Illickthid and get the Magician. Destroy him!" Morgan shouted, trying desperately to get the chaotic beast under control.

I tightened the knot on my new woven Demon carrier and took a deep breath.

Here goes nothing.

Palm up, I knelt down and extended my hand.

Morgan's eyes flashed. "What are you—"

The tiny Duplickity reappeared, its metal leg poised above my outstretched hand.

"No!"

The bird punctured my hand, then pressed her head against my bloody palm, her beak drinking rapidly in the tidal wave of crushing Magick rolling off of Morgan.

Images flooded my mind, too many and too fast to count. The tiny bird unloaded a whirlwind of thought, but one directive resounded above the rest.

We are Flock.

I smiled and wrapped a gentle hand around the bird. "Damn straight we are."

Morgan's Magick split the ground beneath my knees, but with the Duplickity in hand I was invisible, and my ex-girlfriend knew it.

"Ignore the Illickthid and find that Magician!"

Not that easy, Morgan.

I scrambled over the broken ground with eyes for only one thing: the cube. With Morgan's infernal toy detached from Sofia, Harold and I would have another set of arms —or six.

The Duplickity flooded my mind with images of running free, of escape, of disappearing, but I cast them aside. This wasn't my first time bonding with a member of the duplicitous Flock. They push hard to run, and I couldn't fault them, that's what they did, but not today.

Today, we're the heroes. Don't worry, you'll like it.

The tiny bird shook its head, and I tucked it under the soft edge of the Demon carrier, then ducked to avoid another blast of Wild Magick. Between the Reaver's crushing blows, and Sofia's uncontrollable outbursts, the room was coming apart at the seams. Even invisible, I had precious little chance of surviving the melee much longer.

Here goes nothing.

I scooped up a broken piece of the visitor's chair in my free hand and swung it against the infernal cube.

Boom!

Wild Magick mixed with Morgan's clockwork power, and together they erupted like professional fireworks. The Rubik's Cube let go of Sofia and immediately her body returned to normal, insect arms twitching.

Well, close enough.

"What the hell?" The Skeeter rubbed at her head, her jaws still fully unfolded, and hungry for blood.

Morgan's borrowed Magick flared, while beyond her, the sound of more Reaver's screams filled the air.

"You take care of my ex." I pointed to a clearly angry Morgan, only stopping when I realized neither of them could see me. "I'm going to see if I can pump a little life back into my other favorite bug person."

"Gene?" Sofia's wild eyes scanned the room. "You caught it!"

"What can I say, I have a way with plastic animals. Now, I'll see what I can do to talk her into bonding with you, but first, I need you to—"

"Wait, she's your ex?"

"It's a long story."

The Skeeter's stinger quivered in anticipation, while razor sharp fangs glistened in the fleshy folds of her mouth. "Tell me over a drink sometime." Sofia slammed her mosquito arms into the ground and vaulted herself into the air.

I had no idea they could do that.

Morgan had no idea either. She might have been prepared for Sofia's assault before, but she'd been burning through borrowed Magick at an insane rate, and that was taking its toll on her focus.

Boom!

The Skeeter slammed into my ex, knocking her body to the ground with the force of a whip crack and sending that clock-work Magick spinning.

Reavers roared, once again no longer controlled by Morgan's borrowed Magick, their blood-hungry cries echoed through the building.

Run.

The tiny bird flashed more images of escape, but I pushed them aside.

We've got a job to do.

It was hard to tell, but I could have sworn the flamingo sighed.

I know, buddy. We'll find you a nice marathon runner next.

Morgan scrambled to keep Sofia's stinger at bay, the fleshy appendage snapping at the air just above her neck, while

Magick swirled from the black metal ring. She was pulling in enough power for an impressive counterpunch.

Oh, no, that's enough of that. It's Gene's turn.

I dipped under the Reaver's outstretched arms and rammed my knees into Morgan's wrist. The sudden jarring motion knocked her hand free and gave the Skeeter the opening she needed. Sofia's stinger plunging deep into Morgan's flesh. My ex flailed wildly, but the Skeeter's insect arms lanced her body and pulled in the suddenly limp Magician like a spider with its prey.

"Keep her alive," I said, sliding the ring off Morgan's finger.

Sofia ignored me, her fleshy jaws pumping blood like mad from Morgan's pale skin.

"You want to join the Flock?"

The young woman hesitated, her eyes trying to find me in the room.

"Then I suggest you do what I say."

The Skeeter removed her stingers and let those folded jaws reseal against her face.

"I need to know what she knows."

Crack!

Harold's strong exoskeleton snapped against the Reaver's body, but his talons remained solidly embedded in the beast's flesh.

"Harold, can you move?" I shouted, leaving Morgan and dipping under one of the Reaver's many arms.

The Illickthid shook his angular head. "I can't feel my legs."

"All of them?"

Harold grunted and pushed his claws deeper into the Reaver.

"I'll take that as a yes. What can I do?"

The Illickthid's mandibles twitched against the Reaver's knotted flesh. "Remember me."

"I'll do you one better," I said, scampering up the mantis's knobby back. "How about we put this one to bed together?"

"What are you doing?"

"Making sure you eat your Wheaties." I squeezed the Dead Man's Tongue in my palm. I wasn't about to put the ring on, but I figured I could get a decent amount of power just from holding it—I was right.

A dark and violent Magick surged into my hand and raced up my arm. The Duplickity wiggled against my chest, struggling to free itself from the soft confines of the net.

Bad! Bad! Bad!

More images came, visions of a twisted landscape, with tall trees and misty moors. I tried to shake them away, but the pictures kept coming. They weren't from the Duplickity, they were from the Dead Man's Tongue itself.

Drop! Drop!

The Reaver swung Harold and it took all I had to stay attached to the Illickthid's back.

The swamps disappeared, only to be replaced with the faces of Magicians, so many, they raced past like the pages of a pain-filled yearbook. Each one died a more gruesome death than the last, and each at the hands of someone, the same someone on the other end of this ring. Magick pried out of them and stored, pulled into the ring-bearer's body like some sort of malevolent reservoir of death and pain.

Crack!

Harold's back snapped, and with it went the visions. It didn't matter where they came from, or whose power it was, because right this instant, it was mine.

"Fortis!"

Magick spilled out of the Dead Man's tongue and rolled over me like a chilling wave. The power twisted into Harold's skeleton, fusing joints and restoring the strength behind them.

"Better?"

"Ah!" The Illickthid broke free of the Reaver's grasp and in a single motion split the chaos beast in two, the bloody and muti-lated remains collapsing on the floor in a twisted mess.

Eugene Law...

I dropped off Harold's back, my mind again flooded with images of that dreary place.

Bad! Bad! Bad!

The Duplickity twisted against the carrier's straps, but I ignored her, and focused my attention on a thin and shadowed figure standing in the middle of that swampy vision.

Who are you?

The thin form exploded into a murder of crows, the black birds filling the misty sky.

Cling!

The ring fell from my fingers, while the vision's parting words echoed in my head.

Soon, Eugene Law. Soon.

27

BUG KING

*A*Reaver's scream brought me back to the present.

"Harold?"

The Illickthid was already half-way through the door, his scratch-covered carapace squeezed against the jagged opening. "The children!"

"Without the ring—"

"Come on, Magician. Glory awaits!"

If by glory you mean soul-crushing pain, and almost certain death, then yep, it's right there for the taking.

"Sofia?"

The Skeeter's insect arms held Morgan to her chest, my groggy ex-girlfriend's eyes unfocused and confused.

"She's not going anywhere, Gene," Sofia licked at the blood on her lips, "but I won't hesitate to devour her if you fail to deliver the Duplickity."

The tiny flamingo was gone. No longer tucked to my makeshift Demon carrier, and with exceptional invisibility—the bird could be anywhere.

Very little chance of that.

"You got it, Delia."

The angry Skeeter hissed. Her jaws rippled briefly before closing again. It was clear that Sofia didn't know what sort of power I wielded and wasn't interested yet in finding out.

Let's hope that lasts.

"Now, when she's functional, find out who gave her the Dead Man's Tongue."

Sofia's insect arms squeezed Morgan. "The what?"

The sound of Harold tearing free of the confining door-frame reminded me that I was running on borrowed time, and so was the Illickthid. Strength Magick only lasts so long, and there's always a price to pay.

Really should have mentioned that.

"Just ask, she'll know what you are talking about. How long does your saliva last?"

"Magician!" Harold's booming voice echoed from some-where down the narrow hall.

"Long enough." The Skeeter turned her attention to the stinger's rapidly healing wound.

"Dead Man's Tongue," I said again.

"Go."

I stepped over the rapidly fading bloody mess of broken Reaver, the last vestiges of it sublimating into an angry red mist. The Demon carrier loosened, and I tightened the knot keeping an unconscious Stewart strapped to my back.

"Magician!"

"I'm coming."

Deep breath, Gene.

* * *

"How many are there?"

Harold's massive mantis body filled the hallway in front of me, his claws leaving long gouges in the polished vinyl floor.

"I smell one at least."

163

"Well, that's a relief," I said, trying to figure out where to position myself to not be in the way of Harold's many legs. "We need to wrap this up quickly."

"Indeed, there are children visiting family. I can hear their heartbeats. They are scared."

"Hell yeah they are. I am too, but there's something you need to know. The Magick I—"

"There!" Harold stopped at what appeared to be a reception desk, the wide counter-top almost destroyed beyond recognition. Crushed computer screens flickered and cast an eerie light over the mangled bodies of what had at one time been nurses and doctors.

Morgan, what did you do?

Harold's slashing arms cut the air. He pointed to the double-door entrance to what I assumed was some sort of playroom. "The Reaver is inside."

"Harold, wait." I tugged at the Illickthid's claw. "There's something you need to know. The Magick I used to knit your shell, its—"

"Magician, I know I'm dying."

"But the—"

"That's not what's important now. What's important is to know that I truly lived. Give me this last time. Let me revel in the twisted blood of my ancient enemy. A seat at the great harvest awaits me on the other side, as does my wife. She waits patiently and I have dallied for too long. I need a win, Magician. For me the sun is setting, but there are young ones beyond that door whose morning hasn't begun to break."

The Illickthid's broken eye stared back at me, an oozing reminder of the last Reaver we'd crossed paths with, but it was his words that struck a chord.

The chitinous beast from a long past era was right. It didn't matter what stood in my way, or even if certain death awaited me on the other side. My daughter was out there, all three of her, and I'd made a promise.

Cathy's wild hair whipped in the Hellgate's flames in my mind's eye, only to be replaced by the same young woman coaxing beautiful notes from a violin's strings. In an instant, both of them vanished, and in their place was the Wild Reaving, the Calamity of fire and death.

I had to find a way to put them back together, or die trying.

I took a deep breath and was pleasantly surprised to find a little Magick still swirling around in the deep recesses of my body. "Screw it. Let's do this."

"That's the spirit, Magician! You would have made a good Soul Weaver."

"Hardly, I can't sew for shit."

Illickthid claws snapped in and out. "Yeah, neither can I. Trust me, this is more fun."

"I'm not certain your definition of fun holds up in translation."

Harold tilted his angular head.

"It's nothing. We need a plan if we are going to—"

The massive Illickthid swung around and charged the double door, his talons out and snapping like a maniacal pair of hedge trimmers. "For the blood of our ancestors!"

Harold ripped the doors off their hinges and exploded into the playroom.

"Or we could just barge in. That works too." I tightened Stewart's carrier and called up what Magick the House was willing to part with. "For the blood of our—screw it— for Cathy!"

Yeah, if those kids weren't terrified before, they sure as hell would be now.

* * *

I RUSHED into the room behind Harold and immediately wished I'd been able to convince him to hold up for a plan. This Reaver was much larger than the other one, and far more aggressive, if that were possible.

Bent and misshapen arms swung in wild angles, shattering already busted furniture and tearing through plastic children's toys in the process.

Kids? Where are the kids?

I found them tucked up in the corner of the room behind a broken loveseat, the jagged springs sticking out like coiled spikes.

Bingo.

Harold's claws clacked in the air, and he wasted no time slicing into the Reaver's chaotic body. "Get the children. I will take the beast."

"Works for me." I ducked under an erratic haymaker and cut a path through the wreckage.

Hooked claws left deep gouges in the Reaver's flesh and expertly drew most of its attention away from me and the children, but the chaos beast had quite a few eyes and at least one of them didn't buy the distraction.

Boom!

A wild swing from the monster caught me across the back and sent me sprawling across the hard floor.

"Look out!" One of the kids cried.

I rolled to my side just in time to see a Reaver foot leave a deep indentation in the exact spot I'd previously enjoyed.

Thanks, kid.

"Get the children," Harold cried, his claws furiously digging into Reaver flesh.

"I'm working on it!"

The Illickthid hooked his claws around one of the Reaver's many arms and slammed his head into the beast. "Work on it faster."

"Don't overdo it. You only have so much Magick—"

Crack!

A wide gap split down the Illickthid's exoskeleton. The Magick was already fading.

If Harold noticed, he didn't seem to care, his claws continued digging deep gouges in the Reaver's flesh and drawing the beasts attention away from the broken loveseat and children hiding behind it.

Shit.

I scrambled up and across the room, narrowly avoiding wild Reaver swings in the process. "Okay, kids. It's time to go."

Three small children huddled behind the splintered wood and bent springs, their eyes rimmed red with tears, and their little hands visibly shaking.

"We're gonna be fine. Who here likes bugs?"

A small girl raised a shaky hand.

"Great, you see that bug. He's like the king bug. He likes kids—"

"He's going to eat us!"

Crack!

Harold's exoskeleton popped again under the Reaver's unrelenting fists.

"No he's not. He doesn't eat children."

One of the kids looked disappointed. "What does he eat?"

Reaver blood oozed across the floor, but the Illickthid wasn't going to hold up much longer, his claws were slowing by the second.

"I take that back," I said, finding an opening in the melee. "He totally eats kids. Yum, yum! Now, if you don't want to get eaten by the bug king or squished to jelly by the—"

"Playdoh monster!" the young girl cried.

I like this kid.

"Yeah, if you want to get out of here you'll run as fast as those little feet can carry you on my count."

The children cuddled up against me, their little fingers clutching to my borrowed flannel and muddy denim.

"All right, on three, ready? One, two, th—"

With a swinging double punch, the Reaver sandwiched Harold's angular head and crushed it like the insect it resembled. The Mantis collapsed where he stood, his once formidable claws limp, and what remained of his head dripping onto the hard floor.

28

GRAFFITI GIRL

The Reaver turned its hellish attention to me and the rest of the tiny trio.

"Ok, guys. Change of plans. Does anyone have a crayon?"

Tears streamed down confused faces.

"Color doesn't matter, just need a crayon."

A wild and soul-chilling scream shook the focus of my little group. "It's okay. Just one crayon."

"Marker?" The bug-loving young lady held up a thick, red felt-tip.

"Yahtzee!" I snapped the top off and dropped to my knees. "Help me clear out a spot.

Panicked eyes and frightened faces pointed to the approaching monster, their words not much more than unintelligible cries. That was except for marker-girl. The pigtailed blond scampered up next to me, her tiny fingers pushing debris out of the way and giving me a wide spot to work with.

"Nice job, kiddo!"

"My name is Sarah."

"Right, keep it up, Sarah." I shoved the open marker into her hands and pulled the crying duo close. "Draw me a circle around all of us."

"I love circles."

Amen, kid, so do I. Especially when they save our collective asses.

Sarah hopped to her tiny feet and dragged the marker along the vinyl floor like a pro. It wasn't long before she had us surrounded.

"Great, work," I said, taking the marker from her. "Now, get your buddies there and hold hands."

"But they're boys."

The Reaver grabbed Harold's broken body and threw it aside.

"Trust me, Sarah. In a few years you'll totally want to hold boy's hands, and I promise you, your dad won't like it one bit."

The little marker girl did exactly what she was told. She grabbed those boys' fingers like her life depended on it, and for all we knew it did.

"Okay, everybody, do not leave the circle." I grabbed the marker and slashed at the floor. Swirling lines and whorls danced from the end of that felt tip in bright and vibrant red.

"It's coming!" Sarah shouted, her little fingers white against the crying boy's hands.

"Working as fast as I can."

The Reaver tossed aside furniture and crushed what remained of Harold's carapace.

One of the boys made a run for it. His wet fingers slipped out of Sarah's hand, and in the next breath he was up and over the torn loveseat.

"Stop!" bug girl screamed, but he was already running for the opposite corner.

Come on, really?

I jumped over the circle's edge and slipped the carrier off my back, then pushed Stewart into Sarah's open arm. "Hold the baby and do not move."

"Uh—"

I slammed my hand into the ground and let the power of the Void surge through me. The House wasn't what it was, but it wasn't dead yet—not by a long shot.

Magick roared through my fingers and into the haphazard seal. Morgan had used something similar once before, when a Reaver she'd purposely brought had turned on her and the rest of us. I just hoped I'd gotten it right.

Boom!

Reaver fists crashed against the blinding light of the sigil's Magick. I ducked out of the way of the now thoroughly destroyed love seat and let the Seal's power do its thing. The ornate lines and whorls focused like a magnifying glass and took the Reaver's heavy hands.

Blow after blow rained down, but the Magick didn't budge.

Hot damn!

My excitement was short lived, as it didn't take the Gloom-beast long to figure out there was a child outside the seal's protective barrier.

The Reaver turned its attention toward the young boy. Blood-mad eyes and twisted mouths screamed in hungry anticipation.

I motioned to bug girl to stay inside the circle. She got the message and squeezed Stewart tighter.

Oh, he's so gonna love that.

I scrambled over the broken pieces of playroom couch, but the Reaver had already reached the boy. It had him pinned between a set of broken chairs and a smashed coffee table.

I reached for my Magick, but it was already pushed to the edge keeping the Seal intact and I didn't dare drop it.

"Hey, stupid!" I shouted, waving my hands in the air like a moron. "Over here."

The Reaver's many eyes ignored me, and instead focused on the easy meal.

Damn it.

I grabbed a broken chair leg and tossed it at the monster, but it bounced off harmlessly. "Run, kid!"

The little boy didn't budge. His tiny legs stayed rooted to the ground, while all the color drained out of his face.

Shit.

I scanned the room, looking for something, anything, I could use. Harold's claws lay limp only a few feet away.

Well, I've done crazier...

I wrapped my hands around one of those hooks and was surprised to find it lighter than I expected. "Fortis..." I whispered, hoping I could bleed just enough Magickal strength without losing the Seal's dome in the process.

Snap!

With a sickening pop, Harold's arm detached from his body. I knew it wasn't what he would have preferred, but I thought the sentiment would have resonated with the old Illickthid.

"For Harold!" I shouted, embedding the razor sharp claw in the Reaver's back.

The beast swung around, turning its full attention on me.

Well, that worked.

"Run, kid!"

The boy snapped out of his deer-like stare and made a break for what remained of the double doors.

Okay, now what's the plan, Gene?

I took a few steps back, the very angry Reaver directing its full fury at me.

You really need to start thinking about complete plans. These half-assed ones are totally going to get you killed.

I ducked a Reaver fist only to catch my foot on a matchbox car. The tiny four wheeler shot out from under me and took my balance with it.

And this is how it ends?

The chaos beast's haphazard limbs and broken faces filled my vision.

A miracle would really be nice right now.

The tiny orange beak of an undersized plastic bird appeared between the Reaver's legs.

Good enough for me.

"We are Flock!"

The little bird shot out, and not a moment too soon. Her little metal legs bobbed along the broken floor and into my outstretched arms.

Come to daddy.

A hailstorm of fists rained down from angry Reaver, but thanks to my membership in the Flock, they missed me entirely. I rolled over with the little plastic bird pinned to my chest. The Duplickity sent images rolling through my head almost too fast to count.

Works for me.

The tiny bird bobbled its head.

"Yeah, yeah, don't get cocky."

I tucked the bird under my arm like a football and slipped behind the raging monster. Harold's mantis claw remained wedged in its back, while more images flashed in my head.

"I get it. Do you know how crappy the chances are that actually works?"

A large chalk board of complex equations appeared in my mind.

Bird math, great.

I grabbed the elbow end of the embedded arm. "I'm glad you've done the math, but pardon me while I question just how good you are at... at whatever the hell math that would even be."

An annoyed image popped in my head and I shook it aside— I needed my concentration if this was going to work.

The Reaver must have felt my hands against Harold's claw, as it turned the moment I pulled.

Now or never.

The little bird nodded.

Damn it. You focus on the invisibility. I'll focus on the Reaver.

I reached for the Seal's Magick. The shimmering dome protecting the crying boy and his white-knuckled girl-friend flickered.

Please be right.

The chalk board returned and I shook it off.

Here we go!

I formed a human bridge, not unlike that time I caught my hand on a live wire and became the conduit between the electric company and the wet ground, except this time I was pumping all the Seal's expanding dome-like awesomeness into Harold's embedded claw.

Not crazy at all.

The Duplickity bobbed its head.

No comments from the peanut gallery.

The dome vanished, leaving Sarah, a painfully squeezed Stewart, and the boy with what was sure to be crushed fingers completely unprotected.

Come on...

That Magick roared back into me and from there into Harold's claw. Once inside the Illickthid's appendage, it expanded like a balloon animal, the shimmering walls of cosmic power splitting flesh and ripping sinew.

Huh, it worked.

The tiny bird sighed.

Reaver skin rippled under the pressure and a wild yell echoed from its many mouths. The beast collapsed against the ground, dead and broken.

I set the Duplickity down and wasn't ready for the crushing hug from bug girl. She let go of the other boy, who promptly ran for the door, and plowed into me. "You didn't leave."

"Of course, I—" That wasn't Sarah's little voice. It was tired and far too old for her tiny body.

The House.

The young girl handed over a still quiet Stewart, then placed her hands on her hips. "It's starting, Gene."

29

DEAD MAN'S TONGUE

Sirens wailed in the distance, their piercing noise a welcome relief, but I had no interest in being here when they arrived.

"Get out of her." I looped the tiny Imp's carrier of soul strands over my shoulder. "She's just a kid."

A thin line of blood trickled down Sarah's nose. "Which is what makes all of this so much more difficult—kids fight like crazy."

"Don't—"

The House crossed her little arms. "She'll survive, Gene. Your bigger concern should be whether I survive. I see the Illickthid is dead."

I dropped Harold's broken claw. "Harold. He had a name."

"And now it doesn't matter."

My hands squeezed into white-knuckled fists. "It *does* matter. He died saving these kids, one of which you are currently walking around in."

"But don't you understand, Gene? It doesn't matter who he was, or what he did, if you don't stop what's coming for me. Do I have to remind you what happened to God's Tears?"

My chest tightened at the memory of that wind-swept place. "No."

"Good. Now, where's the Chinthe?"

"Chinthe?!"

Sarah bobbed her tiny head. "Yes, I didn't send you here to buddy up with a cancer-ridden bug man. I sent you here for the dog. I need a way to get you on the battle field before things get out of hand—if you haven't noticed, I'm running out of Magick."

"I've noticed."

The Chinthe... Angela!

"Where's the dog, Gene?"

"I don't know."

The little girl slapped a comical hand to her forehead. "Are you serious?"

"It's gone."

"Well, you better figure out a way to get it back." Sarah kicked at the Reaver's bloody remains. "Because things are heating up."

"Morgan is here."

The young girl twirled her pigtail in a tiny hand. "Yeah, I figured that out, but she's not calling the shots."

The Dead Man's Tongue.

"Who is?"

The House's young eyes caught sight of something behind me and turned back to me in a panic. "Find the Chinthe and get back to me. There's not much time left."

Against my better judgement I grabbed the little girl's arm. "Wait, who? Who is calling the shots?"

Tears streaked like rain down her terrified face.

"Sarah?"

The young girl's fragile voice broke up between bouts of crying. "It's really, really scared."

The Void is afraid.

I wasn't quite sure how to process this, but I didn't get much time to.

"Gene, you've been holding out on me."

Sofia.

I spun around to find the Skeeter standing in the broken remains of the playroom doors. The distant sirens were getting closer, but none of that seemed to phase the hairless, tattooed woman.

"What do you mean?" I asked, gently sliding Sarah behind me.

The ring.

The Dead Man's Tongue reflected in the flickering light.

She found it and put it on. Damn it.

"Sofia, you don't want to do that. Whoever is on the other side of that ring—"

"Has power, lots of power. I used to think you were the toughest dog on the block, but now that I've tasted this." She held up her clenched fist, blood dripping from the polished metal. "You aren't on top anymore, Gene."

"I never was."

Sofia clenched her fist tighter. "Like hell you weren't. It's been a long time since you and I first met, and in all those years you know who I hear about, you know whose name is on everyone's lips?"

"Ed McMahon?"

Sofia ignored my poor attempt at a joke. "Yours."

"That's just because I owe them money."

Something brushed against my leg—a brief flash of pink.

The Duplickity.

"Don't play the fool, Gene. I may still look young, but I've learned a lot."

I gently pushed the bird between my legs.

"Well, obviously you haven't learned enough. You haven't figured out when you're being used. Hint, it's right now."

Sofia ran a pale finger around the Dead Man's Tongue. "It's worth it."

"No, it's not. Whoever they are, they are just using you like a tool in their belt, just like they used Morgan. I promise you, they won't follow through with whatever it is they're offering—it's all lies."

"No, Gene. Lies are your speciality." The Skeeter's insect arms unfolded from the open sides of her leather vest.

Sarah's tiny fingers clutched at my borrowed shirt.

"I never lied to you."

Sofia's jaws rippled. "No, you did worse. You had a chance to save my father, and you crushed it with your fingers. The Duplickity's egg is pure potential, a touch of infinity. It's the closest we come to salvation in this bleak world and you destroyed it. You shattered the egg and with it any chance I had to undo the hell that Deacon had wrought."

"I had no choice."

"There's always a choice, Gene. You just took the selfish one. Tell me, how is Porter? How is that lovely wife of yours that you just had to save?"

I saved her and never gave a second thought to your father...

"I don't know." I placed a hand on the whimpering young girl behind me. "Is that what you want to hear? I gave up knowing. I gave up everything that ever meant anything to me. Infinity has a price—Magick demands sacrifice. What are you willing to sacrifice, Sofia?"

The Skeeter's jaws unfolded like a fleshy flower lined with sharp fangs. "Sacrifice? I am sacrifice, Eugene Law. I am the living, breathing embodiment of loss. The difference between us is that I have embraced who I am." Sofia's arms stretched wide. "I have lost everything, and in doing so I've gained more than I could ever have imagined possible."

"What did you do to Morgan?"

The Skeeter's serrated stinger licked at her blood-red lips. "I did what I do best. Isn't that what you wanted?"

"No!"

The thought of Morgan at the end of Sofia's twisted lips was almost too much to take—no one deserved that.

"You left her with me. Part of you had to know what I would do."

"I asked you to get information—that's all."

"And that's what I did." Sofia held up the ring. "Your ex was a fountain of wisdom. She told me everything. Who you really are, and what makes you tick. Most importantly I learned what this is, and who is on the other side."

The Dead Man's Tongue glowed on Sofia's finger, and from it Magick flooded the room.

There was no reasoning with the Skeeter, whoever was powering that ring had pumped her full of false hope, and that made her deadly.

"Sarah," I whispered. "Do you like birds?"

"Ye... Yes..." The little girl pressed her face into my shirt.

"Great, this next part's going to hurt a bit, but I promise afterwards you'll be fine."

What are you doing? She can't be more than seven. You can't have her join the Flock. Those birds will destroy her mind.

Sofia's insect arms spread wide. "Tristan sends his best."

If the Skeeter had split me in two with those wicked arms, she'd have shocked me less than those four words did.

Tristan! Was it possible? Had that high school kid somehow amassed enough Magick to out swing the dying Void?

I shook my head.

It didn't matter if Morgan's nephew was on the other side of that ring or not, whatever was there would mow down Sarah and me without wasting a second thought.

I pressed my leg against the invisible bird. I knew she was there, and the images that flashed in my head reminded me as much.

Run!

I shook my head and sent back images of my own, pictures of the young girl, clutching the bird and vanishing into the wreckage.

The Duplickity hesitated, its hive-like mind full of uncertain images.

Do this for me. We are Flock.

Images of a confused and broken young woman flooded my mind and I had to fight back against the churning in my gut.

Do it.

"Ouch!"

Sarah's yelp drew the Skeeter's attention. Sofia's eyes flared at the sight of the tiny pink flamingo lapping at the blood on the young girl's leg.

Forgive me, Sarah.

"Okay, sweetheart, pick up the bird and run. Don't stop running until you find your mom and dad. Whatever happens after that, I'm sorry."

Sofia hissed, her wide jaws quivering in frustration. "That Duplickity is mine!"

Sarah hesitated. "I…"

"Pick it up and run!"

The young girl let go of my shirt, her tear-streaked cheeks bringing back memories of Cathy clinging to the fiery edge of the Hellgate.

How many more will have to suffer?

Sofia's insect arms tore through the broken bits of the play-room. "Give it to me!"

"Pick up the bird, kid! Pick it up now!"

The tiny girl's tear-streaked face vanished, winking out of view moments before the first Skeeter claws stabbed at the air where she'd been.

Please forgive me.

30

INTO THE WOODS

*S*ofia screamed in frustration, her insect arms grasping hopelessly in the empty air. "No!"

"Run, Sarah!"

The Skeeter turned her blood-red eyes on me, the Dead Man's Tongue on her finger putting out enough Magick to ripple the surrounding air. "We will destroy you."

"Get in line, sister." I tightened the Demon carrier to my back. "You think you're the first person to try and put me in the ground?"

Think, Gene.

My worn-out brain cells weren't firing on all cylinders at this point, and I was decidedly short on options. I was beat, and I was pretty sure Sofia knew it. The Reavers had taken their toll, as had the Seal, and the House—the Magick I'd come to rely upon was coming to its end and I had no idea how much was left in the tank. Sadly, Tristan didn't appear to be suffering from that problem.

Damn, I hate that kid.

Sirens roared, and the bright blue and red lights of more

emergency vehicles than I had any interest in meeting, splashed across Sofia's hairless body.

The Skeeter's tattoos lit up with borrowed Magick courtesy of the Dead Man's Tongue. "It ends now."

Yip! Yip!

An orange puffball hit Sofia like a hairy missile, his tiny claws tearing minuscule gouges in her cheeks. "Argh!"

"Gene?"

"Angela!"

Adam's mom leaned against the jagged edge of a broken couch, her sunburned face and wind-blown hair a shock to the system. "That's a new one. Adam never told me about—Oh my God, Gene, are you okay?"

I pulled Angela up and held her hand. "I am now. Call the dog and let's get out of here."

"I don't know his name."

Sofia's insect arm yanked the furry orange beast off and tossed him to the ground.

Yelp!

"Bobbin, his name is—"

It turned out I didn't have to say much more than that, the tiny dog had taken quite a shine to Angela, and was more than happy to hop back into her arms.

"Let's go!" I shouted, squeezing the older woman's hand.

Sofia's borrowed Magick crackled like a firework display.

The tiny dog panted in Angela's arms. "Uh, how do I make him go? Mush? Scoot?"

"I have no idea. Marco always just did what he wanted to when he wanted to."

Sofia and the rest of the shattered room vanished in a blinding blur of white.

Yeah, just like that.

* * *

Sunlight slipped through the dappled leaves and cast a warm glow on the earthy forest floor. The distant sirens had been replaced by the cheerful call of effervescent song birds, their warbling cries filling the air with the pleasant cacophony of life.

Lick, lick, lick.

"Ugh." I pushed the footstool dog away from my face. "I'm up. I'm up. Angela?"

A gentle breeze worked its ways through the dense canopy, its soft kiss a welcome relief.

"Angela?"

Yip! Yip!

"Present." The older woman pushed herself up on dirty elbows. "Where are we?"

"I haven't figured that out yet—" I grabbed at the Demon carrier that was no longer wrapped around my chest—"Where's Stewart?"

"I have no idea."

Bobbin ran to a nearby tree and barked at something in its branches.

"We can worry about the squirrels in a minute, buddy. We need to find the Imp."

"Gene." Angela pointed up. "There he is."

Hanging at least two dozen feet in the air was the still bundled Stewart, the Illickthid's net holding him like a tiny hammock in the monstrous oak's branches.

"How did he get up there?"

Angela shrugged her shoulders. "You know, for a Magician, you really don't have as many answers as people think you do."

"I've been saying that for years." I ran my hands along the thick bark looking for a hand hold. "It's nice to know at least someone's been paying attention."

Adam's mother pointed to a gap in the tree. "Use that knot."

I hesitated, not entirely sure what might be making a home in that black hole.

"They don't teach tree climbing at Magician school?"

"Actually, no." I put my hand in the knot, and was pleasantly surprised when nothing bit it. "First, there's no such thing as Magick school, and second—"

"Seems to me you could really use something like a Magick school. It would really solve a lot of problems."

I pulled myself up far enough to grab a lower branch. "No Magick school."

"Suit yourself. Branch on your left," Adam's mom said, waving at me from the ground.

"Thanks, I—"

"Now put your feet there."

My muddy feet scrambled for purchase on the damp bark. "Thanks, but I think I've got—"

"No, not there." Angela scooped up the tiny dog in her hands. "Over there. You keep putting your feet on the mossy patches. Is this your first time climbing a tree?"

I gritted my teeth and wiped the thin sheen of sweat off my forehead on the borrowed flannel. "No, it is not my first time climbing a tree."

"Really?" Angela moved under me, the tiny dog licking her hand. "Because I feel like I'm having to tell you everything."

I hoisted myself onto a narrow branch. "That's because you won't stop telling me what to do. I assure you I am perfectly capable of climbing a tree without your assistance."

"That branch is weak."

I leaned against the thick trunk and wrapped my hand around a jutting branch closer to Stewart's dangling carrier. "It's fine."

"No, it's weak and if you pull on it, it's going to—"

Crack!

The limb gave way and crashed into the muddy ground, taking with it a smattering of Spanish moss.

"Told you."

Deep breath, Gene.

"Angela?"

Adam's mother tickled at the tiny dog in her hands. "Yes, honey."

"Which branch should—"

"On the right."

I reached out with my hand.

"No, your other right. My right which would be…"

I switched hands and caught the wider limb with my fingers. "This one?"

"Yup."

It took a few more minutes of back and forth for Adam's mother—obviously a tree-climbing professional in another life—to guide me to Stewart's branch.

"There you go," she said, taking a seat on a nearby fallen log. "I think you've got it from here."

Sigh.

"Thank you."

"Don't mention it, sweetheart. I do the same thing for Adam all the time."

And that explains so, so many things.

Stewart's carrier drifted gently in the cool breeze, the Soul Weaver's strands caught around the stem of a twig-like sucker that was already bending under the tiny Demon's weight.

Nice and slow, Gene. Nice and slow…

I straddled the branch and grunted at the unpleasant crushing sensation around my man parts. Ed's jeans might have been tight, but straddling an oak tree branch took their unpleasantness to a hitherto unknown level.

"Now just shimmy down the branch."

Thank you, Angela.

"I got it."

"Right." Adam's mom played with the tiny dog's fur. "Mr. Magician knows all about trees, doesn't he?"

Yip!

"Yes, he sure does."

I wiped sweat with the back of my sleeve, oddly surprised it still smelled like peanut oil, then shimmied a few inches closer to the dangling Demon.

"Almost there," Angela said, placing the dog down and standing up to get a better look at my progress. "Don't over compensate. If you lean too far—"

My hand slipped off the damp branch and I almost came off the tree completely. "Stop talking! Please just stop talking."

Adam's mom clamped her mouth shut.

Deep breath. You can do this, Gene.

I scooted a little closer, but Stewart was still too far away to reach, and to make matters worse, the branch beneath us was starting to bend precariously.

Okay, new plan.

I laid flat against the thick limb, Ed's flannel pressing up against the damp bark, and reached for the Illickthid's Net.

Almost... there...

My fingers grazed the soft strands.

Come on.

Below me Angela's fingers pinched at the air.

So close.

A gentle breeze twisted the tiny hammock, and I caught it in my hand. "Gotcha!"

"Great job," Angela cried, waving her hands. "I knew you could do it!"

I pulled Stewart into my chest and sat up. The tiny Demon looked so fragile in the soft folds of the soul-strand net. "The things I do for an Imp, right?"

"Imp!"

A booming voice shook the tree.

"Angela, what—"

"Gene, behind you!"

I turned around to find a face protruding from the mossy bark of the ancient oak. Eyes from knots and a thick beard of straggling suckers, the great tree cast its angry view on me. "Imp!"

The branches shook, and I struggled to keep a grasp on Stewart.

"Gene, toss him to me," Angela cried, her arms wide.

"Catch!"

Stewart didn't fall more than a few feet before narrow vine-like twigs wrapped his still body.

Shit.

"Gene, get down!"

More thick limbs, like jungle snakes, crushed me to the branch I'd been straddling. I wasn't going anywhere, even with an expert tree climber calling out ill-timed suggestions from below.

"Imp!" The tree boomed.

Crap.

31

WHERE THERE'S SMOKE

"Gene!"

Yip! Yip! Yip!

Angela's words and the tiny dog's barks slowly faded beneath the thick blanket of leaves and branches. It wasn't long before all that remained was the rustling sound of grinding limbs.

The arboreal cocoon echoed like a broken record. "Imp, Imp..."

"Stewart's a pain, but he didn't do anything to you."

Branches squeezed tighter, their narrow limbs cutting off the already dappled light.

"Listen, we've got a case of mistaken identity. That Imp isn't whoever you think it is. Sure, he's kind of a jerk, but he's my jerk. Let me go and we'll leave, scout's honor."

The face returned, its eyes and mouth forming not unlike the Defiler's proxies, a mosaic of leaves, branches, and dripping sap. "Searspit must die."

"Whoa, whoa, whoa." I pushed back against the crushing walls of green. "He already did, and at my hand."

The great tree hesitated, and I slapped my hand against the

wide branch I'd been straddling. "Feel that?" I asked, hoping there was a little of the House's Magick still swirling around in me. "I speak for the Void, and unlike that bastard I don't lie. Searspit is dead."

"Lies."

Sharp twig-like branches scraped at my skin. "Hey, I already told you, I don't—argh!"

The tree pulled my hand inside the bark, bringing with it pain, and the immediate memory of the Withering. My wife's young face, and then her faint heartbeat floated past as vivid memories, but the tree pulled me further. I stood at the edge of the Hellgate again, Cathy was just beyond my fingers, her hair twisting wildly in the fires of Hell. My words vanished in a sparkling shower of Hell Fleas, and in an instant I was back in that dirty bathroom off the interstate, the bloody body of a Minor Demon at my feet. A reflection in the mirror drew my attention.

Little Ed?

The Demon Hunter's son stared at me, confused and unsure. "Gene?"

"Eddie, is that you?"

The reflection of the junior Demon Hunter scratched at his head. "I don't know."

I wiped dirt off the smeared glass. "What happened?"

"Happened? Nothing happened. I have always been, and will always be. My roots go deep, and my branches reach for the heavens. My children know no end. They are as uncountable as the stars in the sky."

"That's got to be tough—kids can be a real pain."

A sharp snap of pain in my hand brought me back to exactly what sort of danger I was in.

Fewer wisecracks, you moron.

"Little Ed, it's me. It's Gene. Kaylee's your mom and Ed's your dad? I mean there was a staff and all, and I have to be honest I don't understand how any of that even worked, but you're their son."

The mirror and the young man's reflection in it vanished. I spun around only to find myself laying on the hard concrete floor, while above me Evil Gene glared menacingly.

"Yeah, I remember him—snappy dresser, total jerk."

Little Ed stepped out behind the evil half of my soul. "He is part of you."

"Yes, he is. I can't deny that. Still, I wish I had half his fashion sense."

Evil Gene sprung to life and had his hands at my throat, those malevolent fingers squeezing the blood in my neck. "How? How did you come out on top? You are weak. You are nothing. How did you possibly win?"

"I've got... friends..." I said, my words barely slipping out against the evil soul's crushing grip.

"Friends?" A confused Little Ed vanished again, along with Evil Gene and the rest of the peanut vending shed.

"Eddie?"

The clink of plates and the glorious aroma of breakfast food washed over me.

The diner.

A sassy waitress dropped off yet another plate of pancakes and eggs, our table now full to the brim, the white porcelain wobbling precariously. Little Ed's face appeared through the twisting steam.

"I get it, you want to take a trip down memory lane. That's really wonderful, but I don't have a lot in the way of time. My daughter is right about to kick off the apocalypse, and since she's way too much like her old man, she doesn't know what the hell she's doing."

Little Ed turned his attention to the open seat next to me, except it was no longer open. Kaylee smiled and held my hand. "Oh yes, we've been married a long time."

"No, kid. That's a lie. She's covering for me with a Leprechaun. It's not what it seems."

"Lies…"

The diner darkened, fading away in the wispy steam of uneaten breakfasts.

"Yes, white lies. Listen, that was your mom, she just was trying to keep me out of trouble. I promise."

The Green Swamp stretched out just beyond the edges of Sturkey, its muddy ground holding me firm. Kaylee's root Magick twisted around my legs.

"Kid, no, listen, you aren't getting the right parts. You can't jump around like this, you're missing context. There's a reason why she's squeezing the life out of my feet."

Little Ed stepped out from behind a narrow pine. "Explain."

Kaylee's tear-stained face cried out in pain, and in her hand she held the tiny plastic compact. The Soul-Splitter was inside, bound up in powerful Magick. Cosmic power I'd spent years on was about to be undone by a damn pocket screw driver.

Delia.

No longer in her prime, the ancient and withered Skeeter leaned against the heavy oak staff.

"This was it, kid," I said, tugging at my numbing feet. "This was when your mom did the unthinkable for you."

"My mom?"

"Right, I know it's hard to believe now that you're old man oak and all, but you have a mom, and that's her."

Little Ed took a step toward us, then hesitated.

"Give me the mirror!" Delia screamed, her overweight body pressing against the staff. "I break this and your little wooden boy is gone."

"Don't do it, Kaylee." The words escaped my lips without me saying them.

Tears streamed down the Swamp Witch's face. "I have to, Gene. Don't you understand?"

I didn't then, but I did now. Now I understood only too well. We do things, so many things, and not all of them good, for the ones we love.

Cathy.

Delia's cackling laugh brought me back to the unfolding memory. The staff snapped, and a shock wave of pain tore apart the vision. Trees vanished and the Swamp Witch blew away like a column of smoke. In the end, it was only me and Little Ed.

"I died."

"No, you didn't. You want to know why? Well, get in line, because even I don't understand it, but you are missing the best part."

Kaylee returned, crouched over the body of her son. "Eddie…"

The green stem of a new staff erupted from the ground like a hungry sapling, it's many stalks twisting into a single woven core.

"This." I held up the Magickal tap root. "This is what a parent's love can do, and this is what she did for you. You survived damn it, and you went on to sacrifice yourself for those you loved."

The staff vanished in the fires of the Five Star Toaster, a roaring wall of unholy flame that surrounded us.

"There!" I pointed to the writhing bodies of the tar-stricken Ed and Donnie. "You saved them. There are only two people I've ever known that held the toaster's handles and lived, and as far as I know they are both here right now."

The reflection of Little Ed appeared, his back against the broken pavement, and in his hands the infernal toaster. "I… remember."

"Hot damn, kid—whoops," I said, noticing the imaginary fires. "What I meant was, it's great to have you back. Now, let me and the Imp go, and we'll figure out a way to get you back to your family."

"I can't do that, Gene."

"Why not?"

The imaginary flames roared higher. "My children need me."

"Huh?"

Little Ed tossed the toaster aside and pointed to the distant horizon, where a burning red glow filled the darkening sky. "I did not have a word for them before, but now I do."

"What is it?"

"New Dead. An unstoppable army of the Damned with their ashen bodies and eyes of hate-filled tar are destroying my family."

The Calamity will not stop with Hell.

"Eddie, I'm sorry. I..."

"My roots go deep." Little Ed's body twisted into the bark of that ancient tree. "I have seen more things than you can comprehend. The one you call the Calamity is only one part of your daughter. They are all connected. To destroy one may end them all."

"No, that's not how—"

Little Ed's eyes faded into tiny knots in the rough bark. "The trunk cannot survive without the roots, and the branches cannot survive without the trunk. They are all connected."

"Wait, Eddie, what do I do?"

The great oak vanished, and in its place was the House, 69 Mallory Lane. It loomed in front of me, its power waning. The windows rattled, and the door shook. Someone stood on the porch. It was me, a tired and broken Eugene Law opening the door and stepping inside. Behind me, standing at the edge of those steps like three stoic sisters were the shards of Cathy.

Sacrifice.

The vision faded away, and I found myself back on the ground. Angela and the Chinthe hovered over me. "Gene! Are you okay? That was one heck of a fall. I should have climbed the tree... Gene?"

Lick! Lick!

"Gah!" I pushed away the tiny dog. "I'm fine. What happened?"

"You tell me. One minute you are holding the carrier, and the next you are falling out of the tree."

"Stewart?"

Adam's mother smiled and held up the net-bound Minor Demon. "I played stickball as a kid."

"Angela." I rubbed at my sore head. "Do you smell something?"

Adam's mother took a deep breath and her eyes went wide. "Smoke."

"Yeah, that's what I was afraid of."

3 2

HOME

*H*azy white smoke drifted between the distant trunks and shrouded the trees in an unhealthy blanket of foreboding.

Angela pulled me to my feet. "What happened, Gene?"

"The Calamity."

"Did you see her?"

I shook my head. "Not directly, but Little Ed showed me what is coming, and it has the ashen fingerprints of the Calamity all over it."

"Little Ed? You mean the nice young man from the diner? Whatever happened to him?"

"You're standing under him."

"Huh?"

I pointed to the oak tree. "Angela, this is Ed Lovely Junior, also known as Eddie."

"What?"

"When he caught the Lost Button it took him here. In the time since, he has taken root, and spread himself to become this forest."

"I don't—"

"Listen, Angela, I don't understand it myself, but it doesn't matter, because New Dead soldiers are coming, and they aren't visiting for tea."

Crash!

The boom of a distant tree falling echoed through the thick forest.

"What do we do?"

"We leave," I said, gently scooping up the dog and handing him over to Adam's mother.

"Where? Are we going back to Hell?"

I took a deep breath and gently laid my tired hands on the dog. "Not yet, I have one last stop. I have to say goodbye."

Angela coughed in the thickening smoke. "Where are we going, Gene?"

Trees shivered around us, the forest was moving and I didn't want to be here when the New Dead arrived.

I'm sorry, Little Ed.

A lone acorn lay on the ground. I picked it up and shoved it in my pocket.

"We're going home."

* * *

PLUSH red carpet flowed like a grand river beneath my feet. It trickled down stairs and cut a twin path through a potter's field of auditorium seating. Beyond the straight-back chairs, long curtains hung from impressive pillars like gaudy velvet dresses across a distant stage.

The stage...

Even in the dim light, it was impossible to miss Cathy sitting in the first chair, her violin in hand and a focused look on her face.

My breath caught in my chest—it was my daughter, but it wasn't. She looked so different, so grown up, so mature. The young woman I remembered would have fought tooth and nail before she'd given in to wearing a dress, but this one carried it with a grace and beauty that hit me like a hammer blow.

Catherine Law.

She twisted at the tuning pegs, turning them back and forth gently with each pluck at the strings. All around her other members of the orchestra did the same. The mild cacophony of pre-show preparation filled the auditorium.

"Gene." Angela grabbed my arm. "Where are we?"

I scanned the room until my eyes settled on them and I had to grab onto Adam's mother in turn to keep from falling over. "Porter."

She was dressed to the nines in a long black number I'd never seen before. Her hair up, it showed off the graceful curves of her neck—I missed that neck, and the head that sat on top of it. A stray hair teased at her bare shoulders. The entire ensemble brought tears to my eyes, but I couldn't turn away.

Like a man dying of thirst, I drank it in, all the pain, all the sadness, and all the memories. My wife turned her head to say something to the woman next to her, and I caught the edge of her eyes and the sly smile I'd long ago tattooed on my heart. Even if could stare into those distant eyes and loving smile forever, and it would never be enough to fill the aching hole in my chest.

No amount of Magick was worth this—infinity paled in comparison.

"Is that your wife?" Angela asked.

"Yes."

"She's beautiful, Gene."

"She is, and I gave her up. I gave all of them up."

Kris.

He'd grown up more than I believed possible. The last time I'd seen him he was playing with blocks and leaving toy cars on the floor for his father to step on. The young man fidgeting in his seat was a far cry from that little boy. His small sport coat did little to hide the surprisingly lanky frame he'd must have inherited from the rest of Porter's brothers. He tugged at the tie his mother had undoubtably made him wear and toyed with a folded program.

He's still my Kris.

The tiny dog growled in Angela's hands and turned a number of unhappy heads in our direction.

Angela pet the Chinthe's fur and stepped back into the shadowy corner of the upper level. Her own eyes misty, it was clear she missed her son, and I'd kept her from him for too long.

I gently directed her toward the entrance doors as the lights began to dim and she shook her head. "No. I have a feeling you are going to do something terribly self-destructive, and I cannot live with myself if I don't let you at least hear her play, even if it's just once."

I stopped, the weight on my shoulders lifting just a bit. "Thank you."

Angela wiped a tear from her eyes with Bobbin's fur. "Pardon me, Gene, but this whole thing sucks."

"Shh…"

Angela glared at the women and she immediately turned back around.

I like you, Angela.

"We don't always get to pick what happens to us," I said, the lights fading.

"So don't settle for what happens to you."

"Huh?"

"Gene, I'm not going to tell you how to be a Magician, and I'm certainly not going to tell you how to be a father. I'd say you are one of the best I've ever met. What I will tell you is this. When life gives you lemons, you throw them back —hard."

The woman a few rows ahead of us turned around to glare

again, but Adam's mom gave her a hand gesture that even in the dark had exactly the intended effect.

"Angela..."

"Hush, Gene. Your daughter's about to start. Close your eyes and soak it in. Life goes fast, and if you aren't careful, one day you'll be at the end of it, and wondering what the hell happened. You've given my son a purpose, a father figure, and a genuine role model. You've earned this. Now shut the hell up and enjoy it. Whatever insanity is out there, it can wait."

I closed my eyes and leaned against the felt-covered wall. Exhaustion soaked muscles slipped into quiet contemplation in the cool dark. Angela was right. This was a moment I'd never get back again. I owed it to myself to enjoy all I could.

The conductor tapped at his stand and the instruments went silent. The audience held its breath as the first notes swelled to fill the wide room.

"First chair? Impressive," Adam's mother whispered.

"Thank you."

Angela's hand found mine, and she squeezed it. "She's starting. Oh my God, Gene. She's amazing."

The first notes hit my ears, and I had to open my eyes. Cathy dragged the bow across those strings with a precision I didn't know was possible. Each note blended effortlessly with the one after it, a music wide and haunting, yet at the same time full of life and love. There was something else hidden in that melody. Something I hadn't noticed at first. It danced between the notes, soft, pure, and strong.

Magick!

It wasn't much, but tucked somewhere inside the stirring grace of my daughter's solo was the cosmic power of the universe.

I didn't get to focus on it though before the door beside us slipped open. Multiple figures filed through, quietly drifting down the plush red aisles, the open sides of their jackets easy to see even in the dim light.

Skeeters.

"Gene," Angela squeezed my hand. "Something's not right…"

Growl…

"I know."

33

SWARMING

I let go of Angela's hand. "Stay out of sight, these guys aren't something you want any part of, trust me."

"What are—"

"Mosquito people." I pushed up the sleeves of my borrowed shirt and hastily slipped out of Stewart's carrier. "Nasty bastards. It appears Sofia's expanded her swarm."

Black shapes set up at the end of each row.

They're boxing them in.

"Angela." I handed over the hammock-wrapped Minor Demon. "Hold on to Stewart and stay out of sight until I give you the sign."

"Gene?"

"You'll know. Trust me, you'll know. Let that furry little missile go when I give you the sign."

Adam's mom swung the carrier over her shoulder with the practiced grace only a mother possessed. "Gene, there's more than a dozen of them. What are you going to do?"

"Improvise. I'll figure something out—it's sort of what I do." I ducked down behind the seats and scrambled toward the far corner of the room. "I signed up for this. My family didn't."

"Gene!"

I had barely made it half-way down the outside aisle when the first scream punctured the pregnant air and stopped my daughter's solo cold. The voice that followed brought with it a crashing wave of memory.

"Ladies and gentlemen, if I may have your attention."

Deacon!

He was older now, his skin stretched taut like the head of an overly tightened drum. Still, the Skeeter hadn't changed his preferred attire. He remained dressed head-to-toe in a black wool suit that represented the best in Mr. Evil fashion. Without a hint of compunction, he leapt onto the stage and let his frightening insect arms extend out to their maximum width.

Deacon was a showman, and center-stage was exactly where he wanted to be.

Boom! boom!

Doors slammed shut as over-sized Skeeters sealed us in, while the rest of Deacon's swarm blocked the aisles, their claws unfolding with deadly precision in the dim light.

"Excellent. Now, if I may." Deacon's clawed arm picked the baton out of the trembling conductor's hand and tapped it on the music stand. "Welcome one and all to the beginning of the end. How many of you woke up this morning and thought you'd have a front-row seat to the end of the world? Well, not you in the back, sorry, but you only paid for the cheap seats." The Skeeter swung his insect arms wide enough to take in the confused musicians. "Beautiful music, am I right?"

No one spoke, but a dull murmur echoed through the crowd.

Deacon shook his head, the seam of his jaw unfolding just enough to set off a smattering of gasps among the audience. "Tough crowd. I can appreciate that, but it would appear you aren't grasping the gravity of the situation. Let me help you with that."

The hairless Magician's insect arms shot out like the jaws of a coiled snake and impaled the helpless conductor. Deacon lifted his lifeless form up like a trophy for all the crowd to see.

Skeeters hissed and their jaws rippled with excitement, while the rest of the audience descended into pandemonium.

"That's better." The man-in-black tossed the corpse to the ground. "Now that you understand what is at stake, we can begin. Each of you should consider yourself blessed this evening —well, except for that gentleman. You are in the presence of greatness."

Confusion and panic raced through the auditorium like wild fire, but the Skeeters kept the crowds pinned into their rows. One of the concert goers pulled out a gun, rising from his seat and pointing it with trembling hands.

Damn it.

The man opened his mouth, but never got a word out, nor did he discharge the tiny pistol. The closest Skeeter's insect arms flashed and sliced the man's arm straight through to the bone. The weapon tumbled to the ground.

No!

I squeezed the edge of the seat back, but there was nothing I could do, not yet at least. Deacon was too far away, and I was in no condition to take on a dozen Skeeters at once—I'd barely survived Sofia.

More fresh blood sent the Mosquito people into a frenzy. Faces peeled apart in the dim light, their glistening fangs and serrated stingers quivering in hungry anticipation. An unholy chorus of hissing shrieks cut through the room like a cold wind.

The man clutched at his sliced wrist and tried to stem the bright red flow of blood while the closest Skeeters swarmed over the seats toward him.

"See!" Deacon shouted, his insect arms pointing right along with his fingers. "That was what I was trying to avoid."

Flared jaws hissed in excitement.

"But he's left me no choice." Deacon shook his hairless and pale head. "Do it."

Skeeters descended on the would-be hero. Hungry jaws and insect arms reduced the man's screams into a bubbling mess of fleshy pulp.

"Do we have any more heroes?" He spread his arms wide. "How about you, sir? Are you a hero?"

"No..." an elderly man in the front row shook his head.

"Excellent, and you ma'am? Are you are a hero?"

The well dressed woman next to him clutched at her purse and followed suit. "No."

"Splendid. The Defiler has come for the lost sheep, just like you. Just like all of you. His darkness is the great embrace."

I took a deep breath and reached for my Magick, only to have the sharp nails of a well-heeled socialite grab my wrist. "It's happening. You are wasting valuable time, and Magick!"

The House.

Her grip was strong, but the eyes behind it weren't. She was weak and tired, a dying Void. The House was ending, and now even I could feel it—the waning edges of an infinite power collapsing like a fading star. I didn't pay much attention in school, but I was pretty sure that always ended with a rather large explosion. I had no interest in front row seats for the supernova that would come afterwards.

"Let go of me."

The elderly woman's vise-like grip held firm. "You signed the contract."

"And you promised to keep my family safe."

More screams erupted throughout the wide room.

"Do they look safe to you?" I pulled back on the House's cold fingers. "You do your job, and I'll do mine."

"Gene—"

"Magick, now!"

The House glared and the sweet taste of cosmic power swelled in my body. "Don't make me regret this."

"I won't."

The Magick slowed to a trickle.

"Hey, don't hold out on me."

"Get creative," the House said, pulling back its hand. "And you better be there."

"I'll be there at the end. I promise."

The woman shook her head and blinked her eyes as if coming out of a daze.

I wouldn't miss it for anything.

I slid down another couple rows, inching closer to Deacon while trying to stay out of sight. The hairless Magician frowned and snapped the baton in his insect claws. "We can do this the hard way, or the easy way. In either case, Asaroth the Defiler will get what he wants."

Mosquito people corralled the panicked crowd and kept them in the rows. Porter and Kris's face appeared in the crowd, then vanished just as quickly.

"I don't want to let my men feast on you, but I will if I don't get what I've been sent here for. It's that simple."

Don't say it...

"I have come for Catherine Law. Give her to me, and I will make sure at least half of you survive to see the dawn."

The crowd hesitated, confused looks on their faces.

"How hard is this? Is it so difficult to help me find one person?"

A low mumble rolled through the concert-goers.

Deacon's insect arms snapped out and shattered a nearby cello, that same claw passing through the flesh behind it like it were tissue paper. The musician collapsed, his hands unable to keep blood in his punctured body.

"We can do this all night, or you can tell me which one of you is Catherine Law."

My daughter placed her violin in her lap.

No, no, no! Don't do it.

"I'm Catherine Law."

"Cathy, no!" Porter jumped to her feet and reached for her distant daughter.

Skeeters rushed the stage and surrounded my child. Black and twisted insect arms separated Cathy from the rest of the musicians.

"Is that you, Porter?" Deacon tilted his head and used a hand to block the stage light. "It is you."

"What do you want with my daughter?"

"Oh, Porter," Deacon used his segmented arms to prop himself up like stilts and descended from the stage to hover in front of my wife. "It is you. The Defiler said you wouldn't remember me, but I wasn't sure I believed him."

"I'm not letting you take Cathy." Porter's tiny fists tightened.

"You see, there was a time when that would have concerned me. When your husband's deal meant you were under the protection of a force even I steer clear of, but not anymore."

"My husband died years ago."

Deacon laughed, a giddy and sickening sound. It echoed in the quiet hall. "No, I assure you, your husband is very much alive, but he won't stay that way for long."

I KNOW

ead? I'll show you dead.

Magick swam in my chest, but it was far from the inexhaustible power the House had been doling out over the last few months, this was bottom of the bag, chip dust Magick.

How am I supposed to work with this?

Skeeter claws held my daughter tight, the hairless men's jaws fluttering with excitement.

"All right, boys. It's time." Deacon raised his arms. "You know what that means."

Skeeters swarmed the seats, almost at random, but it didn't take long for me to figure out what they were doing. I knew it because I'd seen it before, in the fiery Gloom all those months ago.

The Conjuring Sigil...

Back then it had been Tristan's doing, but this design was no different. Skeeter claws sliced through patrons like sheep, their blood falling on the upturned chairs and forming the pattern that would bring Asaroth the Defiler.

Do something!

There wasn't enough Magick for a frontal assault, but I had

to do something. My eyes caught the distant pistol's metal lump and I had an idea.

Please remember, honey. Please...

I dug deep and pushed away the pain, and the screams of the dying. I pushed for whatever Magick was left, the tiny, drifting energy the House had left me. I didn't need much, just enough for a simple toss.

Please remember, Porter. I know you've fired a gun before, please remember how.

"Leva," I said, letting the tiniest amount of precious Magick slip out between the seats and loop around the fallen gun.

Barely visible in the dim light and commotion, the black metal stock wiggled.

Come on...

I pushed more Magick into it, willing the stupid gun up and into Porter's distant hand.

"What are you doing with my daughter?" My wife cried, climbing over one seat only to be pinned to the next one by one of Deacon's insect arms.

"Me? Nothing. The Defiler? Well, he's got his own plans. Who am I to question the great darkness?" Deacon swooped down to hang above my wife. A single claw lay embedded deep within her beautiful shoulder and kept her fixed like a cataloged butterfly.

The gun slid a few feet, but in the wild commotion of flipping seats and slashing Skeeter arms Porter didn't seem to notice.

Damn it.

There wasn't enough Magick to get the gun back to me, but maybe there was enough for one last push.

I took a deep breath only to have the wind sucked right out of my sails. The summoning was working. Against all odds, the sigil had enough power to bring a very willing Asaroth into this world.

Fire erupted above the orchestra, the disjointed flames quickly forming into a circle, a circle that brought with it a crushing memory.

My daughter's face against a backdrop of flames was too much to take. I'd lost her once, and in doing so torn my life apart. I wasn't going to lose her again.

"Leva!" I shouted, pouring everything I had into the Magick. "Leva! God damn it!"

The gun flipped up off the ground and tumbled end over end in the air only to land next to Porter.

"Gun!" I shouted, my out burst drawing the attention of the Skeeters. "Gun, Porter. Shoot him!"

My wife didn't have to be told twice. She scooped up the gun and pointed it at Deacon.

Boom!

The gun's blast echoed in the wide room, its bullet tearing through the hairless monster's flailing jaw.

Before Porter could fire again, the Skeeter pounced. His serrated stinger impaled itself on her neck.

"Porter!" I shouted, backing away from the outstretched arms of Deacon's men. "Shoot him again!" But my wife's face disappeared beneath the Skeeter's hungry jaws.

Insect arms cut the air, and I jumped up on the back of a newly emptied seat. I needed more Magick, and I needed it now.

Damn it!

Porter's eyes glazed over, her fighting fists falling gently to the side.

"Run, Kris!"

More Skeeters raced down the aisle toward my son, their long black insect arms throwing people aside.

"Now, Gene?" Angela asked, stepping from the shadows, the Chinthe fighting in her grip.

"Yes!"

The little orange ball of fur shot down the aisle and sunk his tiny teeth into the monster closest to my son.

"What the—" the black arms and the rest of Deacon's henchman vanished along with the tiny dog.

Okay, that is kind of awesome.

"Run, Kris."

My son hesitated.

There was another Skeeter coming, and there was no Chinthe to suck him up into God only knows where, there was only me.

I ran across the arms and seat backs, throwing my body into the massive Mosquito man's back before he could reach my son.

Boom!

The Skeeter hit the ground with me on top of it. Long black insect arms rattled against the nearby seats while I slammed his head against the hard concrete a couple times for good measure.

"Kris!"

"Eugene Law." Deacon's serrated stinger licked his torn jaws, while his insect arms dropped Porter and pulled my young son close. "What a pleasant surprise. The Defiler will be pleased I saved him the trouble."

"Kris, it's gonna be fine."

Tears streamed down my boy's confused face. "Who are you?"

"Quite a sacrifice, Gene. You gave all of this up for the Void's power—impressive."

"I didn't do it for the power."

Deacon tilted his head. "What did you do it for?"

"He did it for me!"

Cathy!

My daughter fought against the grip of the Skeeters pulling her toward the fiery gate. Flames licked at the edges of her dress, while something massive twisted in the inky depths in the center of the yawning hole.

"You remember!" My stomach dropped while my heart soared.

"It doesn't matter now." Deacon yanked my son into his bloody and quivering jaws. "The Defiler is coming, but he never said anything about a son." The hairless Magician's arms tore open Kris's shirt. "What do you think? Wouldn't he make a great feeder?"

"Deacon, if you—"

"If I what?" The Skeeter's stinger drifted toward my son's neck, the color draining from Kris's panic-stricken face. "You don't understand, do you Gene? You are done. It's over. I have your daughter. The Defiler is coming, and when he's finished, I'll add two feeders to my swarm." One of Deacon's insect arms drifted back to caress my wife's bloody face. "Or, perhaps a Blood Queen?"

I reached for my Magick and dug as deep as I could go, but there was precious little there.

"Dad!" Cathy screamed.

Tentacles of inky blackness poured out of the gate. Long arms reached for my daughter. The Skeeter arms holding Cathy let go, their owners beating a hasty retreat from the Defiler's destructive touch.

Magick! I need something to work with...

Cathy's violin and bow lay on the floor not far from her.

That's it!

"Cathy, the violin, play it!"

My daughter turned her confused head toward me, the rest of her trying to stay one move ahead of the grasping arms. "What?!"

"Play it!"

Cathy ducked the Defiler and scooped up the instrument. "What do you want me to play?"

"You can play Twinkle, Twinkle Little Star for all I care, just play something, damn it!"

Cathy bit her lip and dragged the bow across the tiny instrument's strings.

"It doesn't matter." Deacon used his remaining insect arms to hoist my son up into the air. "Asaroth comes!" The Skeeter's serrated stinger pierced Kris's neck.

"No!"

Cathy's bow cut a jagged and fear-filled path across the violin's string, while the Defiler's tentacles snaked around her. "Dad!"

Dad.

The simple sound of it filled me with hope, and in that moment, I refused to lose my children to the darkness again. "Play, sweetheart. Play like everything you've ever loved depends on it!"

The first few notes of that nursery rhyme echoed in the great hall, bouncing off the walls and rising above the Skeeters' hiss and the confusion. A cosmic power beyond logic and reason, it pushed back against the Defiler's corruption. Its Magick swelled both familiar and at the same time very different.

I reached for it, willing the Wild Magick of my daughter's music into something more.

"Gene!" Angela's startled cry shattered my concentration.

Skeeters had Adam's mother surrounded, their insect arms hovering mere inches from her face.

"You see, Gene." Deacon retracted his stinger, blood trickling down Kris's chest. "You cannot stop me. You cannot stop Asaroth. The dark embrace is without end."

"What the hell?" A startled and clearly confused Stewart shot into the air. His wings restored and his body showing no signs of the Reaver's crushing blows. "Gene? Where are the Reavers? Or the bug girl? Oh, they come in bug men too. Look at that."

35

STELLA MORTEM

"Stewart!"

The tiny pink Imp swooped between the Defiler's writhing tentacles. "Yeah, boss."

"A little help here."

Stewart's rubbery body shifted to a malevolent purple. "With pleasure." The Minor Demon folded his wings like a hawk, zeroing in on the hairless Magician and Kris. Tiny claws flashed and with a wet slap the diminutive monster slammed into Deacon's eraser-like head.

Smack!

The Skeeter tumbled backward, letting go of Kris, and turning the bulk of his fury on the frustrating Imp.

"Kris!"

My son hit the ground hard, his arm awkwardly slamming into the seat back, while his head rocked against the concrete.

No!

Cathy's violin and its shaky notes fought against the Defiler's power, but it wasn't enough. Deacon was right, Asaroth's darkness was too great. The rest of us depended on the Void for our Magick, but not the Defiler. He existed without the Void's help.

His Magick was his alone, and the dark embrace of those inky tentacles was coming whether we were ready for it or not.

"Kris," Cathy cried, her melody coming to a stuttering halt.

"Keep playing!"

My daughter shook her frightened head. "I… I can't."

The Defiler's tentacles swept through the room, and wherever they touched destruction followed. Seats melted and curtains dissolved. Anything caught in Asaroth's dark embrace disintegrated before our eyes.

"You can. I know you can. I know because I've seen the Calamity's eyes. I know because I know my daughter."

"But Dad—"

"Play, Catherine. Play for me, play for your mother, and play for Kris. Play!"

My daughter closed her eyes and pulled the bow across the strings. The simple melody returned, but this time with conviction. This was not the shaky and broken version we'd been hearing, these were the perfect notes of a twinkling star.

A star…

Magick swam in Cathy's melody, a power born of the Void, but different somehow. It danced above the cacophony and pushed back at the Defiler's tainted evil. My daughter's Magick was beautiful, powerful, and best of all, Wild as the day is long.

I reached for that Magick, tugging on its mental strings and plucking at those notes with my mind.

"Stella," I whispered, my soul yearning for the cosmic glory deep inside her music.

A small, white ball of intense heat winked into existence above the Defiler's fiery gate. A star was born, and its glorious radiance was more than Asaroth's tentacles had planned for.

"Gene!" Angela shouted, pulling me away from the Magick. "Help!"

Skeeters had Adam's mother surrounded. The closest one's jaws flared wide and its hungry stinger probed the air.

"Call the dog!"

"What?"

"Call the dog. He listens to you."

"Bobbin, here boy!" Angela shouted, ducking an insect arm aimed at her head.

Yip! Yip! Yip!

The little orange terror appeared in the aisle, its fur soaking wet. It shook once, then shot down the red carpet like an angry badger.

"Gene—" Angela's cry was cut short by the piercing tip of a spear-like arm.

The tiny dog didn't hesitate, in one instant the black-clad Skeeter was there, and in the next it wasn't. The Chinthe whisking it off to who knows where.

"Dad?"

"Kris!"

Blood trickled from the hole left by Deacon's stinger, but whatever was in that saliva appeared to undo the memory loss the Void had imposed.

"Dad." My young son pressed a bruised hand to his neck, then pulled back his bloody fingers. "Dad?!"

"Keep pressure on it." I scooped my hands underneath his arms and helped him up. "Can you walk?"

Kris swayed gently, his still very young and weakened body pressing against me. "I don't—"

"There." I pointed to Porter's slowly stirring form. "Get your Mom and get out of here."

My son hesitated, his fingers not willing to let go of my hand. "Dad, I—"

"I'm not going anywhere without you. I promise." I pushed him toward his mother. "But Mom needs you. Go!"

Kris had only stumbled a few feet before Stewart shot past, flung by Deacon's insect arms. The bald Magician pulled himself out of the tangle of seats, his flared jaws torn and bloody, while his face bore the numerous claw marks of a very annoying Minor Demon.

The tiny star glowed in front of the Defiler's gate, its purity and power fighting back against the rising tide of darkness.

"Flagellum!" Deacon shouted while Magick born of the Defiler's embrace erupted from his hands like black and inky tentacles of corruption. Deacon's whip-like strands struck Cathy, cutting off her music mid-note, and with it forcing the star to flicker and shrink.

"Cathy, don't stop playing." I scrambled over the seat backs toward the Magician.

Broken notes snapped in and out from my daughter's instrument, Deacon's whip-like Magick pulling on her arms.

"Stewart!"

The purple Demon scrambled up from behind a distant seat. "Huh?"

"I need you to screw up some Magick, now!"

"But last time it didn't—"

"Do it, Stewart!"

The tiny Imp clawed his way onto the seat back and cracked his tail like a bullwhip. A shock wave of Magickal manipulation rocked the wide auditorium, twisting and perverting the Skeeter's whips, but also setting the baby star on tilt.

Deacon's black whips froze solid, the soft and inky tendrils becoming dense like electrical wires, and crashing to the ground all around my daughter.

"Cathy, look out!"

An errant wire knocked the violin from her hand.

"It worked!" The Imp's tiny face swelled with pride.

Shatter!

The beautiful instrument exploded against the ground, its strings tearing apart the tightly bound wood.

Stewart slapped a clawed hand to his face. "Oh, crap."

Without my daughter's Magick to push back against it, the

Defiler's tentacles poured into the room, and like a malevolent plague they passed over the crowd, reducing everything they touched to ash.

"Damn it, Stewart." I ducked the path of an errant tentacle.

"I know, I know." The purple Demon was airborne again and twisting between the Defiler's arms.

"Keep Kris and Porter safe," I shouted, jumping up and over another of Asaroth's arms.

Stewart tucked in his wings and dropped to avoid a black tentacle. "What are you going to do?"

The small white light flickered above the Defiler's portal, its power waning.

It's dying...

"I'm going to kill a star."

"What?!"

I pointed to Kris and Porter huddled between the seats. "Get them as far away as you can. We're about to implode."

"Boss, that's not the best idea—"

"Now, Stewart!"

The purple Demon swooped out of the way of yet another Defiler arm, this one crashing into the seats between us and instantly turning them to dust.

"Dad!" My daughter's small fists pounded at Deacon's insect arms with little effect. The hairless Magician had reached the stage and held her up like a trophy for his master.

"It's too late, Gene. The Defiler has won. Soon he will have your daughter and after that, the Void."

Cathy's tiny star flickered, its power all but spent.

"Gene," Porter cried, her distant and tear-filled eyes full of memory. "I remember now. I remember everything. I may have forgotten, but I never stopped loving you. I know that now."

The star flickered and twirled, its light fading in the unholy darkness of the Defiler.

Cathy kicked her feet and clawed at Deacon's long insect

arm, but the hairless Magician only pushed her closer to the gate. The fiery edge burned behind her whipping hair and brought with it memories too strong to push away.

We were back there again, back in the parking lot, the Defiler's tentacles destroying cars and cutting a path of torrid destruction. Cathy hung by her translucent fingers. Her spirit clung helplessly to the fiery gate. "Don't let me go, Dad!"

It's happening again.

A flare in my hand smoldered as a reminder of the past, of my mistakes, and their consequences.

Boom!

The unexpected bark of a handgun report pulled me back to the present. Porter ripped off a round into Deacon's body. It wasn't much, but it was enough to get him to drop Cathy.

"Sing!"

My startled daughter scrambled to her feet. "Dad?"

"Sing, Cathy!"

Her faint voice wavered in the face of the Defiler's power. "Twinkle, twinkle..."

Is it enough?

I reached out and found it, a single drop of Magick that drifted on those broken notes. It wasn't much, but sometimes it only takes a tiny amount to tip the scales.

Come on...

The twinkling star spun, shuddering against the Defiler's darkness. I pushed the last drop of power into that collapsing ball of glowing plasma, only to have it wink away in the Defiler's clutches.

"No!"

Rumble...

"Boss," Stewart cried, his tiny claws trying to pull Porter and Kris back from the yawning portal. "You did it!"

"Huh?"

"You just killed a star."

36

WE'VE GOT HISTORY

*I*mplosion!

Tentacles flailed wildly, the Defiler's cursed touch destroying everything in his path in an attempt to fight back against the pull of the collapsing gate.

"Stewart!"

The tiny Imp flapped his wings against the strong suction of the fiery portal. "Don't blame me, this was your idea."

"Get them clear." I pointed to my wife and son.

Porter's hair came undone and whipped in the maelstrom of swirling Magick. "Cathy!"

"On it."

I'm not losing her again.

I vaulted over the remaining seat and made a break for the stage, my body being pulled forward by the same closing portal dragging my daughter. "Cathy," I cried, reaching for her hand. "Give me your hand!"

My daughter's fingers clutched the edge of the stage as folding chairs and bits of broken instruments rocketed past her and into the swirling gate. "Dad! Don't let me go."

Flashes of that day rolled through my mind. It had all

happened before, and I would be damned if it was going to happen again. I buried those dark thoughts and lunged for Cathy's hand. "I've got you."

My fingers stopped just short, caught up by the black insect arms of an angry Deacon.

"Not so fast." The Skeeter pulled me away from the portal and my daughter. Dark tendrils of the Defiler's power feverishly tried to repair his broken body, but Asaroth's influence in this world was waning, his tentacles and their Magick were returning to Hell.

For a date with the Calamity no doubt.

"Dad!"

A serrated stinger shot out from Deacon's torn jaws and made a break for my neck. It was fast, but not fast enough. I caught the fleshy appendage with my hand. Its sharp edges peeled away skin like a pairing knife.

"Gotcha!" I yanked the twisted man forward, using his stinger as leverage. The Skeeter stumbled, insect arms flailing wildly against me and the pull of the closing portal.

Cathy's hair whipped in the wind like a hurricane flag, while her fingers skidded along the stage's edge toward the closing gate. "Dad!"

Blood dripped down from my hands, but still I yanked harder, anything to pull his arms away from Cathy. "Just hold on."

"To what?!" My daughter slid past chairs and whipping sheet music. An unclaimed cello rolled over her only to vanish into the unholy dark.

Deacon's flesh bit into mine. "Find something," I cried, blinking back at the pain and my sore muscles.

My daughter grabbed the edge of a billowing curtain, its thick red fabric stretched taut in the gate's pull.

"You cannot win," Deacon sputtered, his words breaking with the flapping of his unfolded jaws. "The Defiler is eternal.

He will have your daughter and with her he will break the Calamity."

I twisted the Skeeter's probing stinger against my bleeding fist. "He already has a Cathy, how many does he need."

Deacon's wide eyes told me all I needed to know. They brought with them a reminder of Ed's words.

That's not your daughter, you can't trust Asaroth.

He was lying. He didn't have one of my daughter's shards, but if he got one, then what?

The great oak's words hit me like a lightning bolt. "They are all connected, you cannot destroy one without impacting the others."

He's going to take down the Calamity with her own sister.

I hesitated just enough for Deacon to spot his opening. The Skeeter's insect arms shot out and tore through his own stinger. The fleshy worm writhed in my hand, while Deacon twirled onto the stage, his insect arms digging into the hard polished oak.

"The Defiler will have your daughter!" Deacon's jaws flapped wildly as blood streamed down his ruined face.

"Not on my watch." I tossed the twitching stinger aside only to have it vanish into the closing gate. "Hold on, Cathy!"

My daughter whipped at the end of the billowing curtain, her hands sliding down the thick fabric and the edges of her feet getting dangerously close to the swirling gate. "Dad!"

"I'm coming!"

Rip!

The heavy red fabric tore in the whipping power of the gate.

Of course it tears, why wouldn't it?

"Stewa—"

"On it!" The Minor Demon shot past like a streaking comet.

"Don't let her go!"

Stewart hit the twisting column of fabric like a hawk. His

diminutive claws knocked the thick curtain aside and wrapped tight to my daughter's hands. "I've got you."

It was all happening again, my daughter, the Defiler, and even Hell itself. I'd come so far—too far—to end up right back where it all began.

History will not repeat itself.

I pulled myself onto the stage. Deacon's insect arms blocked my path. He couldn't risk using more than a couple, lest he be caught up in the closing portal's pull.

"Is there something you don't want to meet on the other side, Deacon?" I said, crouching down to keep from being pulled into the vortex.

"The Defiler will have your—"

Boom!

A bullet tore through the Skeeter's skull, shattering bone and exploding flesh. His arms went limp and his body tumbled backward.

"Porter!"

My wife tossed the gun and ran for the stage. "I suddenly remembered how much I hated that thing."

Angela and Kris huddled against distant chairs along with the rest of the remaining audience as the Defiler's tentacles withered whatever they touched. Dark and frustrated, they swept the room in an anger-fueled rage. Chairs, Skeeters, and anything else the Demon's dark embrace touched melted away into dust, their ashes joining the cloud of destruction being sucked up by the closing gate.

"Look out." I ducked a sweeping arm before it turned me into spent ash. My wife lunged forward at the same time, narrowly missing her own grazing hug of death.

"Stewart, don't—"

"Let her go, I know, I know." The Minor Demon's wings flapped like mad in the portal's fury, "I can't help but feel like we've been here before."

Another tentacle shot out, this one hitting the stage and causing the wood to peel away like an over-ripe fruit.

"Cathy, don't let it touch you." I jumped back from the disintegrating wood.

"Dad, I'm slipping," Cathy's hand spun free of Stewart's clawing grasp.

"Stewart!"

"I'm doing everything I can." The tiny Demon pushed harder, his undersized muscles stretched to their limit.

Just a few more seconds.

The portal was now just a fiery sliver. In seconds, it would close completely, and with it take away any worry that the Defiler would get my daughter.

"Just hold on!"

"Gene." Porter jumped up on the collapsing stage and grabbed on to me. Together all we could do was watch as the final moments ticked past. "You did it. She's going to make it!"

The wind died down, and with it the Defiler's portal. Tentacles retracted into its inky depths, vanishing one by one. Stewart's wings finally gave out and the little Demon drifted gently onto what remained of the broken stage. My daughter landed with him, her hair windblown and her shoulder's slumped.

"You did it." Porter threw her arms around me in the final moments of the closing gate. "She's—"

Crack!

A final tentacle erupted from the razor thin portal, its inky darkness slamming into my daughter and knocking her to the ground.

"Cathy!" Porter screamed and pulled away from me only to watch her child's legs melt like a popsicle in the sun. "Gene! Do something!"

The portal slammed shut, and I froze, unable to look away.

This wasn't supposed to happen.

We'd saved her.

We'd kept her from the Defiler's clutches, yet there she was melting before my eyes.

Cathy!

My daughter's scream pulled me out of my haze. "Dad!"

"Gene, do something!"

I reached for a Magick that wasn't there, while my wife crawled over the missing stage to reach her fading child. "Cathy! No, no, no!"

"Don't touch her!" I shouted, but Porter wasn't listening, eyes focused on only one thing. Thankfully, Stewart was. The tiny Demon held my panicked wife back, keeping her away from a dying child with everything left in his tank.

The net!

"Angela, the net!"

Adam's mom raced down the center aisle, the flowing strands of a Duplickity net and Kris in tow. "What do I do?"

"Throw it on her."

The Defiler's dark embrace raced up my daughter's waist and then to her chest, everything it touched fading away like the edge of a burning paper.

Porter clawed at Stewart's wings, her eyes red with tears. "Cathy!"

Angela and Kris unfurled the great woven soul-strands like a cast net and tossed them over my dissolving child. The Illick-thid's weaving swept over her body, and in that final agonizing moment before it reached the stage, my daughter melted away to dust, her sad eyes and silent scream burned forever on my heart.

ROUND TWO

"Cathy!" Porter screamed, throwing the tiny Demon aside to kneel at the dusty remains of our eldest daughter. "No, no, no!"

A single tear sparkled in Stewart's dark eyes, his skin gently shifting to a pale-green hue. "Boss, I didn't see the..."

I collapsed against the stage, my body tired and my soul spent. "I know."

I failed.

Sirens wailed in the distance and I ignored them. It didn't matter what happened next, nothing did.

With this Cathy gone the others were sure to follow—Little Ed had said as much. The three shards of my daughter, a trinity of emotions, had just lost one of its members.

A two-legged stool cannot stand.

I pounded my fist on the broken wood. My blood stained the floor an angry red.

"Gene..." Angela extended a hand toward me. "What do we do?"

I pushed her away. "Nothing. There is nothing left to do. I did everything... No, I didn't do everything. Everything would have meant making the sacrifice mean something. Everything would have meant giving up my family so they could have a better life. Everything would have meant my dust on the ground, and not hers—never hers."

Porter swung around, her tear-streaked face a mixture of rage and sadness. "Better life? What kind of bullshit is that? Better life my ass. Families don't work without their fucking members, Gene. You gave us up—"

"To keep you safe." My voice broke. "I gave you up to bring back Cathy and to keep you safe. That's all I've ever wanted. Don't you understand? Without you three my life is a train-wreck. You know the things that darken our door, and what they bring." I pointed to Cathy's dusty remains. "That. They bring destruction and death. I'm a magnet for the world's evil, and all the pain they represent."

"Pain!" Porter pounded her tiny fist on my chest. "You want to talk about pain? Good, let's talk about pain. You put a hole in our hearts wide enough to drive a truck through. How's that for pain?"

"The House promised—"

"I don't fucking care what that damn thing promised. I know what happened. You think just because we couldn't remember you meant we didn't know something was missing. Do you know what it's like to live every day with a hole in your heart and not know why?"

"No…"

"Of course you don't, because you were out there doing something." My wife swung her arms wide. "You were out there. You got to do something about it, while the rest of us got our heads pushed into the sand. How do you think that felt?"

"But I wanted you safe. Don't you understand? I did it all for you."

Porter shook her head. "No, you did it for *you*. Let's not mince words here, Gene. You took the deal for you, not for all of us. You couldn't live with yourself. You couldn't stand seeing us suffer and you took the easy way out."

"Easy! I gave up everything for each of you. I gave up who I was. Do you know what my life's been like?" I held up my bloody hands. "This is not the only blood on these hands—not by a long shot—I've done terrible things, truly terrible things, and all of them I did for you."

"We'd have found a way."

I shook my head. "You were a wreck. You never left the hospital, and Kris," I pointed to my son, "Kris was coming apart at the seams. I couldn't stand it. I couldn't stand to see you suffer. Does that make me a terrible person? I couldn't just sit back and watch the only thing that mattered in my life turn to dust. I had to make it right, no matter the consequences. I couldn't live with myself knowing what I did to you."

"But you didn't do it to us—that damn thing did." My wife pointed at the scorched remains of the stage. "And then you decided to make it right by tearing the ones you love apart? What sort of person does that? You put the family back together only to rip it to pieces all over again. I love you, Eugene Law, and I signed up for this. Why won't you get that through your thick skull?"

"But Kris, and Cathy…"

My wife nodded. "They did too. We all did, damn it. We are a family, and we succeed or fail together. We need all the legs of this stupid table or it topples over."

Three legs…

"The House promised, and I never meant—"

"Of course you never meant to, but you did. We may not have remembered you, but that didn't mean you weren't missed. This damn family doesn't work without you and without her."

"But, the hospital… Do you remember what it did to you, and to Kris?"

Tears streaked my son's eyes.

"And this was a thousand times worse! You goddamn idiot, you wrecked us. You fucking wrecked us."

And now I did it again.

Porter collapsed against me, her anger descending into quiet sobs.

Stewart gently lifted the edge of the Illickthid's net only to have movement beneath it send him springing into the air. "Boss!"

The faint translucence of a flickering soul shined beneath the gossamer threads.

"Cathy?"

"What?!" Porter spun around, her eyes on the pile of dust. "What do you see?"

"He sees Cathy, Mom," Kris said, confusion in his eyes.

You see her?!

"Kris, can you see her?"

My young son nodded.

"Gene, what is he talking about? Is Cathy here? I don't understand," Porter asked, her eyes frantic.

Cathy's faint soul shifted gently beneath the net.

"Stewart, don't let her—"

The tiny Imp was already way ahead of me. He gently tucked the edges in until the shard was perfectly trapped in the narrow mesh.

"She's not gone."

"What!?" Porter reached for the dust but I pulled her back.

"No, not completely. Stewart has what remains of this shard in the net. I just hope it will be enough."

"Shard? What are you talking about?"

"When Cathy fell into Hell the first time, her spirit shattered and created three different shards." Stewart's claws tied off a knot on the newly twisted sack. "I tried really hard. I'm so sorry about it."

"Why didn't you—"

I hugged Porter to me. "I didn't tell you because I didn't think it mattered. Think of them like three legs of the same stool. With one destroyed the rest would follow, but it would appear destroying a shard is a lot harder than we thought."

"So, there are more of her? More of my daughter?" Porter pushed back, hanging on the tiny Demon's every word.

"Well, I've only met one of them, and she's basically become the warlord of Hell," the Imp said.

"What?!"

Stewart bobbed his head. "Yeah, the Calamity. She's kind of a massive pain in the ass, but scary as all get out."

"My daughter is a warlord?" Porter folded in my arms. "I don't understand."

"She is, and she's going to ride right over Asaroth and into the Void, and in doing so, she'll become the infinite source of all Magick."

"I don't understand what you are talking about." Porter pushed me away and got to her feet. "I want some answers."

"There's no time." I pointed to Stewart and the net. "Suit up and do not let that go. You understand?"

"Completely." The Imp cinched the net around his body like a baby carrier.

"Good, Angela, get the dog."

"Dog?" Porter spun around, the sounds of sirens and angry voices closing in on the destroyed auditorium. "What dog? Gene!"

"Bobbin!"

The tiny orange ball of angry fur skipped down the center aisle, his little cheeks red with Skeeter blood.

"There's a dog?!" My wife threw her hands up in frustration.

"It's a really long story." I grabbed my wife's hands and pulled them close. "And one I promise I'll explain completely one day. Now, I need you and Kris to get far away from here."

"Where are you going?"

Stewart flapped his bat-like wings and hovered in the air. "We're going to Hell. Ha! It sounds so funny to say that."

Porter ripped her hands away. "Oh no you're not, not without me."

"Or me." Kris clamored to stand next to Angela.

Outside sirens blared.

"It's too dangerous. You don't know what's on the other side. I can't possibly protect you both—"

Porter picked the gun up and ejected its magazine to check how many rounds remained with a practiced precision I'd all but forgotten about. "We can take care of ourselves."

"Porter—"

Stewart landed on my shoulder. "Boss, we've seen this one before. At least this time we know where she is."

Police burst into the auditorium.

"Angela, now!"

Adam's mother grabbed the tiny Chinthe, and we huddled together.

"Okay, this might hurt just a little."

The searing pain of all my cells splitting apart was the last thing I remembered before the world went white.

38

VANTAGES

"This is Hell?" Porter kicked off her heels and walked barefoot on the muddy hill. "I was expecting more, you know, fire?"

"It's a long story, and as Ed likes to say it's different for everybody—but I think he's full of it."

A hard wind swept across the desolate hill, bringing with it the acrid smell of smoke and ash.

"Maybe that's your fire." I pointed to the nearby summit.

Kris raced off ahead of us, his fancy shoes squelching in the deep mud.

"Kris!"

My son came to a halt the instant he reached the top. His excitement visibly curtailed.

I jogged up next to him, Stewart on my shoulder, and Cathy's shrunken and faded soul still wrapped in the Duplicity's net. "You can't do that here. You've got to…"

"What is it Gene?" Angela asked, clutching the tiny dog and up to her ankles in the dark mud.

"It's the end."

"What?" Porter climbed up next to me, the gun in her hand. "What do you mean the—Oh, my."

Laid across the valley in front of us and stretched to the very edges of the horizon, was an army of an almost uncountable number. Smoke and ash drifted between the distant bodies, but it wasn't the leavings of spent campfires—this army didn't eat, it didn't sleep, and it didn't suffer the living.

New Dead.

A swelling sea of the Damned filled the valley, their bodies clanking together in armor built of old street signs and broken highway barriers.

"Gene, is that…" Porter's words drifted off, her voice shaken.

"New Dead, yeah."

My wife impulsively re-checked the magazine of her borrowed handgun.

"If you want to go back—"

"No. My daughter is here, so I'm here." Porter took a deep breath and switched off the safety. "Besides, I have a score to settle with the Damned. Now, where is she?"

I nodded, not interested in standing in the way of a mama bear, especially *that* mama bear. "There's something you need to know about the Cathy that ended up here."

"Right, right, the 'warlord'…"

"Obelleron," Stewart whispered, his tone a mixture of fear and awe.

I tried to follow the tiny Demon's gaze but his eyes must have been better than mine. "Where?"

"There."

Black horses jostled for position, their bright and fiery hooves spitting sparks against the distant ground. At their lead was a single magnificent stallion, its broad and muscled chest propped up by six equally powerful legs. The terrifying and majestic beast demanded a wide-berth and the rest of the Damned gave it one, except for a single soldier.

"The Calamity," Stewart and I said together.

Porter located the distant horse, and my usually vocal wife went suddenly very still. "Is that... Is that her?"

Our daughter's elaborate helmet sat high on her head. A great plume of long dark feather's erupted from its crest, while the fangs of no less than a dozen Major Demons graced a string around her neck.

"Oh, Catherine. What have they done to you, my baby girl?"

Stewart shook his tiny Demon head. "It's not what they did to her. It's what she did for them."

"I don't understand," Porter said, tears biting at the edges of her smoky eyes.

Stewart's wings opened and closed slowly. "Cathy swept across Hell like a hurricane."

"My daughter? How is that even possible?"

"Hope." The Demon let the word hang in the air like a bad fart. "There's a reason why we had Dante put together 'The Inferno' the way he did. 'Abandon hope all ye who enter here' wasn't just a marketing slogan. We needed to keep that stuff out, and well, you know something, Cathy brought it just the same."

"She gave *them* hope? New Dead? They're the Damned. They don't deserve hope, they don't deserve her." Porter spit her words out with a venom that startled her son.

I placed a gentle arm on my wife's shoulder. "She gave it to them anyway, whether they deserved it or not."

"But, she knew what they did." Porter's knuckles whitened against the gun's gnarled grip. "She knew what they did to me, to us..."

"And she did it anyway—Cathy did what she had to do to survive."

My wife frowned and swept her hand across the assembled army. "This doesn't look like survival to me."

"That's because it's not anymore." I took a deep breath and shook my head. "She's got bigger ambitions now. The Calamity has reached out to other worlds and cut them down like a winnowing fan. Our daughter with an army of the Damned at her command has become the most destructive force I've ever seen."

"Gene, she's just a kid."

"Not here she isn't." I pointed to the distant cavalry. "Here she's grown up. Here she's a woman with a lot of ambition and very little to stand in her way. Do you see any Demons?"

"No, but I—"

"Exactly, she's driven them all into hiding."

"Or destroyed them." Stewart sprung into the air.

"Cathy did all that?"

The Minor Demon twirled around and stopped in front of Porter. "No, the Calamity did. I'd recommend you do not attempt to call her anything else—should we survive long enough to speak to her that is."

Porter pushed the Imp aside and scanned the wide valley. "What is that?"

"What is what?" I said, following her gaze.

"That. It looks like… it looks like your car?"

"The Dad Wagon," Angela and I said in unison.

"Adam? Do you see Adam?" Mrs. Grayson pressed the Chinthe into Kris's hands. Neither my son nor the undersized ball of fur were quite sure what to make of each other, so they settled on an uneasy stand-off.

Stewart swooped down the hill a little way, his bat-like wings catching the hot wind. "Hey, there he is. Did you guys leave him in a Phase Knot?"

"A what?" Angela asked.

"Stewart, are you sure?"

The tiny Demon brought a hand to his forehead. "Yep, I'm sure—looks like a pretty tight design too. That kid's gotten a lot better, Gene. I mean, he might give you a run for your money one day."

"Is he okay?" Angela's worried hands clutched my arm.

"For now. I expect the Calamity has more important things to do than break him out of that protective cocoon. Do you see Ed?"

"You mean the vile Demon Hunter, Edwin Lovely?"

"Yes."

Stewart sighed.

"Yes, and he's still alive," the tiny Demon said with very little happiness in his voice.

"Is he—"

"He's in the Phase Knot with your apprentice. I can't say he looks comfortable—so I've got that going for me at least."

"What about Kaylee?" I asked, squinting at the haze. "Do you see her?"

Porter brushed at stray ash. "Who's Kaylee?"

I frowned pushing away motes of spent embers on the soft breeze. "Ed's ex-wife—the Swamp Witch—there's a lot you don't know. I've been gone a while. I'll catch you up."

"No, you won't."

Kaylee!

Ed's ex-wife stood behind us, along with an armored contingent of New Dead, their ashen skin flaking away in the hot wind, and their tarry eyes black with hatred.

"Kaylee, what are you doing?"

The Swamp Witch pulled up the edge of her mud-streaked shirt to show off a burning patch of ashen flesh where the Soul Ripper's claw had pierced her skin.

No, Cathy!

"Is that her?" Porter asked, her finger already on the trigger.

"Stop!" I pulled my wife's hand back. "It's her, but something's happened, Cathy—"

"The Calamity will be pleased. She's been waiting for you." Kaylee motioned to the New Dead soldiers. "Take him."

"What about my family?"

"She didn't say. I'm guessing it doesn't matter."

"Gene…" Porter took a cautious step back, pulling our son with her. "What's going on?"

"Kaylee, it's me. It's Gene. Remember? I had the awesome pants. We stopped the Midnight Riders and pissed off a lot of Alligator Men in the process?"

"Honey, I don't think she remembers." Porter pulled Kris close, her finger back on the trigger but her hand switching from one target to the next.

Yip! Yip!

The tiny Chinthe barked at the approaching New Dead, my son unable to keep him under control.

"Oh, I remember just fine. You're Eugene Law, the man who gave my only son the Five Star Toaster and taught him how to use it—"

"Gene!" Porter's voice jumped up a few octaves.

"And then, when he was a blaze, you tossed him a Lost Button."

"Gene, you didn't… did you?"

Stewart hovered in the air and tightened the Duplickity net around his chest. "This is all news to me. It sounds like I missed a lot. Midnight Riders? Alligator Men? You do all the fun stuff without me. Plus, you had Lost Buttons all this time, and you never told me?" The tiny Demon shook his head. "I'm disappointed."

"Listen, Kaylee." Porter turned the gun on the Swamp Witch. "I'm sorry, my husband tries, but sometimes he makes mistakes."

The fiery eyes of the Ed's ex-wife didn't hesitate. "I don't. Kill them and take the Magician."

39

INSPIRATION

The Calamity's New Dead sprung into action, their hammered-rebar blades raised high and razor-sharp in the drifting smoke, while behind them a mounted Kaylee pulled hard on the reins to keep her Demon horse in check.

"Porter!"

My wife didn't hesitate. She pulled Kris against her chest and covered his other ear, then unloaded two rounds into the closest soldier.

Boom! Boom!

Ashen flesh erupted. Steel slugs tore great holes in the creature's armored body, while the startling sound of gunfire echoed down the hillside and brought back with it unwanted attention.

"Gene!" Stewart pushed himself above the fray. "More of them are coming."

"Go! Get away from here and keep Cathy's soul safe. I'll deal with the Calamity."

The tiny Demon didn't need to be told twice, his pink and rubbery body vanishing in the ash-filled haze.

"What do we do?" Angela squeezed my arm and backed away from the advancing soldiers.

"You take my wife and son, and you get the hell out of here. Use the Chinthe and go somewhere safe. I'll find you when this is over."

Rust-covered blades cut the air in front of us.

Angela didn't let go. "What about Adam?"

"I'll save him, I promise."

"Like you saved my son? Or your own daughter?" Kaylee's fiery voice cried out from behind the advancing soldiers. "The Calamity will unmake Asaroth and then turn her attention to the Void. She will become Magick without bounds, and the Wild Reaving will consume this world in righteous fire. The dead will know victory, and it will come at the hands of the Calamity. Soon your son will join the fold." Kaylee held up her shirt again to show the newly restored skin of the damned. "The Blessed will welcome him, as they welcomed me."

"The Blessed?" Angela tilted her head.

"I'm guessing she means New Dead. Don't listen to her. I'll take care of Adam."

"Your powers are coming to an end!" Kaylee shouted.

"Gene?" Angela's wide eyes stared up at mine, red-rimmed and confused. "What is she saying?"

Damn it.

"I…"

"Ask him." Kaylee pressed forward. "Ask him where his power has gone. He spoke for the Void, and now it's dying, and with it so is Magick. This is the end of an age, and a better one will rise from the ashes of this ruined place. The Calamity will put an end to our suffering. No longer the Damned—we are the Blessed."

A New Dead soldier lunged forward, his blade swinging in a tight arc and zeroing in on my son's head.

"Porter!"

Faster than I expected, my wife pulled Kris out of the way, but even she couldn't get the gun barrel up quick enough. The rusted blade rammed down against them both, but stopped short, clanging against an invisible shield. A shower of sparks rained down on the muddy ground.

What the...

"Gene." Porter dragged Kris and the tiny Chinthe to the hill's edge. "What's going on?"

Something metal flashed beneath the sleeve of my son's sport coat. It had been so long I'd all but forgotten about it, but the Magick I'd left in that charm hadn't. The rest of them were gone or destroyed, but there was still one last Logic Loop, and it was doing its job.

Frustrated New Dead swarmed my family, their blades swinging wildly against the invisible barrier only to be repelled again and again by the protective Magick of that precious charm.

Ashen hands grabbed me, the fiery touch of anger hot against my skin. "Kris, use the dog. Ask him to take you all away. Ask him to take you home."

"Gene, we aren't leaving you again!" My wife swung the gun left and right trying to get a clear shot in the unholy melee.

"Do it, Kris. Ask the dog. He'll listen to you."

My son's confused eyes met mine through the hailstorm of rusty metal. "Dad!"

"Do it."

Yip! Yip!

The Chinthe nipped at the New Dead, but to no effect, their ashen bodies and wicked blades continued to press the assault. I didn't know how much longer the simple charm could hold up under the constant pressure.

"Do it, Kris!"

My wife and son disappeared beneath the surging horde, a

showering of sparks every few seconds the only reminder they were still there.

"Do—"

My words were interrupted by the clarion call of a distant horn. It echoed across the wide valley and reverberated against the distant peaks. This wasn't the beautiful cry of the Centurion's horn when he swooped down to pick up Maurice, this was something far darker. It rattled my nerves and set the hairs on my arm on edge.

"Stop!" Kaylee shouted, swinging her spear and reining in vengeful soldiers. "It has started—look! Asaroth has come to die. The Calamity mounts Obelleron. Soon the Wild Reaving will wipe this world clean of the great slug's taint. Listen, she blows the horn of Stilchore!"

New Dead soldiers pulled back from my wife and son, their tarry eyes no longer focused on my family, but instead taking in the valley below. Ash and fiery hooves of distant black steeds reflected in the pools of those unforgiving eyes.

It started small, almost imperceptible against the hazy horizon, black shapes that slipped between the smoky clouds. Bat wings, far wider than anything my Imp possessed, emerged from beyond the distant hills. At first there were just a few, but their numbers quickly multiplied, expanding like the swelling thunderhead.

"What are they?" Angela's fingers clutched my arm.

"It can't be…" I wasn't sure I believed my eyes.

"What?!" Porter swung the barrel of her gun from side to side, keeping it trained on the hesitant soldiers. "Would someone please tell me what is going on?"

"It looks like—"

Stewart's rubbery body re-appeared from the low-hanging smoke, his wings beating furiously. "Gene, he did it. The Defiler has woken the Selemour. The Selemour are fighting for him."

Porter squeezed Kris and the dog close, unwilling to take her eyes off the ashen soldiers. "Someone please tell me what is going on."

"Asaroth has woken the Selemour!" Stewart shouted again, as if saying it another time would convince Porter of its significance.

"What is the Sele—"

Stewart threw up his tiny hands in a fit of frustration. "Arch Demons of Hell."

"Arch Demons? You mean like monsters from Kris's video games?"

A great plume of flame lit up the distant sky, followed by another, and still another. There was no denying Cathy's power, but was the Calamity prepared for something as ancient and deadly as the Selemour?

Are any of us?

"Yes, just like Kris's video games," I said, not believing my eyes. "Except a thousand times scarier, and without saved games, extra lives, or cheat codes."

Porter's gun dipped slightly. "Catherine..."

A new black shape appeared on the horizon, but unlike the Selemour it had no wings. It rolled like the burning edge of a curling paper over the mountain top. Black and oily, its long slug-like body scraped at the muddy ground and cast aside the broken remains of long dead trees.

"It is him." Kaylee's tone took on suddenly somber timbre.

This time Porter risked a glance behind her, only to lower her gun barrel completely. "Is that—"

"Yes, that is Asaroth the Defiler."

"Gene, he's huge."

"We're in his world now. Here we see him in his true form."

"No!" Kaylee tried to rally the suddenly concerned New Dead. "This is not his world, not anymore. Who is Wild Reaving?"

A mumble of confused voices didn't respond, their black eyes lost on the swelling tide of darkness.

"Who brought you hope?"

"The Calamity," one of the soldiers said, turning his face away from the massing forces.

"Who drove out the tormentors?" Kaylee cried, rallying her troops.

"The Calamity!" A second soldier joined the first, his voice stronger.

Can she do it?

"Who rides the Demon Steed Obelleron?"

"The Calamity!" Now more than half of the assembled New Dead joined in the cries, their apocalyptic armor clanging with each shout.

"Who will take us to our rightful place?"

"The Calamity!"

Kaylee raised her spear, a hot wind from the distant Selemour giving Ed's ex-wife the same wild hair her warlord master enjoyed. "Asaroth the Defiler is coming, and who will meet him?"

"The Calamity!"

Kaylee swung the great spear above her head. "The Calamity will take the field on the back of Obelleron. The Demon Steed rides again, and it is only fitting he rides against the Selemour. An ancient feud will see its end this day at the gleaming edge of the silver blade and trampled under the great stallion's pounding hooves."

Porter backed slowly away from the exuberant New Dead. "What does all of this mean?"

"It means the Calamity is in for one hell of a fight."

"Gene, she's still our daughter."

"I know…"

But what I don't know is if I want her to win.

40
GUILTY PARTY

*K*aylee pulled tight on the black horse's mane, its fiery hooves sizzling in the loose mud. "Finish them—the Calamity awaits!"

Confused New Dead soldiers tried to shake off the distant glory unfolding on the field below.

Oh, hell no.

"Angela," I whispered, her head close to mine. "Get my family out of here. The three of you need to use that dog and go. I promise I'll save Adam, but I can't do that if I'm focused on keeping you all safe."

Adam's mother hesitated, her eyes drifting back to the valley, and her son. "Gene, I…"

"I swear to you on everything I've ever cared about. I will not let him die. Your son and I will walk out of here together. Now, go!" I shoved Angela into Porter and Kris. The sudden push caught all of them off guard. "Go!"

Porter and I locked eyes briefly, and then they vanished.

It's just you now.

Stewart flapped his wings and landed on my shoulder. "So, just us now, eh?"

"What happened to keeping Cathy's soul away from them?" I whispered.

Stewart bobbed his tiny head and rubbed at the net-like sash. "Trust me. I've got this."

New Dead surrounded me, their black and tarry eyes full of excitement.

Kaylee extended a hand, her hair wild in the hot wind. "The Calamity awaits."

I accepted the Swamp Witch's help, and climbed up on the black horse, its muscled body warm to the touch. "What do I hold on—"

Kaylee tugged on the mane and we exploded off the mark hard enough that I had to wrap my arms around her tiny waist or risk being left in the mud with the rest of the Blessed. Stewart sprung into the air, his wings filling with the hot and angry breeze.

The distant camp loomed large, but beyond it, and far more ominous, was the Selemour, and past them, Asaroth himself. The slug-like body of the Defiler consumed the horizon. My fingers brushed across the ashen skin of Kaylee's restored flesh and I pulled them back, afraid whatever power the Calamity held over the Swamp Witch would find a way to get to me.

Oh, Cathy. What have you done?

NO SOONER HAD we reached the front line than the Swamp Witch and her horse dumped me in the hot mud.

"I could have gotten off on my own," I said, wiping the hellish muck from my face.

"Excellent work."

Cathy!

The Calamity's armored boots stopped in front of me, while a slender hand offered to help me up. "Have you come to try and stop me? Or are you here to see me bring an end to Asaroth once and for all?"

It may have been my daughter's hand, but it was hard to see the Calamity as Cathy. She'd changed too much. The fires of Hell had smelted her like stubborn metal, then in the darkness, hammer blows of pain, regret, and sadness had shaped her into something different. They'd tried to break her, to make her one of them—they'd failed.

The Damned...

There was no ash on that slender hand, and no tarry eyes stared down at me. This place tried to take her apart, but it hadn't counted on her fighting back.

It hadn't counted on hope.

Magick demands sacrifice, but it doesn't hold a candle to hope.

I accepted Cathy's hand, and she pulled me to my feet.

"How did you know he would come back?" Kaylee asked, pulling on the mane to keep her powerful horse under control.

"How did I know?" The Calamity asked, Private Petty's gleaming saber at her waist, and an elaborate helmet under her armored arm. "Tell her, Gene. How did I know you'd be back?"

"Lucky guess?"

Cathy laughed, it wasn't the beautiful sound I remembered, this was the hard and painful laugh of a tired soul. "Nothing here has happened by luck. Nothing. Did Obelleron agree to join me because of luck?"

"No!" A chorus of New Dead shouted back, their ranks stretching out beyond us in tremendous numbers.

"That's right. He did not. He came because I am the Calamity."

"She is the Wild Reaving. The destroyer of worlds and the hope of the Blessed. She is the Calamity, and she has come!" New Dead voices shouted in the hot wind, their chilling cry rattling my already frayed nerves.

Has she really done it? Can my daughter take on the Defiler and win? And if she does, can anything stop her from taking the House?

"But, Gene didn't come for those things, and he didn't come to help us." My daughter swept her armored hand toward the black shapes massing on the horizon. "He didn't come for you, and he certainly didn't come for me—at least not how you think. Tell them, Gene. Tell them why you came?"

"I came to save you."

More laughter, except this time it came from the ranks of the Blessed. Their haunting voices filled the air with a chorus of gut churning sound.

"Do I look like I need saving?" The Calamity smiled, her dirt-streaked and feral face giddy with anticipation.

"No..."

"They can't hear you, Gene. Do look like I need saving?"

"Cath—Calamity, that is the Selemour, you may not know what that means, but the rest of Hell does, and there's a reason why they fear them."

My daughter raised her hands to the soldiers behind me. "Who do we fear?"

"Nothing!"

"Do we fear the tormentors? The Demons and dark ones that led us to this valley of pain? Do we fear the ones that burned our skin raw and filled our eyes with the tar of regret?"

"No." New Dead voices rocked the valley. "We fear nothing."

"You don't understand." I pleaded with my daughter. "The Selemour are beasts of a different time. They are an ancient power far greater than you understand. You ride into battle with them and they will mow you down, and if they don't, then the Defiler surely will."

"Why don't you tell them what you really came here for?" Cathy's hard face reflected in the saber's blade. "Why don't you tell them who you work for?"

"I came for you."

The Calamity shook her head and pressed the tip of the gleaming blade against my neck. "No, you didn't. Tell them who you came for."

"The House."

My daughter nodded and snapped the blade back like a coiled snake. "He has come to protect the Void in its final moments. He has come to stop us, to bring an end to our destiny. Can he do that?"

"No!" New Dead voices shook the ground.

"And why not?"

"Because we are Blessed!" The horde shouted back.

"Don't do it." I pointed to the distant Selemour and the even larger slug-like bulk of the Defiler. "It's suicide."

"You left me here to die, old man. I should think you would want me to ride into that battle, let them finish what you started."

"I never meant for any of this to happen. Don't you understand? I wanted you to be happy—I've never wanted anything else. I just wanted my family to be safe and happy. I didn't ask for this."

"How many times have you had the opportunity to say no? To live a simple life?" My daughter brought the saber up again. "And each time what did you choose?"

"I—"

"Did you choose for me? Did you choose your wife? What about your son? Did you choose him?"

"Ca—"

"No, you didn't. Let me help you remember. Each and every time you had a chance, you chose Magick. You are an addict, a helpless addict willing to put all of those around him in danger to get your fix." My daughter snapped her blade out to the side and the assembled soldiers pulled back, showing me a cobbled together Dad Wagon, and the swirling shield of a very well designed Phase Knot.

Adam knelt inside the shimmering globe, unmoving, while a frustrated Ed held his hands up in a comical display of frozen anger.

"This is how you treat your friends. You abandon them, just like you abandoned me."

Adam, Ed...

"I didn't abandon them, and I didn't abandon you."

The Calamity pointed to her soldiers. "You did. You may fool them, but you don't fool me. You held Ariadne's Thread." She swung the blade back to point at my hands. "Your fingers, your hands. You held my life in those hands and you let it go. You let me go!"

My heart sunk, along with my tired shoulders. "It was the hardest thing I've ever done, and I don't think I'll ever forgive myself for it."

"I won't." The Calamity motioned for her horse.

The immense Obelleron pushed through the assembled New Dead like they were toy soldiers, his neck bending in the presence of the Calamity.

I can't let her do it. I can't let her get on that horse and ride into certain destruction.

"Stewart, throw the net on her. Trap the shard!"

249

41

THE BEST OF US

*T*he tiny pink Demon shot out of the low-hanging haze like a bird of prey, the net in his claws and unfurled just enough to cover the Calamity.

Yes!

Cathy unsheathed Private Petty's blade impossibly fast and in a single motion sliced the Duplickity net in two before the first threads touched her skin.

No!

Stewart scooped up the remaining fold and trapped the shard inside, but wasn't paying attention when Obelleron's wide snout headbutted the tiny Demon out of the sky and sent him and what remained of the net into the muddy ground.

"The Void is more important than your own daughter?"

I reached for Stewart, but the wicked edges of hammered-rebar blades kept me at arm's length. "No, you are the most important thing to me. You all are, each one of you."

The Calamity hesitated, her eyes transfixed on the dim soul that flickered inside the scrap of net. "That's... Why do I know her?"

"Because it's you," I said, hoping to find a chink in the

Calamity's hard-won mental armor. "Not all of you, but a part. That's why you are so full of pain. That's why you kick and scream. That's why you did this." I pointed to the army of the Damned. "You are missing a part of your soul, and without it you'll never be whole. Let me help you. Let me show you the woman you were meant to be."

Private Petty's blade dipped slightly, its gleaming tip stopping just above the black mud. "That's a part of me?"

"Yes, it is. It's the part of you that loves and knows what it means to be loved. It's the part of you that makes beautiful music and appreciates the world for what it is. It's the part of you—"

My daughter snapped Private Petty's saber up and rammed it into the flickering soul, the blade passing through without hesitation. The light inside winked out and disappeared in the black blood that poured from Stewart's punctured gut.

"Cathy!" My knees collapsed and my hopes with them.

What did you do?

"There is no part of me worth saving. I have told you before, old man. Catherine is dead and buried, and you killed her."

I pushed the rebar blades aside and pulled Stewart into my arms.

"Boss…" His tiny claws pressed against the net, and the wicked hole beneath it. He tried desperately to hold back the steady stream of dark blood. "I tried. I promise I tried."

"I know, Stewart."

The tiny Demon's pink skin lightened to a pale gray. "I know I'm not supposed to say this, but you actually are a good guy. I tried so hard to get you to take the bad path, but you know what, I think I failed—"

"Stewart."

"No, I did." The Demon's eyes drifted. "I totally failed. I figured I'd turn you into a monster eventually, but it didn't work, instead you turned me into something else."

I pressed on the wound. Stewart's black blood stained my muddy palms. "A pain in my ass?"

Stewart shook his small head. "Yeah, there was that, but you rubbed off on me." The tiny Demon's claws loosened. "I'm glad I got to know you, Eugene Law. You are one of the good ones, and maybe, thanks to you, I can be one of the good ones too."

"Stewart, stop. That's an order." I pressed my hand against his stomach. "You hear me. We'll get through this, just like before. We'll find a way. I've got to introduce you to those Alligator Men, and show you how I made Animated Pants, trust me, you're gonna love it."

The diminutive Demon's eyes closed and his tiny claws fell away.

"Stewart!"

The pale Demon's wings curled. "I wonder if I'll get a ride…"

"If anyone deserves one it's you." Tears blurred my eyes.

"Goodbye, Gene."

A final breath escaped Stewart's tiny body, and his head went limp in my arms.

No!

The Calamity held the black-tipped blade up for all her army to see. "Who has drawn first blood?"

"The Calamity!" they cried, their voices strong and fueling the rage building up in my chest.

I laid Stewart on the ground and gently closed his eyes. "Goodbye, Stewart the Amazing."

"Who am I?" Cathy shouted, thrusting her blade in the air again.

"You are the Calamity!"

Wild cheers rained down on the woman that had ceased to be my daughter.

My hands shaking I stood to face her, pushing away the rusted rebar blades of hungry New Dead. "Why? Why did you do it? What did he ever do to you?"

My daughter swung her blade in the air. "He wants to know what do we do with Demons?"

"The tormentors must die!"

The Calamity raised her other hand in a fiery salute. "Who are we?"

"We are the Blessed."

My shaky hands tightened into fists. "Cathy, this isn't you."

Private Petty's blade snapped back, its tip against my throat. "I told you. Catherine Law is dead."

The black tipped blade cut into my skin. "I see that now. You aren't my daughter."

"I never was."

"Do it then." I pushed against the biting metal. "Do it. Kill me now. That's what you're good at. Killing is who you are, and it's all you are. The Calamity is nothing but a murderer. So, go on, what's one more?"

Magick swirled in my chest. It came out of nowhere. In one moment the well was dry, and in the next it practically boiled over.

The Calamity smiled, her feral eyes hungry like the Damned that surrounded us.

"Do it, now!" she shouted.

New Dead soldiers pulled me away from the Calamity.

"Do it before we lose it again."

I reached for the Magick and opened my mouth only to find rusty metal shoved between my lips.

What?!

One of the Damned pulled my arm straight while another rammed what looked like a rail road spike between the bones of my hand.

Blinding pain hit me like a gut punch. I staggered a few feet before my knees collapsed against the muddy ground.

"Don't bother fighting it." My daughter pulled on the chain

that tied my bloody hand to my wrapped mouth. "Obelleron's bridle, forged in the fires of Hell and unbreakable."

I tried to speak, but I couldn't get words out against the hard metal.

"You want to know why?" The Calamity yanked me forward. "After all this time I learned something. While I hated her, Morgan was right, you are the best battery ever created."

I tried to pull the spike out, but a sharp crack of Magick forced me to yank my hand back.

"I know the Void is dying, but unlike you, I learned that before the finale it's going to pour everything it can into you, and you know what?" The Calamity pointed her sword to the Defiler's distant and swelling mass. "I know exactly what I'm going to do with it."

New Dead soldiers kicked at Stewart's body, and in the hot wind, the torn pieces of Harold's net rolled away, and with them my hopes.

"Don't be so sad." Cathy slipped a hand under my chin and pulled my face up to meet her wild eyes. "You are about to see the end of Asaroth. Just think, you'll be remembered forever."

My daughter tossed the chain to the closest soldier. "Put him in the car and get ready."

Obelleron dipped his wide head for the Calamity to climb on.

"What are we?" she shouted, holding the tarnished blade high.

"We are the Blessed!" her hordes cried back, their blades clanking against makeshift armor. Long tongues licked at ashen lips, while black eyes hung on her every word.

"Look in the distance. What do you see?"

"The end!"

"Is this the Defiler's Hell?"

"No!" The ground shook.

"Whose Hell is this?"

"The Calamity!" An uncountable number of blades and spears raised high in the air. Their owners screamed in the hot wind.

The Wild Reaving.

My daughter pushed her helmet on, the dark visage frightening against the backdrop of her army.

Her army...

Selemour filled the distant horizon. Black wings swelled large enough to block out the cloud-filled sky, and beyond them, the great mass of Asaroth consumed hills.

The Damned dragged me to the cobbled together Dad Wagon. Their ashen hands burned hot against the forged steel of Obelleron's bridle. I reached for my Magick, but it ignored me, lost to the bonds of enchanted metal.

One of the soldiers pulled open the door and shoved me in the backseat.

Slam!

The Calamity raised her sword in one final salute, and the Demon Steed beneath her reared up to match its rider.

"Today we finish what we started. Today we cleanse this world and make it ours—to the end!"

"To the end!"

New Dead piled into the front of the Dad Wagon and the throaty engine roared to life.

To the end, Catherine—for one of us.

PART III
WELCOME TO THE END

42

FURY

The old Mazda kicked up mud and raced over the broken ground like a jackrabbit. With a wild yell, the ashen driver poured on the gas and the engine roared. I had to hand it to the Calamity, she'd certainly figured out how to put the very best mechanical New Dead talent into working on the Dad Wagon. In the entire time I'd owned that car, it'd never sounded this good. Then again, it had never been driven by New Dead directly into the winged fury of the Selemour.

Arch Demons, she's going to take on Arch Demons...

Obelleron thundered alongside us. His large hooves threw up mud with each powerful blow. My daughter rode high atop the Demon Steed, the feathery plume of her helmet giving her an almost banshee-like appearance in the smoky haze.

My daughter...

Catherine Law was dead and gone—long live the Calamity.

No, you can't quit, damn it. There's a spark in there, you saw it, even if it was just for a second. You saw it. She's still your daughter. You know what you have to do.

"You sure about that, Gene?"

The House.

A worn and tired Jenkins appeared in the seat next to me. His pale skin somehow even more distressed and spotted than I remembered it. "Thought you could use an inspiring figure from your past. You know, someone to keep you motivated. Viktor was a pain, but damn did he know how to make a sacrifice."

I opened my mouth to speak, but the strong metal kept the words solidly trapped.

My old mentor shook his head. A few wispy hairs of snapped in the hot wind. "Well, it's good of you to actually show up. Would have been a lot better for you to not be bound and gagged, but maybe that's asking a lot."

A little help here?

The House coughed into his bone-white hand. "I've given you all I have." The old Magician pressed a strong finger against my chest. "All of it's right there, and what are you doing? Joy riding? Gene, this is the end. Don't you understand? They're all gunning to take my place, and my best hope is wearing a metal bridle like a moron."

I'm not a moron.

"Say that to me out loud."

Gah!

"You can stare daggers at me all you want, but the truth of the matter is you're trapped. You've got yourself in quite a bind, and you have no real plan for getting out of it."

I'm working on that.

Jenkins leaned against the door and pointed to the sky where black-winged Selemour, like fiery molten rock with sharp claws and ferocious teeth, filled the air with clouds of burning ash. "Well, you better work faster. The Selemour are no joke. Stupid guys may look annoying, but there's a reason why they are the Dukes of Hell. Asaroth may have stirred them up, but I am guessing he has very little in the way of control over them. Speaking of control, where's the Chinthe?"

I sent him with my family. I told them to go home.

"Yeah, that sounds like something you'd do." The old Magician shook his head and returned to staring at the approaching wave of molten death. "I was on the fence with you—even in the beginning—you care too much. I thought it might have been the winning formula. Find someone strong but willing to think beyond themselves."

Boom!

The first Arch Demons landed. Its wide body much larger than Obelleron. The Demon Steed looked like a child's toy in comparison to the two story monsters, but Cathy remained undeterred. Part of me had to admire her ferocity.

"She's what you could have been."

The Calamity swung Obelleron to the side, his hooves cutting hard in the thick mud. Our New Dead driver followed suit and the Dad Wagon rumbled behind her.

"Whoa." Jenkins grabbed the door handle. "Where was I?"

I sighed and held up my spiked hands.

"Oh right. I was lamenting the fact that I put nigh-infinite power in your fleshy little frame in the hopes that you'd see me through the rebirth, but now I'm really starting to question that decision."

Private Petty's sword flashed from Cathy's side, its bright blade muted with the tarnish of Hell.

"I mean, let's take your daughter—bang-up job there by the way. Sure, she's basically brought Hell to its knees, and is only seconds away from leading a suicidal wave of the Damned against the Selemour and Asaroth, but what happened to the innocent Magician underneath? What happened to her, Gene? Where's the real Cathy?"

My teeth ground against the hot metal.

You did this to her! You created the Calamity!

Jenkins shook his head. "I didn't make the deal. That was your lawyer—you really should pay for counsel, Gene. At least have someone look over it before you sign. Still, here we are, certain death for all of us only seconds away. You with my nigh infinite power swirling around in your chest, and me, moments away from a rebirth I'm pretty certain I won't see the other side of. We're a matched pair, you and me."

A fiery sword roared to life in an Arch Demon's hands.

All around us the rest of the Calamity's horde rumbled over the desolate ground. Mounted and on foot, the wild cries of the Damned echoed across the valley, while around them Arch Demons landed, their own voices bone-shaking.

Cathy pulled hard on the Demon Steed's mane and guided him toward the descending Selemour. Obelleron snorted and sparks erupted from his nostrils.

"Yep." the House frowned. "Looks like this is how it ends. Well, shit. I did get to see fire in Hell one last time, so there's that."

Cathy!

My daughter stood on the Demon Steed's back, her hair flying wildly and Private Petty's blade raised high.

She isn't going to make it.

"Nope."

The Arch Demon's jaws opened wide. Bright red flames poured out like molten stone.

"It's been fun, Gene."

Cathy, no!

My daughter pointed her free hand at the Dad Wagon. New Dead in the front seat spun around and grabbed the spike wedged in my hand, then pulled it forward. Before I could fight back, ashen hands jammed it into a gap in the center console.

Magick exploded—the blackened steel pulled like a Dead Man's Tongue on steroids. Cathy had a plan for the Selemour, and it was breathtaking.

"My Magick!" the House cried, his frail body flickering in the bridle's pull. "Gene, you need that. Stop it, stop the—"

Everything poured out of me: love, pain, joy, and heart-ache. A lifetime of emotions and moments condensed into a stream of Magick beyond understanding. The cosmic power of a thousand suns ripped through me and into that black steel. Glorious pain crashed like a tidal wave, the edges of my vision dimming in the onslaught. The Calamity took it all, everything she could get her hands on and then some. The Magick surrounded her body like the wings of a great bird, their fiery tips raised up to the bleak heavens.

The Dad Wagon hit the brakes and cut hard to avoid the fiery blade of an Arch Demon, and as it did, half the contents of the trunk tumbled into the second seat, but the spike kept me pinned to the console. New Dead soldiers screamed in wild fury, their ashen bodies surging in waves against the monstrous Selemour. Great flaming swords cut the Blessed down like tall grass, but the dead didn't stop, they never stopped.

They came in waves too many to ignore. Their voices raised in a single cry, a unifying and unholy scream.

The Calamity has come.

The ashen hands and tarry eyes scrambled over one another to blunt their blades against the fiery Arch Demons.

Boom!

The largest of the great monsters dropped from the sky, its monstrous wings unfolding wide enough to cast aside dozens of the Calamity's men in a single pass. A great crown topped his head, burning gold and gleaming in the light of his flaming sword.

I'd read the books, but never thought I'd see him in person.

Revelore the Dark had come to heed the Defiler's call.

The King of all that Burns was here.

The Monster's blade cut a wide arc and mowed down scores of New Dead in the process. The Damned were no match for Hell's royalty, let alone the Defiler.

The Dad Wagon turned hard again, bouncing across the

broken ground and avoiding the fiery tip of yet another Sele-mour blade to stay as close to the Calamity as possible. She needed my Magick, the power of the Void itself, if she was to have any shot at survival.

Obelleron surged and my daughter climbed atop the saddle. She stood tall, her hair whipping in the hot wind and Private Petty's blade held high. Magick poured into the Calamity, and with it, glowing wings swelled from her back as she took flight.

My daughter was no longer Cathy, Catherine, or even the Calamity.

She had become the embodiment of destruction, an angel of damnation, a dark-winged Fury with eyes set on one thing—total victory.

43

ON ANGEL'S WINGS

C lang!

The fiery edge of a Selemour blade caught the Dad Wagon's hood and sent us spinning in the soft mud. The New Dead driver and his partner-in-damnation did whatever they could to keep the four wheels upright while I bounced like a pinball in the backseat. At some point, we caught on a rocky outcropping and sheared off at least part of our rear bumper. Yet through it all, we kept up with the Calamity.

My daughter shined like an angry comet against the molten skin of Revelore the Dark. The gleaming edge of Private Petty's blade was the lone bright spot in a sea of destruction.

The Arch Demon's booming voice shook the Dad Wagon. "I am Revelore the Dark, Scourge of Hell, and Devourer of the Nine."

My stomach pulled in on itself like a collapsing star and I was only in the back seat, the Calamity had front row seats for that mental lashing.

To her credit, my daughter never flinched. Those wings of pure Magick unfurled behind her and swelled with a pride all their own. "And I am the Calamity. These are my people, and this is *my* Hell."

Revelore's fiery blade cut a chilling line through the ash-filled sky, and slammed into Cathy.

No!

The swirling pull of Magick threw me against the console as Obelleron's bridle sucked down the Void's power in great gulps.

Pling!

Private Petty's blade caught the Arch Demon's sword and didn't waver. Somehow the diminutive saber and the tiny woman weilding it held their own against the King of Hell's wrath.

"I am the Calamity!" My daughter cried again, lunging forward, her counter-strike catching the Arch Demon off guard and drawing a fine line of its own across his burning flesh.

She's doing it. My daughter is taking on Hell itself... and she's winning!

It was tough to swallow my pride, but the Dad Wagon made that easier by sliding in the soft mud again and giving me something else to worry about. I bounced against the seats as we narrowly avoided a fallen Demon Steed and their rider to stay within siphoning distance for the Calamity.

"You are a fool." The Arch Demon smashed into Cathy with the back of his hand.

My daughter's wings vanished and she plummeted like a stone.

No!

The horde held its breath. The wild screaming of the Blessed went silent as their champion tumbled from the sky.

You can do it, Cathy.

Something had broken in my daughter, but that didn't mean I stopped loving her.

The Calamity's wings exploded open moments before she

hit the ground, wide and graceful, they caught the air and with them she raised the morale of her soldiers.

"The Calamity has come!" the Blessed shouted. Their cries echoed across the valley and sowed confusion among the Selemour.

This wasn't what the Damned did.

They didn't have hope, they didn't believe, and they certainly didn't work together. It had taken someone unique to see past the failures and mistakes. It had taken someone just as misguided as they were, but with the sincere belief she could make the world—any world—a better place.

It had taken my daughter.

The Calamity streaked between the Arch Demon's legs. Private Petty's blade left a flurry of gouges in his fiery flesh.

Wild cheers from the Damned spurred her on, and Cathy's wings swelled with pride and bravado. She shot up the Arch Demon's backside only to come streaking down his chest. My daughter dodged the swings of his sword and used Private Petty's to leave more destruction of her own. She swooped over the Dad Wagon, her eyes wide with excitement.

My wife's fiery passion burned in those eyes.

She's going to do it.

My daughter swung around, the wings of Magick pushing her back high into the air. Revelore lunged, but before he could make contact, the Demon Steed slammed into his shin, knocking the King of Hell off balance. His fiery blade split the ground in front of the Dad Wagon and sent great globs of mud raining down on the already dirty windshield.

Gah!

The Damned driver yanked the Mazda hard, but even he wasn't fast enough. We caught the trailing edge of the Hellfire blade and that was enough to send us airborne. My ribs smashed into something in the dash and my head whipped around hard enough to detach the buckle on that infernal chain.

The world spun in a muddy blur, and for the second time since I'd gotten here I found myself on the headliner, except this time I was pinned in place like an unlucky member of some inquisitive kid's butterfly collection, the spike solidly wedged into the roof's folded metal.

Shit.

The New Dead driver and his copilot had only begun to assess the situation when the fiery edge of the Arch Demon's blade removed the front half of the Dad Wagon from the back. In a blinding flash, the Mazda was finally, and truly, dead—and that was the least of my problems.

The Calamity seized the advantage and beat her luminous wings, then shot across Revelore's molten face. Private Petty's blade cut a tight gash in the Arch Demon's cheek, but not before he wrapped a fiery hand around its wielder.

Whoosh!

The dark Fury's wings vanished in Revelore's fist. The Calamity struggled to free herself, but the King of Hell's fingers clamped down tighter. Fiery Selemour Magick raced back through the spike, its unholy rage leaving blisters on my bleeding skin.

Cathy's heart beat pulsed in my hands. Anger and frustration had fueled her fight, but even they were wearing down in the great monster's grasp. Deep down there was pain, but there was also something else, something hidden between the folds of an anger that cut to the core.

My daughter was still in there, some part of what made her the little girl I bounced on my knee, and the same girl I lost at the gates of Hell was still hanging on.

Cathy was there, and I knew it.

Let her go. If you don't she'll come for you, and for the House. The Calamity won't stop until every world rests under her power.

I knew what I should do, but since when was being a father about doing what you should do?

I squeezed my hands together and took a deep breath. "Let her go!"

The Magick swirling in my chest, the Void's power twisting and turning to avoid the spike's pull. I wrestled it into position and forced it into the bridle's spike, unleashing the House's special brand of Hell.

Cathy faded beneath Revelore's fiery skin, the last strands of her wild hair disappearing in the wavering heat.

"Let her go!"

New Dead soldiers held their breath, an army that had fought valiantly hesitated, their hopes pinned on the young woman lost within the Arch Demon's fist. Even the Demon Steed Obelleron paused, his great hooves mute in the wet mud.

Come on, you can do it.

Revelore held up his hand for all to see. The King of all that Burns' commanding voice echoed across the wide valley like a rolling thunder. "The Calamity is done! You have failed. The Wild Reaving is no more."

Come on...

New Dead soldiers stopped mid-strike, their swords falling limp in their hands. The rampaging power of the Selemour cut through them like a winnowing fan. The Damned fell in waves of hopeless destruction beneath the blades of the massive Arch Demons.

Come on, Cathy!

My daughter's voice boomed in my head, angry, proud, and not willing to give up. "I told you. Never call me that name. I am the Calamity!"

Magick erupted along the seam of Revelore's fingers. The borrowed power of the Void itself, bright green and a stark contrast to the Arch Demon's fire.

The Calamity would not be contained.

Crack!

Revelore's laughter came to an abrupt end, the Arch Demon stopping to stare at the cracks in his massive fist.

Boom!

In an explosion of molten rock and flesh the Calamity roared to life. Her great wings of Magick beat like a drum and launched my daughter along with private Petty's blade on a collision course with the Arch Demon.

"What?!" The confusion on Revelore's face was short lived. The Fury, my angel of destruction, hit him like a comet. The flickering tail of pure Magick vanished in the Arch Demon's fiery bulk, and with it my daughter.

New Dead cheered, their voices raised in a soul-chilling chant.

"The Calamity has come!"

My daughter, wrapped in the power of the Void, exploded from the back of Revelore's wide body. The King of all that Burns shuddered, his flesh crumbling like a doused ash. The golden crown on his head tumbled to the distant ground and shrunk to the size of Cathy's head.

My daughter swooped low and grabbed the golden metal, then spun in the air, her wings wide for all to see.

"Selemour! I am the Wild Reaving, and now, I am your king!" Cathy tore off her helmet and placed the crown on her head.

More wild cheers erupted from her men as the Arch Demon crumpled to the muddy ground. Great boulders of spent monster landed around me, sending up blasts of super heated dirt.

I covered my eyes only to have a broken bit of stone strike my head and turn the world black.

The Calamity, King of the Selemour? What have I done?

44

DEALS

*M*agician...
         An alien voice tugged at my mind and pulled me toward an unpleasant consciousness.

Wake up, Magician.

I blinked my eyes in the acrid smoke. "Who?"

We do not have time. The Calamity is coming. I will make you a deal.

I knew that voice. I'd heard it before, in the proxied form of dozens of fish-headed Demons.

The Defiler...

Asaroth's twisted words rattled in my skull.

She is coming, Magician. Your child has become strong, too strong —but you know where she will go next.

Searing pain roared up the base of my head, and with it came a flood of images. The Calamity stood at the door of 69 Mallory Lane. The House was a broken memory of scorched wood and melted glass. An all-consuming flame surrounded her, bringing with it the power of the Void.

She has done it?

The Defiler's power pressed in upon me, the deep darkness

of an unknowable mind.

No, this is one of a number of possible outcomes, but none of them are good for you.

The image shifted and brought with it the field of battle. Ed, Adam, Angela, and even Kaylee lay dead at my feet, their bodies burned and broken, victims of the Calamity.

"No, she wouldn't do that. She's still my daughter—"

The Defiler's strength squeezed the words from my throat.

She will not stop until everyone you have ever loved is ash.

"I don't believe you."

Believe this...

The Demon filled my mind with more images, each one more powerful than the last. Private Petty's blade cut through my family like a silvery thresher, while behind it the golden crown and the wild eyes glowed in a malevolent red.

"What do you want me to do?"

There is still one more shard of your daughter. I will tell you where she is and how to get to her, if you remove the spike.

The spike, its pulsing metal burning my flesh, and taking with it the ebbing power of the Void.

"You want me to throw the fight."

I want you to realize what is at stake. You and I exist because we must exist. It is how the great wheel turns. You cannot know the light without the dark.

"You're afraid."

Soft and translucent hands caressed my face. My daughter, the caring young woman I lost to the gates of Hell, hovered in the hazy smoke of the broken Mazda. "Dad, you've got to do what he says."

My stomach churned at the illusion's touch.

"You aren't real!"

"No, I'm not. Asaroth lies, but he tells the truth now. He knows where the last shard is, and will tell you if you stand down."

I kicked at the drifting illusion. "What does it matter? She ran the other Cathy through with Petty's blade. I cannot put them back together. A two-legged stool cannot stand."

Cathy gently shook her translucent head. "She isn't gone."

"Oh yeah, how?"

Images popped into my mind, memories of the Green Swamp and Private Petty. The Darkling's blade pressed against mine, and in that blade something reflected back at me, something I'd never noticed before—the soul of a young man who only wanted forgiveness.

The blade. If Private Petty could survive inside it, could she? Is Cathy inside the blade?

The Defiler's pressure returned, a suffocating blanket of darkness that squeezed my mind like a vise.

But she will not survive me. I promise you, Magician. While the Calamity will win, you will lose. You will lose the one thing you care most about in this world.

The shattered blade appeared in my mind—Private Petty's broken saber laying twisted in the dark mud. That image shifted until it became the spike embedded in my hands.

The Calamity comes, Magician. Do what I ask and you have my binding word. I will ensure the sword remains unbroken.

"What about the Calamity?"

Asaroth's suffocating power pressed the air from my lungs like a great bellows.

She must die.

* * *

Yip! Yip!

"Gene!"

Soft hands tugged at my arms, while a very frustrating tongue licked at my cheeks, the two of them pulling me toward a pain-filled waking state.

"Gene, please dear God no…"

Slap!

The same soft hands smacked my face hard enough to rock me back to the land of the living, or at least what counted for it.

Asaroth!

"Porter." I blinked my eyes at my wife and the tiny Chinthe. "You… you came back?"

"Hell yes I did." Porter's gun lay in a holster at her side. She swung a tiny backpack around and unzipped it before turning all of her attention to the spike driven through my bloody hands. "Did she do this to you?"

I shook my head trying to remember everything that had happened.

Do not forget my offer, Magician. The Calamity comes…

"The Calamity." I coughed and tried to pull my hands away. "She did it, Porter—our daughter did it. She killed Revelore, the King of Hell."

My wife pulled my hands back. "Gene, you're feverish and bleeding."

The black spike pulsed in time with my heartbeat and drained Magick with each frantic tick.

"Don't take it out," I said, trying to sit up in the fractured remains of the Dad Wagon. "Without it she won't survive."

Porter pulled me up and pointed to the distant horizon. "Gene, it doesn't matter."

"What do you mean?"

The haze slowly cleared on a Hell destroyed. The Selemour lay in ruin, their molten bodies twisted and broken, while all around them the hordes of New Dead rolled toward me like a pale-white and ashen plague. At their lead was my daughter. No longer a dark Fury of Magick, but now a warrior goddess of destruction. Revelore's crown gleamed from the head of a proud woman atop her Demon Steed.

"She's coming, Gene. I've got to get you up."

"Coming? What about the Defiler?"

My wife shook her head. "Gone. She has beaten them all. Our daughter rides triumphant. She's coming for you. She's coming for the Void. You've got to take the spike out. For your own good, and for all of us."

"The sword. What about her sword?"

Porter shook her head. "It doesn't matter. None of it matters if you don't pull out the spike."

Defiler!

I kicked Porter away.

"Gene!"

"No, I'm not buying it, Asaroth. This is just another illusion. You want me to give up my daughter because you're afraid, because you know you cannot win. The end comes for us all, even you."

"What are you talking about, Gene? You're feverish." Porter scrambled for the spike. "I've got to get this out of you."

"Fine," I said, calling the monster's bluff. "Here, remove the spike. Pull it out."

Porter's fingers hovered over the dark metal. "Are you sure?"

"What are you waiting for? Pull it out now."

My wife's fingers traced the bloody lines on my hands.

"Come on, Asaroth, what are you waiting for? Do it."

The tiny Chinthe growled in the smoky haze.

"Half a second, Gene. I need to—"

"You need to go. This is the end and I will decide how the final notes are played."

Porter faded into ash, and the tiny Chinthe vanished with her, until all that was left was the wreckage of the Dad Wagon.

My hands bled, and the spike pushed at sore bones already rubbed raw. Magick trickled from that wound, and from my soul.

The Defiler's blackness filled the horizon, a terrible and formless mass of evil, but it wasn't the same. An undercurrent of fear flickered in that ancient malevolence, a fear I knew all too well.

I crawled out of the sheared-off Mazda. My elbows and knees dragged in the mud but my eyes remained focused on the army in the distance, and on my daughter. Cathy rode high on Obelleron, the crown of Revelore on her head, and Private Petty's saber in her hand.

Here goes nothing...

I pushed myself up, the black metal spike still wedged in my hands, and held them high for the Defiler to see. "I speak for the Void. I hold your life in my hands. The Calamity will cut you down. You have never faced someone like her, and you may never again. I make you this one offer. Accept banishment from this place and I will use the Void's power to send you far away from the Calamity and her hordes."

You would banish me?

The Defiler's voice rattled in my head, along with someone else's.

"No! You do not speak for me. The Defiler is mine!"

Cathy!

"Do you take the deal?" I cried, pushing the Calamity out of my skull.

Darkness without form twisted and undulated like the tide.

He was confused. Asaroth had never faced a power like the Calamity before. He'd never faced hope, and it scared him.

"Do you accept?" I pushed my hands to the sky.

Yes.

One word.

A single syllable of focused thought drove me to the ground and with it set the Magick in motion. The distant Calamity turned her Demon Steed toward me, fiery eyes like tiny suns, and her sword raised in angry protest.

The Calamity is coming... heaven help me.

HOPE

*A*n old man in his bathrobe shuffled up behind me.

"Gene, what are you doing?" Jenkins asked, his frail hands tight against my shoulder. "You do realize this is it, don't you?"

"Yes."

The old Magician-shaped House let out a long, slow sigh. "I'm pretty much down to the end now, kid. You and the wild one have burned through the last of the reserves."

The thundering hooves of Obelleron threw sparks against the muddy ground, while atop him the Calamity swung Private Petty's saber in a wide arc. An uncountable horde of New Dead rolled like a pale wave behind her, the Blessed and their ashen bodies scouring the land like the threshing floor.

"What comes next?"

Jenkins pulled down his tinted glasses to reveal swirling eyes of infinite color. "That all depends on you."

"Me?"

The Void nodded. "Turn around, Gene."

Just beyond the melted wreckage of my favorite car stood the House, 69 Mallory Lane, in all its seething frustration, the wide porch and peeling paint, the windows that remained hidden behind gossamer curtains, and above all else, the door. The key that old Magician had given me still in the lock.

You can't back down. You've got to do it, for all of them.

"Gene, before you get carried away with this idea of yours to take my place, I've got sad news for you."

I took a hesitant step toward the derelict house. "Wait, what?"

The old Magician pressed his glasses back over his eyes. "Part of the rules. You get to protect the Void, but you don't get to *become* it."

"I don't?"

Jenkins chuckled, his halting laugher barely escaping between great bouts of coughing. "No. That would really be silly, wouldn't it? I mean, what sort of all-powerful-eternal being would I be if I hadn't made that rule a part of the process. Good grief. What is this, amateur hour?"

As if in answer to the Void's question a chilling horn blast echoed across the wide valley.

"And that would be your daughter."

The Calamity's thundering horde broke over the distant hill, the Wild Reaving and her Demon Steed at the lead.

"I... Shit."

Jenkins nodded. "Yeah, pretty much."

"What do I do?"

The House pointed to the spike and its trailing chain. "Well, for starters you can let me pull that siphon out."

I bit down on the metal and yanked it out, then tossed it into the muck.

"Much better. Now, I'd suggest you get ready, because your daughter appears to mean business."

"She's like her mom."

"Oh, right? Like her mom. Look at her, Gene. Look at the Calamity. If you haven't guessed, she's you. She's what Eugene

Law could have been. She's everything you aren't. Where you hesitate, she strikes. Where you question, she answers."

"Yeah, just like her mom."

The old Magician shook his head. "Well, if she doesn't get you, the others will."

A derelict piece of the Duplickity Net floated past in the smoke-filled breeze. I grabbed the thin fabric and wrapped it around my bleeding hands. "Others?"

Jenkins took a seat on the front steps, his hands folded, and his face to the rolling wave of pale destruction. "Yeah, your daughter's pretty impressive, but she's not the only one you have to worry about."

"Tristan."

The old Magician tilted his head. "Is that what he's going by now?"

"My daughter's old boyfriend is no match for the Calamity, or me. I'm not worried about him."

Jenkins shook his head. "You should be. In fact, I'd say he's the only one you should worry about."

"I don't understand."

"You will, soon enough."

"No, I want to know—"

Jenkins broke into another fit of coughing, this time leaving a thin trickle of blood on his narrow lips. "I don't have time for a history lesson, kid. I'm at the end of this spin at the wheel." The old man paused for a second as if figuring out something he'd never considered before. "Ha! Maybe that's why he calls himself that—funny, how did I never see that before?"

"Who? Damn it!"

The old Magician wiped the blood with the back of his hand. "You're wasting time, Gene. You've got one last request. There's just enough Magick left for a single big push."

"Then what happens?"

The old Magician's folded fingers erupted like a tiny pantomimed explosion.

"You explode?"

"What? No. I meant that's it, poof, then it drops to zero."

"No Magick for me?"

Jenkins shook his head. "No Magick for anyone. The Void will stop pushing out the cosmic go-juice you all so enjoy."

"What about creatures like Obelleron, or artifacts like the Prussian Wedding bowls?"

"Black Beauty and the curse buckets will be fine. In fact, Magick out in the world won't go anywhere, but you Magicians won't have anything to draw from."

I took a deep breath, the hot wind of the Calamity's army at my back. "Shit."

"Yeah, it's a tough nut, but I've been here before. The trick is to hold up through the first onslaught. Most anyone who wants in is going to be a Magician anyway, and, well, they'll be side-lined just like you."

"Tell me again why you chose me."

Jenkins placed a hand on my shoulder. I knew it was really the Void, but it was hard to see past the memories of Viktor. In some odd way, I was glad the House had chosen him at the end.

"I chose you because of who you are, and the potential of who you could become. Now, don't get me wrong, the Calamity out there certainly makes me question that decision, but my gut says we go with you." Jenkins shook his aging head. "Gut decisions—you and I have spent entirely too much time together."

"That I can agree with."

"So." The House clapped its frail hands. "What's it gonna be? Wave of unquenchable acid? How about your own army of fiery soldiers? How are you going to carve them up and keep me together through to the other side?"

The Calamity's forces rolled over the hills like a burning plague, and at their lead the new King of the Selemour swung her shining blade—a blade that held another piece of my daughter's soul.

Little Ed's vision came back to me, the three shards of my daughter bound together, but to do that I needed the sword.

The answer was clear.

"I want the sword."

Jenkins pushed up his tinted glasses. "A sword? That's a rather pedestrian request, but maybe we can dress it up a bit. Which sword are you interested in?"

"No, the sword."

"There are a lot of 'the swords' out there. Are we talking something from the Demon Wars? Maybe Clevnix the Horn Cleaver? Or you could go with Ixthicknin the Unbending? There have been a few monkey swords too. Maybe Excal—"

"I want that saber." I pointed to the fast approaching Calamity's tarnished blade.

"Wait, what?"

"You heard me."

Jenkins frowned. "Gene, that's the brass ring. It's a largely ceremonial saber last owned by some monkey from the late nineties—what's special about that sword?"

Cathy...

"Oh, no. That sword holds a piece of your daughter's soul. Gene, this isn't a game show, you don't get a second chance. You need to throw out this hope of putting your daughter together and get your head in the game. Listen, I'll get you Clevnix. I believe I know where it is. Just give me a second. Oh, and if it demands blood and souls you just say 'okay,' you got it? Swords like Clevnix are very particular."

"Who speaks for the Void?"

Jenkins tilted his head. "Excuse me?"

"You heard me. Who speaks for the Void?"

The old man pulled his glasses down, frustration evident in the swirling infinity of his eyes. "You do."

"You're damn straight I do. Now, nearest I can tell that entitles me to my ask. I've done just about everything you've requested up to this point. I gave up my family and destroyed so many monsters—"

"Monsters I had you destroy so you wouldn't face them today. You understand that right? I mean, we're a team."

"I gave all of it up for you, for the Magick, and for my family, and what did it bring me?"

"Near infinite power?"

It was my turn to shake my head. "No, it gave me nothing and in return it took everything."

"Gene, you don't know what you're asking. That saber isn't going to do a damn thing against what's coming."

"That's where you are wrong. It's going to bring me the only thing that matters."

The old Magician squeezed his fists. "Something to bury you with?"

"Hope."

Jenkins threw his hands up in frustration. "I have chosen poorly. I should have gone after Viktor harder. Maybe Morgan Crowley would have been the better selection? She did survive the library."

"Are you going to do it?"

The old Magician got up from his seat on the House's front step. "It's already done."

"What?"

Private Petty's saber lay in the mud at my feet, its silvery edge, though tarnished, reflected the tired desperation in my eyes.

I hope I know what I'm doing.

"I do too."

I picked up the saber and held it in my hand only to find the old Magician gone.

The Calamity was now only seconds away, without the saber, but still just as deadly.

"Okay, Gene," I said, my hand on the weapon's hilt. "Whatever you're going to do, you better figure it out fast, because your daughter's coming, and she's bringing friends."

46

SEEDS OF CHANGE

The Demon Steed's fiery hooves threw wide clumps of mud high into the air. The Calamity urged him on, Revelore's crown tight to her head. Wild hair snapped in the wind like a banshee's mane.

My daughter, the Calamity, had eyes for only one thing —infinity.

And you're the bright one who decided to stand in her way.

I tightened my hand on the hilt and sent a fresh wave of pain through my tired arms. Magick slipped from my body like water draining from a bathtub. Behind me the House shuddered. Windows creaked and paint peeled. The end was finally coming for the Void.

No Magick...

The trailing half of the Dad Wagon lay in the mud not far from the house, its trunk latch bent in the hazy smoke.

Or not...

I stabbed Private Petty's sword into the ground and made a break for the car. The distant horde was not so distant anymore, the black and tarry eyes of New Dead twinkled in the fiery smoke and ash.

Shake it off, Gene. Focus!

The bent trunk lid jammed beneath my fingers. "Damn it!"

More chilling horn blasts echoed across the wide valley—the Blessed were coming.

I climbed around to the front, where Revelore's fiery sword had expertly reduced my car to a vertical convertible, and crawled into the back seat.

The thundering hooves of the Calamity's cavalry pounded against the ground and sent vibrations through the broken Mazda.

Shit, shit, shit.

I pushed the release and unlatched the back seats. Since the car was upside down, that did exactly nothing.

Another horn blast puckered my butt cheeks.

Come on, damn it.

I yanked the seat forward and tucked my head under the swinging cushion. The trunk was a mess, which should have come as no surprise given the circumstances, but somehow still shocked me. An overturned and cracked Prussian Wedding Bowl lay awkwardly against the steel roof.

"Better than nothing," I said, scooping up the porcelain bowl and shoving whatever I could find in it.

Bastet.

The Soul of Isis lay beneath a morass of jumper cables and bungee cords. Her eyes still covered by the blindfold I'd placed on it years ago.

"Remember when my biggest problems were oil stains from a broken mower?" I asked the silent statue before dumping it in the bowl.

Propelled by the wild yells of the approaching New Dead I raced back over the muddy ground, the Prussian Bowl and its contents bouncing with me. I switched hands long enough to grab the saber, then hit the front steps of 69 Mallory Lane and took them two at a time until I reached the porch.

The Calamity broke over the final hill. Her fiery eyes gleamed along with the devilish ring of gold on her head. Whatever remained of my daughter lay buried beneath that crown, cocooned in a thick fog of hatred.

The Calamity has come.

Obelleron and his rider thundered past the Dad Wagon's remains and tore up the ground en route to the House and a date with infinity.

"Stop!" I tightened my hand on Petty's saber. Blood soaked through what remained of the Duplickity net and coated the sword's hilt. "I speak for the Void!"

The Demon Steed reared up. Four of its six legs carved great fiery trails in the smoky air.

"Let me through, old man." The Calamity pulled back on Obelleron's mane. "You know you cannot stop me."

Dirt-streaked and bloodied, my daughter no longer resembled the young girl I'd loved. Her mud-caked hair and wild eyes spoke of a pain I couldn't possibly understand. With the saber gone, she'd returned to her rusty, hammered blade.

"I'm your father. I can still tell you what to do. That's what dads do."

My daughter raised a hand and the army behind her circled. The Blessed swelled to fill the space just beyond the Dad Wagon's remains. The tar-filled eyes of New Dead soldiers with their jagged armor pressed together like a single sheet of weathered steel and closed us in.

"You left me here to die. Is that what a father does?" Cathy pulled on Obelleron's mane, and the Demon Steed bowed, letting her step off onto the muddy ground.

"I'm warning you, Catherine. I won't hesitate—"

My daughter's cold and vicious laugh cut through me. "You won't hesitate? All you do is hesitate. It's your greatest strength. Tell me, did you have a plan for any of this? The saber? That's your last weapon?" Cathy shook her crowned head and took a gentle step toward the porch steps.

"I'm warning you." I held Petty's sword in shaky fingers.

"You're warning me?" The Calamity swung around and swept her ash-streaked hand over the surrounding army. "I command the single greatest army every assembled. Their ferocity has already stretched into the edges of this world and made great inroads into others."

"So I've seen."

The Calamity stabbed her blade into the mud. "It doesn't have to be this way. Come down from that porch and I'll find a place for you."

"Like you did for Kaylee?"

My daughter held up her hand and motioned to the assembled masses. The Swamp Witch stepped out of the ashen dead, her face a twisted mask of rage-fueled anger.

"Do you want to go back to who you were?" My daughter asked Ed's gaunt ex-wife. "Do you want to return to the life you had before you joined the army of the Blessed?"

"No."

Cathy tilted her head and never once took her eyes off me. "And why is that?"

"I am a child of the Wild Reaving. I serve the Calamity now and for eternity."

"Kaylee." I pointed at the Prussian Wedding Bowl. "Snap out of it. You're no child of the Wild Reaving. You're a mother. A mother who cares about a son—a son I lost. You gave us this bowl to save your ex-husband, remember?"

Kaylee's face remained set like flint. "My son is dead. He is one of the Blessed now."

"No, he's not. I've seen him."

The Calamity spun around to face the Swamp Witch. "Don't listen to him, he's lying. Your son is part of the Blessed now. He will ride with us as we raze this world."

Kaylee's face may have remained unchanged, but something in her eyes shifted.

"My daughter doesn't understand, but I do, and I know you do. You'd do anything for Little Ed."

The Calamity ripped her sword out of the mud. "I do understand. These are my children, as uncountable as the stars, and deadly as a scorpion's sting. I love them in a way you will never comprehend. When the great Demons tortured them, when the rest of the world gave up, I brought them hope."

Hope.

Magick was powerful, but it didn't hold a candle to hope.

"Kaylee, your son lives, and has lived many a year on a Lost Button world of trees. A great forest that stretches to the edges of the horizon."

"Eddie…" A lone tear streaked the Swamp Witch's cheek.

"Stop!" Cathy placed a foot on the first step, her sword pointed at my chest.

"At least he did live when I last saw him."

A hammered rebar blade drooped in Kaylee's hand. "What do you mean?"

"The Wild Reaving had come to his world, and with it came fire and destruction."

The Calamity slammed her blade against the step. "We are cleansing this diseased and broken—"

"Eddie…"

I tucked a free hand into my pocket—it was still there. The acorn I'd picked up from Little Ed pressed against my leg.

"Ignore him. Your son has joined the Blessed, as have you. I brought you back from certain death. The cleansing fire of the Calamity runs through your veins."

"Gene." Tears streaked the ash and soot on Kaylee's cheeks. "Gene, is he… is he alive?"

Hope.

I pulled the acorn out of my pocket and tossed it to her, the tiny seed tumbling in the ashen air.

The Calamity snapped it out of the sky before it could reach Kaylee. "False hope is dangerous, Gene." My daughter dropped the seed on the muddy ground and buried it under foot. "Remember who you serve, and who healed you. Let your son go and join the Wild Reaving."

"Is that what you want, Kaylee?" I pointed Petty's saber at the assembled masses with their burning skin and tar-filled eyes. "Is that what you want for your son? You brought him into the world from dust, but do you really want him to return to it?"

Kaylee's blade fell from her hand and her knees buckled. "No…"

"Then you are a fool, and we will sweep over you like we have swept over the rest of Hell. Nothing will stand in the way of the Wild Reaving."

I tightened my grip around the saber's hilt.

Wanna bet?

47

HATE AND HEALING

he Calamity's rusted blade cut the air in front of me, and if it hadn't been for a little muscle memory from Private Petty, I'd be missing a good portion of my face right now.

Thanks, Michael, wherever you are.

Cathy pressed the attack, her sword arm moving faster than I anticipated. The wailing cheers of New Dead accompanied her strikes like the crowds at a wrestling match. Each swing egged them on to greater heights of crazed excitement.

Sparks showered the front steps of 69 Mallory Lane, but my saber held. "You don't want this, Cathy. I promise you."

My daughter snarled and snapped her blade forward in a powerful lunge. Petty's sword knocked the rusty metal aside, but not before it left a deep cut in my flesh. "Argh!"

"Still think this isn't what I want, old man?"

I clutched my side and swung Private Petty's blade in a narrow arc, just enough to send her back down a step lest she lose an arm. "I don't want to do this."

The Calamity leapt onto the porch, her sword missing my foot, but taking out a wide chunk of the rotting wood. "Then lay your saber down and let me walk through that door. Infinity waits for me on the other side. Would I not be a perfect Void? I am the cleansing fire, the Wild Reaving. Imagine a universe where Magick runs through me."

"I've seen it." I lunged, but my saber missed her by inches. "Little Ed showed it to me, and it was a nightmare."

At the sound of his name, a broken Kaylee sat up, eyes red with tears. "My son showed you this?"

"Really not the time for conversation, but yeah," I said, spending all my energy trying to keep the Calamity from shaving off an appendage.

Petty was right, talking and fencing is damn tough. Sorry, Michael.

"How did he show you?"

The Calamity's sword cut a line across my thigh, again drawing blood and forcing me back toward the door. "Kaylee, I don't know. He's basically a tree now. The little wooden boy is all grown up. He's an oak—heck, he's practically the whole forest—let's just say you have a lot of grandchildren."

"Enough!" Cathy swung her blade in a wide arc. She slammed it against the saber and sent a shock wave through my sore arm.

How long is this reset going to take?

The Magick swirling in my chest was almost gone, and so was my strength. The Calamity knew it.

Clang!

Hammered rebar rammed the saber again, this time stronger than the last. The sword slipped out of my hand and skidded across the rotting porch before coming to a stop far away from the door.

"What's more important to you now? The sword or the House?"

The sword, a shard of my daughter's soul trapped inside it,

was too far away to reach, but to step aside meant the House would be undefended.

Cathy raised her arm for the killing blow.

"Neither." I clutched my side to stem the flow of blood. "There is only one thing that matters to me anymore—you."

My daughter's hand hesitated. "You lie."

I held up my bloody hand. "Do I, Catherine?"

"I told you, don't call me that."

"It's who you are. It's always been who you are. You never stopped being my daughter, no matter what you've done. I forgive you and I love you."

Cathy's sword arm lowered, the inner battle in her eyes ferocious. "No! Fight back."

I let my hands drop. "No. I won't fight you anymore. If you want to take the House you will have to cut me down."

New Dead erupted in wild cheers. The assembled soldiers shouted for my death. "The Calamity has come! Cut him down in the cleansing fire of the Wild Reaving!"

My daughter's hand shook, the hammered rebar unsteady in her fingers. "Step aside."

"No, Catherine. I won't. The only way this ends with you on the other side of that door is with me dead at your feet."

Ashen faces of the Blessed screamed in the hot wind, their voices raised in exhilaration. "Cut him down! Long live the Calamity! Long live the Queen of the Blessed!"

Cathy brought the tip of her blade to my neck. The hot metal pressed against my skin. "This is your last chance."

"No, sweetheart—it's yours. You did what you had to do to survive, and I see that now. Catherine, you turned Hell on its side. You wear Revelore's crown on your head and command the Demon Steed Obelleron, but you took it too far. Somewhere along the way Cathy got lost, and the Calamity was all that remained. The thing is, you may think she died, but I know better. She's still in there." I pressed a bloody hand against my chest. "I know, because she's still in here."

"Cut him down!" The New Dead screamed in voices full of malice and hate.

I laid a tired hand against the blade's rusted metal. "Do what you must, but you have to know I never stopped loving you. Never. The day I lost you to that Hellgate was the day a part of me died. I've spent every moment since then trying to get you back, and if that's not going to happen, then you should just cut me down, because the life I have isn't worth living anymore."

Frustration was apparent on the faces of the Damned. My daughter hadn't done what she'd come here to do. "Cut him down! Cut him down! The Calamity has come!"

The tip of Cathy's blade pierced my skin, just enough to send a faint trickle of blood running down my neck, but that was more than enough to put the New Dead into a frenzy.

"Cut him down!"

"Do what you must, Cathy. I will never stop loving you."

My daughter's hand shook. "Why won't you be the monster I know you are?"

"Because he's not that monster—you are!" Kaylee shouted. She'd left the sword in the mud and stumbled forward to stop just short of the porch.

"Kaylee, wait, there's no Magick—"

The Swamp Witch collapsed to her knees, and ignored my cries, then plunged her hands into the hot muck.

New Dead surged forward. Their ranks broken, they pushed toward the house like a pale wave of death and destruction.

Rumble!

The House shook, the ground beneath it rumbling.

"What is that?" The Calamity cried, trying to stay upright. "Is it the Void?"

"No. It's her son."

Trees erupted from the muddy ground. Great trunks ripped

apart New Dead, and twisted together to form a living dome of thick bark and bright green leaves.

Little Ed.

New Dead caught on this side of the barrier found themselves at the mercy of hungry branches, their sharp tips gouging eyes and thick limbs snapping necks. Snaking vines raced up the porch, wrapping the narrow columns and the Calamity's legs.

"Dad!"

My daughter fell backward, pulled off the porch and wrapped in the thick vegetation. Revelore's crown landed in the mud.

"Cathy!"

More saplings sprouted around the Demon Steed and penned the powerful stallion behind a wall of thorn covered green.

Kaylee pulled aside her shirt and pressed a mud-stained hand against her ashen flesh.

"Kaylee, stop!"

The Swamp Witch dug her hands into the hellish reminder of what she'd become and tore it out. Blood poured from a wound hidden behind the New Dead flesh. The Soul Ripper's claw had left a hole too big to survive for long.

"Eddie, I failed you," a bleeding Kaylee cried, throwing aside the damned skin. "I am here now. Please forgive me. Please!"

New Dead pounded against the arboreal shield, their wild screams from beyond the thick trunks all but deafening.

"Little Ed, let Cathy go!"

"No, Gene." Blood oozed from the Swamp Witch's side, along with the color in her cheeks. "She has to pay the price. She has to pay for what they did, for what they did to me."

My daughter fought against the twisting vines. Sharp thorns cut deep scratches in her skin.

"She lost control of them. It wasn't her fault. It was the

Calamity. She didn't mean it, she was only doing what she had to do to survive."

"Dad!" My daughter's face vanished beneath the twisted vines.

"Eddie, stop! Please stop! We've come too far. I didn't bring you here for revenge."

Kaylee collapsed in the mud, her eyes closed and blood streaming from the wound in her side, while all around her the wall of green shook with the sounds of the Damned.

"Cathy!" I clawed at the vines, my already bloody hands sliced further by the thorns. "Cathy, don't give up! Don't you dare give up!"

"So this is the Calamity? I expected more."

Gaunt and bent, his body stretched thin, a young man condensed from the trapped smoke and ash. His accent was cold and strange, alien in a way I didn't understand. A Dead Man's Tongue ring shined on his bony finger, while deep-set eyes dug into my soul.

Tristan.

48

FULL CIRCLE

ristan, Cathy's first real boyfriend, stood not far from the Swamp Witch, a giddy smile on his gaunt cheeks. "Eugene Law. I've waited so long to finally meet you in person. I'm a fan, a really big fan."

"You aren't Tristan."

The young man shook his head. "What? Has this body devolved too much? It always happens on the tenth turn. The flesh just goes to hell. It's only a matter of time now before it melts away completely. Thankfully, we're here now, and it won't matter in a few moments."

Tristan's body exuded Magick, a pent-up power I couldn't understand, but one I'd felt before at the end of Morgan's fingers. "How?"

"Oh, come on, Gene. You know the Viburna, and you know Jenkins. You think he was the first one to hunger for immortality? Hardly." The skinny young man let his voice drop into the same scared youth who'd spilled his soul in the back of my car all those months ago. "Do you know what it's like to have someone in your head?"

The stark realization hit me like a sledgehammer to the gut. "You've... you've been in him all along?"

"Bingo. You think some kid's going to understand the Magick wrapped up in my book? Or know how to summon the Defiler, and what to tempt him with? You think he'd know how to handle New Dead? You think he'd make sure to send them after your wife?"

If the first revelation had taken my gut, this second one ripped the wind from my sails.

"Ten Spins."

Tristan nodded, his skin stretched tight against a faded skull. "In the flesh."

My tired fingers balled up in fists.

"Now, Gene. Don't waste the final moments of your life trying to do the impossible for the ungrateful. The Void doesn't care about you. Once the rebirth is over do you think it'll just let you live a nice quiet life? Set you up with a little mountain villa?"

"You took everything from me."

"And so will the Void." Tristan bent down to let his thin fingers drift through Kaylee's hair. "I'm proof of that. You'd think he'd take better care of the last speaker of the Void, but you can't expect an eternal being to have much in the way of a retirement plan."

"You're lying."

Tristan pushed Kaylee's head aside. "Why would I? There's no point. Think, Gene. Where's the value in lying now? I served the Void, and in exchange it built me a prison."

"The library..."

The young man stepped over Kaylee's quiet form. "Yes, but it's more than that. He filled it with Magicians, the greatest of your age and mine. Hell, he even got you to throw Morgan Crowley in there —turns out she's a lot more resourceful than the Void counted on."

Magick swelled around Tristan, a Magick not born of the Void.

"How? How are you doing that?"

"Morgan wasn't the first one to steal power. Though I'll admit she was pretty good at it—she survived the library after all. But there is more to it than just bleeding Magicians dry in the moment. You had to find a way to store it, to build it up like a great reservoir. For that you need a body you can throw away when the power is done eating it alive. For that I needed this kid."

Blood rushed to my cheeks. "You cut Cathy's Thread."

"Of course I did—I had to. You were winning. I didn't count on you becoming the speaker of the Void after the fact—high moral fiber and all—but yes, of course I cut her thread."

I reached for my Magick, for the power of the Void, but it was gone.

I used it up.

Tristan stretched his hand above the vine-wrapped Cathy. Magick unfurled from his long and narrow fingers. Vines pulled away from her face.

"Cathy." I yanked at the loosened thorns.

"She's breathing." Tristan pulled his hand back. "And she'll stay that way if I walk through that door."

"But the Void..."

"Gene, why do you care anymore? Do you really think I'd be a worse eternal than the last one was?"

"Last one?"

Tristan's fingers slid down the vines and they pulled away at his touch. "The Void has you convinced he's the only one that has ever been. That's just not true."

"It's not?"

"Hardly, he's the one that broke the cycle. The mantle gets passed, it always has, until this one. Now he wants to hold sway yet again, to take another turn at infinity. Do you really think he'd be better at it than me?"

"I…"

My mind drifted to the evil and destruction perpetuated at the House's command.

Tristan let go of Cathy's vines and put a foot on the first step.

"Listen, it's simple. Just step aside. I have a lot of admiration for you. Morgan was right, you're one hell of a Magician, but more than that, you're a complicated person, and as Viktor used to say, life likes complicated people."

The Calamity's gentle breath brushed across my hand.

He did this to you.

I let go of my daughter's thorn-covered body and stepped in front of the door. "No…"

"You don't want to do this, Gene." Magick swirled around Ten Spins wasting form. "Something tells me you are out of juice."

I reached for my Magick, but the well was empty. There was nothing left to draw.

"Performance problems?"

I swung a fist at that annoying kid's face, content in knowledge that to make contact with his chin would really go along way in curing a lot of what ailed me, except my knuckles never reached him.

My arm froze in mid-strike, my hand unable to pierce the Magick surrounding Tristan.

"Fists, really? I can tell by the look on your face you've used the last of the Void's surge of Magick up. Who could have anticipated the Calamity's one-on-one dust-up with Revelore? That was a surprise to me, but the bigger surprise was you letting her take the last of the Void's power and leave you defenseless."

Petty's saber lay on the distant porch.

"A Soul blade isn't going to do you any good, Gene. I gave up my soul a long time ago."

"No!" I dug deep and pushed with all my strength, but the Magician only laughed.

"Okay, my turn."

Crack!

Tristan's hands moved fast, faster than I ever imagined possible. A flurry of blows hit my body in places I hardly knew existed. They ejected the air from my lungs and left me crumpled on the rotting wood.

"Now, if you'll excuse me. I have a date with infinity."

I clutched at my side and tried to claw at the young man's feet, but he kicked me away and stepped in front of the door.

"Goodbye, Gene. I promise when I'm the Void your death will be quick and painless. Now, your wife on the other hand..."

Bastet's statue lay in the Wedding Bowl next to me, the blindfold still over her eyes.

Please work.

I scraped the fine ceramic likeness out of the bowl with tired fingers. "The Soul of Isis may want to have a word with you. She's laid claim to killing me for more than a few years." I shattered the statue on the rotting porch, and sent a cloud of dust and broken clay into the air.

Tristan lunged for the door, but his hand never made it to the knob. The razor-sharp claws of a vengeful feline stopped him cold.

"As the speaker of the Void and the last Magician to hold you captive, stop him, Bastet, and the Soul of Isis shall dance for no one but herself from here to all eternity. Your freedom guaranteed by my blood."

Half-woman, half-cat, and all deadly, the Soul of Isis held Tristan's wrist with her sharp claws. "Freedom?"

"Eternal."

Hiss.

Bastet's claws cut deep grooves in the young man's withered chest, but she wasn't ready for what came next. Tristan hooked her arm with his hand and twisted his narrow body, then launched her into air and sent the Soul of Isis crashing into the broken wood.

"Kittens!"

The brightly colored hair of a dozen topless cat-women filled the muddy ground. Their claws out and their feline eyes narrowed, they moved with a vicious grace.

"The Soul of Isis, Gene, really?" Tristan's stored Magick surged and more shapes condensed out of the smoky air.

Pale and hairless, with long insect arms that unfolded in deadly precision.

Skeeters!

"Deacon may have worked for the Defiler, Gene, but this young one has found a higher calling."

Sofia stepped in front of the rest of the Mosquito People, her tattoos glowing with the power of the Dead Man's Tongue on her finger. "Gene, I'm so happy we could see each other one last time, and I promise you, this will be the last."

49

CAVALRY

Tristan's hand grabbed the knob, but he couldn't keep it there—Bastet made sure of that. Her claws forced him to let go.

"You can't let him open that door," I cried, pulling the Prussian Wedding Bowl toward me. Redemption and forgiveness were the bowl maker's final gifts, but would they be enough for Tristan, or for any of us?

The cat-woman frowned. "What does it look like I'm doing."

Tristan's furious arms and legs put Bastet on the defensive.

"Just keep up the—"

My words vanished in the stabbing pain of a Skeeter's insect arm. Sofia skewered my shoulder. Her long claw dug in and pressed me against the porch.

"Going somewhere, Gene?" The woman's jaws unfurled like a deadly blossom to reveal an angry stinger and sharp fangs.

I tried to pull off the pinning arm, but my hands were too tired. "Why, Sofia?"

The Skeeter pressed her claw deeper. Blood dripped from the wound. "You lost me my best chance at saving my father in years, and for what? Some kids? Ten Spins has promised me more, much more, if I help him dispense with you."

"Haven't we been over this before? Didn't Delia offer you the same thing? How'd that turn out?"

Sofia hesitated, only for a second, then raised up a single black arm for the killing blow. "That was in the past."

Boom!

The explosive bark of a handgun report rattled the tiny porch. A single round tore through the Skeeter's face and sliced apart her flailing jaws, and took most of her stinger with it. It was an expert shot, and one that couldn't have come at a better time. Sofia toppled over, her neck twisted in the bullet's whiplash.

"What the—"

Yip! Yip! Yip!

The undersized Chinthe shot across the porch and leapt into the air, only to land on the Calamity's vine-bound prison.

"Bobbin, get the rest of them!"

Porter?!

My wife, in full tactical gear, scrambled up the porch. Tight black pants with a myriad of pockets jingled beneath a belt of spare magazine clips. She'd clearly gotten a lot more into firearms in my absence and given our current predicament that wasn't necessarily a bad thing.

Porter rammed the gun in her holster and immediately pressed a hand against my shoulder. "Do you have any idea how hard you are to find even with that damn dog?"

"I told you to go home."

"I did. I got my gun, and then we came back."

"We?"

Porter pulled back her hand. "Gene, you're bleeding like crazy."

"We?!"

My wife nodded. "Yes, we. Angela is working on the rest of them."

"Angela!" I grimaced at the pain in my shoulder. "Please tell me you have a great friend you met at explosives training or 'Expert Shooting for Angry Wives' class that just happens to be named Angela. Please tell me you don't mean Adam's mom."

Porter bit her lip and pulled back her palm. "Why aren't you healing?"

I shook my head. "It's a really long story—no Magick."

"Gene!"

"I'll survive—I think, but you didn't answer my question." I tried to prop myself up but my arm had gone numb.

"Yes Adam's mom—she's persistent and rather scary." Porter hooked a hand under my shoulder and pulled me the rest of the way.

All around us, Kitten claws and Skeeter arms clashed in the dense grove of unnatural vegetation. Jaws unzipped in the dim light that slipped through the canopy, their serrated stingers hungry for blood, while just beyond them the wailing frustration of New Dead slammed against the thick trunks.

"What do we do?" Porter held me up, her shoulder bearing most of my weight.

"I need the saber and I need to be in front of that door."

"What?"

I pointed to Tristan and the ferocious Bastet. "If he gets into the House this all goes to Hell."

My wife unholstered her gun. "We're already—"

"Damn it, woman. Get me in front of the door."

"Enough!" Tristan exploded in a burst of violent fury. His fists and legs moved with an impossible speed and sent Bastet off the front porch and sprawling in the mud. "You want a fight, Gene? I'll give you a fight." The bloody young man jumped down from the porch and placed a hand on the vines and dense foliage surrounding Cathy. "Ignis!"

Magickal flames roared out of the young Magician's hands, licking the green stems and setting the thorns alight.

"Cathy!" I pushed Porter away and pointed to the thorny casket. "She's wrapped in all that. Get her out before she burns to death."

Porter threw me at the door, then leapt off the porch to join her daughter.

"You don't want to do this, Tristan," I said, the weight of my body banging against the closed door. "This isn't you."

"You're right, it isn't him. He was a frail and weak boy. Without me he would have died on the floor of that hospital. He knows that. I gave him purpose."

I stretched a foot out to catch the edge of the Prussian Wedding Bowl.

Come on...

"Purpose?" I coughed, my shoulder throbbing. "This is his purpose? To be your fleshy ride service?"

I dragged the bowl closer. The blood from my shoulder dripped into the bright porcelain.

Almost there...

Tristan took another step and still hadn't looked down. Could I get that lucky?

"He'll have the privilege of bringing me to the threshold of infinity." The young Magician lifted his foot above the lip of the bowl.

Bingo!

I kicked the porcelain under his foot and hoped it would be enough. "Forgiveness and redemption, Tristan. The bowl maker's final gift. I forgive you. Now lets kick this asshole out of your body." I grabbed his hand and let the Magick of the bowl wash over me.

Ten Spins fought back. The power in the Dead Man's Tongue was like standing in front of an open pizza oven. I gritted my teeth and squeezed tighter, then closed my eyes and pushed my way into a very crowded brain.

Tristan!

Ocean waves crashed against a wide beach, white foam rolling over dark blue water. Something floated on the distant tide, pale against the dark sea, it bobbed gently atop the violent surf.

Tristan.

The young man's body drifted aimlessly on the unforgiving surf.

"Tristan." I cupped my hands. "Listen to me. You've got to fight him."

"He can't hear you anymore."

Ten Spins.

Thin and toned like a warrior from an age long passed, the Magician stood at the end of the rolling surf. Bare from the waist up, tattoos traced twisting lines across his pale body.

"That's how you did it? You wrapped yourself in Magick?"

"That's only a single step, the first one of many, so, so many," the muscled man said, his voice calm against the crashing waves. "The other steps make the Viburna pale in comparison."

I pointed to the distant body drifting on the waves. "Like stealing the lives of innocent young men?"

"Innocent? Maybe the definition of that word has changed since the first time I heard it. I assure you, Tristan was far from innocent."

"And that gave you the right to take his life?"

Ten Spins dragged his hand through the foam of a broken wave. "He gave it to me willingly—ten times."

"Tristan," I cried again, stepping into the surf. "Come on, the Wedding Bowl isn't going to last long."

"Only another couple more seconds." Ten Spins blew the foam off his fingers.

An undertow pulled on my ankles, threatening to drag me out into the unknowable depths of consciousness. "Tristan!"

"He can't hear you."

I ignored the Magician and took a few more steps deeper into the crashing surf. I hadn't gone far before a confusion of voices whispered at the edges of my mind. Faint words, barely cohesive, tugged at my thoughts.

Help me.

Mother, where are you?

So much pain...

I give up my tenth turn at the wheel...

I shook them off, but no sooner had I done that than more voices followed. Screams of agony and cries of frustration, they were all here. All the souls he'd taken over the years and all the bodies he'd destroyed on the road to immortality. They were the ocean of his evil mind.

I cannot let him become the Void.

I paused, bracing myself against the next wave and the gibberish sounds that came with it.

Dad...

That voice, I knew that voice. I knew it because I'd heard it ever since it drew its first breath, every crawl, stumble, walk, and run. I knew that voice because it was my daughter's voice.

Cathy... but how?

The sky darkened as a distant squall brought flashes of lightning. The Wedding Bowl was cracking, and each thunderclap carried it one step closer to collapse. Beyond me, the waves brought with them more voices. They washed over me, too many to count, but somewhere in the cacophony was my daughter, her words almost disappearing against the rising tide.

You cannot let him become the Void, Dad.

50

TARGET PRACTICE

I opened my eyes and the ocean vanished. It was lost to the fires of Hell, fires started by the ancient Magician and rapidly consuming what remained of Little Ed.

The Bowl!

Ten Spin's Magick pressed against the power of the Wedding Bowl, an angry fury that burned through the bowl maker's gift like a disappointed in-law.

You're not getting inside this door.

Flames danced across the vines and licked at the house, while just beyond the porch my wife fought to undo the Calamity from Little Ed's thorns.

I wanted to cry out, but I couldn't risk losing my concentration.

Porter, duck!

A serrated Skeeter stinger shot out for her head, only to be detached by Bastet's razor-sharp claws. The vengeful feline had taken up position in front of my wife and was busy shredding whatever got close to them, but she couldn't stop the fire. Bright white flames tickled at the thorny prison, while beyond them smoke poured from the trunks holding back the New Dead hordes.

Ten Spins' Magick yanked things back into focus. The young man's body was giving out, but that didn't stop the ancient Magician from pushing an untold number of lifetime's power through it.

Crack!

The bowl was coming undone.

"Gene!" Porter cried, pulling a multi-tool out of the myriad of pockets that lined her tactical pants. "I can't cut this stuff, and when I tear it, it just grows right back. What do I do?"

Focus, Gene.

"She's going to burn. Cathy's going to burn! You've got to help me."

Crack!

That crack didn't come from the bowl, it came from Little Ed's Magick tree line, the first trunk split, and with it came the grasping hands of the fiery Damned. Ashen arms tore at the widening hole, and beyond them, black and tar-filled eyes sparkled in the dancing flames.

They're coming...

Ten Spins' power swarmed over the bowl, finding the cracks and widening them. The maker's gift wasn't going to hold up much longer.

"Gene! Do something!"

Fire covered the Calamity's thorny tomb, but the bowl's unmaking was imminent.

"Gene!"

Porter tore back thorns just long enough for my daughter's face to appear beneath the flames.

I'm not losing you again.

Ten Spins pushed harder, his stored and stolen Magick too powerful to ignore, but so were the flames that encased my daughter. The fires brought with them memories of Hellgate, and of failure. Maybe it was Ten Spins who had set my personal hell in motion, but I was the one that let her go. My hands were the ones that set the Calamity on her personal path of destruction.

The wounds in my hands..

The spike!

The bloody spike of Obelleron's bridle shimmered in the flickering light.

Saddle up.

"Jam the spike into him!"

"What?" My wife cried, tears in her soot streaked eyes. "But Cathy!"

"Stab him with the spike."

Porter found the wicked metal in the mud and scooped it up. No sooner had she done that than New Dead broke through the tree line. Ashen bodies poured into the fiery prison like sand escaping from an hourglass.

Kittens surrounded my wife and Bastet, their bright hair and sparkling eyes a stark contrast to the wave of pale dead. Claws flashed and swords clashed as the Calamity's forces fought to reach their own.

No!

I pushed back against Ten Spins with everything I had, pulling from reserves I didn't know existed, and willed the bowl to hold.

"Whoa, Gene. Now this is a party."

Ed!

Ten Spins ignored the newcomers and focused on the bowl.

Pain lanced my shoulder, and my arms went numb. Darkness filled the edges of my vision.

Ed... help...

The Demon Hunter surfaced not far from Porter, along with Adam and his highly determined mother.

"Ed." Porter held the spike in one hand and her pistol in the other. "Keep them off me."

"You got it, sweetheart." The twisting threads of Ed's broken stitches flagged in the fiery wind. "Adam, I'm gonna need the Shield of—"

"No Magick, Ed." My apprentice shook his head.

"What do you mean no—"

The ashen bodies of New Dead knocked Adam to the ground.

"Adam!" Angela screamed before I lost her in the smoke.

Boom! Boom!

Porter's gun barked in the haze. The bodies of New Dead erupted in great showers of ash and embers, but still more poured through the burning trees.

Come on, Porter!

My apprentice appeared briefly, his mother yanking the Damned off of him like a professional wrestler, while Skeeters circled around behind her.

Shit.

I wanted to cry out, but I couldn't risk losing my battle of wills with the old Magician.

Come on, Porter...

My wife broke the New Dead line. With the spike in her hand held high, she zeroed in on Ten Spins' back, while behind her the fire consumed the Calamity's thorny prison.

Please...

"Argh!" Black claws pierced Porter's shoulders like fish hooks, yanking her away and sending the gun careening into the dirt.

No!

Sofia's torn jaws flapped like a derelict flag in the hot wind, yet even with her stinger reduced to a bloody stump she still pulled my wife into her claws like a hungry spider.

Fires burned the Calamity's cell, and the Soul of Isis vanished beneath the hellish tide of the Damned.

"Gene!" Porter's voice faded against the pounding of my heart.

"Holy crap, what the hell are you?" My old roommate's face appeared next to Sofia's, his hands doing their damndest to keep him from being ejected like a rodeo clown as he rode the back of the angry Skeeter.

My vision faded, but Ed Lovely didn't.

"Hey, Dead Man's Tongue." The Demon Hunter spotted the ring on Sofia's finger and went after it like a zealous bride's maid. "I'll take that."

Tears streaked my wife's eyes, but she refused to give up. She stretched out with her hand, and the spike for Ten Spins' exposed shoulders.

Black claws dug into Porter's flesh and pulled her back.

No!

Fire reflected in the black eyes of the Damned, and in the glistening Skeeter's claws.

Boom!

The handgun erupted. A bullet slammed into the front porch and blew a hole in the rotting wood. Adam fumbled with the weapon as New Dead crawled over him like angry toddlers.

Boom!

The next round hit the door frame behind me and sent a rain of wood dust and splinters on my head.

"How about you shoot this bug thing." Ed pulled on Sofia's neck and the Dead Man's Tongue.

Yip! Yip!

The Chinthe bit down on the Skeeter's leg, and flickered momentarily, but the black metal ring kept the dog from doing its thing.

Boom!

Mud splattered near the orange fur ball and sent him scampering out of the way.

"This!" Ed held up Sofia's ring hand. "Do you think you could shoot this!"

Ashen hands pulled Adam down.

Crack!

The wild fist of a furious mother smashed the nose of the closest New Dead. Angela followed it up with a few more, raining down her righteous fury on the Blessed.

"Shoot, now!" Ed shouted, Sofia's hand held up high.

Boom!

The bullet tore through the young woman's hand. Skin ripped free from bone, and with it came the black metal of the Dead Man's Tongue. Sofia's insect arms released Porter and twisted around to claw at Ed. The Demon Hunter might not be a Magician, but there wasn't a mortal man alive that knew more about Magick.

My old roommate squeezed the ring in his palm and slapped a hand to the Skeeter's chest. Callused fingers closed the lines of half a dozen sigils tattooed across her body.

Ed knew what he was doing, even if the rest of us didn't.

51

BY THE SWORD

*A*rcs of power crackled between the sigils on Sofia's chest. Magick, driven by the Dead Man's Tongue and pulled from Ten Spins' reservoir, flooded the confusing and nonsensical pattern.

Ed may not be a Magician, but he sure as hell knew how to screw it up.

Lines touched that shouldn't touch and circles crossed that should have stayed unbroken. The jumbled mess he'd created sucked power from the Dead Man's tongue like a vacuum hose, and in doing so, split the young Skeeter's skin in two.

Ed jumped off, but the damage had been done. The sigils etched in her skin burned together like melted plastic, peeling back to reveal the bloody and twisted pulp underneath. Sofia's unfolded jaws flailed helplessly against the fiery Magick. Her insect arms pulled in tight like a dying spider, only to burn away in the violent cosmic power.

Porter broke free of the Skeeter's grasp and raced for the porch. Her tired feet took the steps two at a time, while fires raged across the Calamity's thorn-covered casket.

Do it!

Ten Spins' foot came down and shattered the bowl.

Porter lunged in the final second, her hand extended to plunge the spike home, but the newly freed Magician was faster. He pivoted to the side and snapped a hands out to grab hold of my wife's neck and mine.

Like two sides of an unbalanced scale the ancient Magician held us tight.

My wife gasped, her hands flailing in the young man's powerful grip. More New Dead poured through the burning trunks, filling the muddy field with the howling voices and wild eyes of the Damned.

Porter's face turned red and our eyes locked for a moment.

"Do it," I breathed, willing my mouth to move even without the sounds behind it.

My wife's eyes rolled back in her head and her shoulders went limp.

No!

Ten Spins turned his attention back to me. "I will destroy everything you love if that is what it takes. Your wife, your daughter, your son. Everything and everyone you have ever cared about will fall beneath the power of the Void."

Porter's eyes snapped open and she rammed the spike into his hand. Driven by the strength of my wife's final push, the bloody metal cut through flesh and dug between bones.

Please, please work!

Magick erupted from the ancient Magician's body, then snaked down the bridle's broken chain and into the air. The power swirled like a great tornado, twisting over the splintered porch and past the raging fires. It knew where to go, because even broken, Obelleron's bridle knew where to send it. Just like a bird returning home to nest, Ten Spins' stolen Magick flooded the thorn-bound body of the Calamity.

Please be okay.

Vines peeled away like burnt embers in the tumultuous blast.

The shoots beneath them bent back and exposed Cathy's body to the full effect of the roaring power.

The Calamity has come.

Great wings of Magick returned to Cathy's back and propelled her up and out of the ashen remains of the green prison.

"The Calamity!" New Dead cried, their hands and arms raised in salute to the power that had returned to see them through to almost certain victory.

Bastet and her Kittens pulled back, as did the few remaining Skeeters, uncertainty clear upon their faces. Ten Spins dropped Porter. My wife crashed into the porch, her skin torn and bleeding.

The old Magician brought the spike to his mouth and tried to pry it out, but Obelleron's bridle wouldn't budge.

The Calamity landed on the porch, her feet touching down like an angel. Magickal flame roared around my daughter, her hair once again billowing like the Wild Reaving she was. She reached down and picked up Petty's saber. The soul blade shined in her hand.

"The Wild Reaving has won! Long live the Calamity!" New Dead soldiers roared in excitement, their weapons and armor clanging together.

Ten Spins turned around, his hand still pressed against my throat. "Take another step and your father dies."

"Destroy him!" New Dead cried, their ashen faces and black eyes hungry for death.

"I promise you. I will end him. You may think I have no other options, but I do."

The Calamity raised her sword and my daughter's face reflected in its tarnished edge.

"So be it!" Ten Spins cried, then collapsed against the porch, his body, Tristan's body, dissolving like a sand castle in the heavy surf.

The New Dead surged toward the House, their tar-filled eyes reflecting in the fiery power of the Calamity.

"Dad?" My daughter's soft voice cut through the roaring of the Damned. "What do I do?"

I tried to respond, but I had problems of my own. Ten Spins was master at body jumping, and somehow he'd figured out exactly how to crawl into my head. I opened my mouth to speak, but that bastard took my words. "Nothing, you've done everything you need. I will enter the House now."

No, no! Stop him... stop me!

Cathy placed a hand on my shoulder. "Dad, are you okay?"

"I'm fine, Catherine."

No, no, I'm not fine. Do something!

Confused New Dead shouted from the porch's edge. "Destroy him!"

The Calamity turned to her mother. "Mom, are you okay?"

A face reflected in Private Petty's blade, but it wasn't mine—it was something else entirely. A blend of Tristan and Ten Spins, a blurred and twisted face that churned my stomach.

Click.

The door lock dropped into place beneath fingers I no longer controlled.

Cathy, help me!

A strong current pulled at my mind. The mental images of my wife and daughter faded in the crashing surf of voices and confusion.

"Gene?"

Porter clutched at her cheek. Bright blood trickled from the wound. The assembled New Dead pressed in further, their black eyes reflecting back my confused and blended psyche.

"I'm fine."

The Calamity helped her mother up, while all around her the New Dead called out for blood. "Destroy him! The Calamity must come!"

"Dad?"

The door handle wiggled beneath my fingers.

Help!

"I'm fine, woman."

Porter's head snapped back, panic in her eyes. "It's not him."

A great ocean wave of thought swept over me, and I clawed for the surface. Ten Spins was in control and pushed me toward the opening door. We had only to fall back and greet infinity. My hands broke the mental surface of the wave, while confused and frustrated voices pressed in on me from all sides.

No!

I swam for the light, for the last bits of hope.

The blade.

I fought against the crashing surf, against Ten Spins, and against the weariness in my bones. I fought against every urge to quit, every desire to let go, and every part of me that wished for sweet oblivion.

I'd come too far to give up now, not with my daughter in sight.

I'm here, Dad.

Cathy's voice buoyed me on the rising swells. If she was here, then there was a chance, a chance to bring them all together.

Images flashed in the dark water in front of me. Images of death, violence, and destruction. A chilling and deadly world with Ten Spins at the helm of all Magick.

What do I do, Cathy?

The image vanished only to be replaced with Petty's sword. It stood defiant in my daughter's hand, stained red with blood.

My blood.

I lunged forward, kicking my legs and pushing through the rising surf. The distant light was my only savior. Like a sailor lost at sea, I dug great armfuls of the dark water and cast them behind me.

"That's not him." Porter's voice boomed in my head, twisted and hollow, it echoed against the rising tide.

The Calamity hesitated. "What do I do?"

The current tugged at my legs, while somewhere my fingers pushed open the House's door. The hot breath of infinity, the Void's power, burned at my skin.

"No," I cried, kicking and clawing for the distant light. "No!"

In that instant, I broke through, my hands and arms numb. I stumbled forward on shaky feet, my fingers extended, and my eyes locked in on only one thing.

The blade...

Cathy tried to move her hand away, but in the confusion she wasn't fast enough. I hooked my daughter's arm and drove it, blade and all, into my chest.

"Gene!" Porter's scream mixed with the wild screams of New Dead, all of them washing over me like pounding surf.

The sparkling light in my daughter's eyes vanished beneath that crushing wave. Cold pain and the burning sting of the saber's steel cut me to the core. Darkness drew me down, and in that depth came the chattering voices of so many others, yet only one voice mattered to me, and it was just as sweet a melody as I remembered it.

I love you, Dad.

5 2

TIDES AND TIME

*S*trong hands dragged me from the sea and pulled me to the water's edge only to deposit me on the cold sand. "Cathy?" I blinked my eyes in the dim moonlight.

"Hardly."

The House.

Bathed in the soft light of an alien moon, the House no longer resembled anyone I'd ever known. Gone were the familiar shapes of Morgan, Porter, or even Jenkins, but also gone was the unknowable blur of light and power.

The House was a small man, impossibly old, with a great beard to match. His skin was wrinkled enough to rival an elephant, but his eyes still sparkled with an intensity that put the stars above to shame.

"Is it... are you..."

The Void nodded and took a seat in the wet sand next to me. "I am."

"What happened?"

"He happened."

"Ten Spins?"

The House pulled aside the edge of a wool tunic to reveal the spot where his heart should be—all that remained was a hole, a bleeding hole of withered flesh. "I'm done, Gene."

"What does that mean?"

"For us? It doesn't mean much. You killed yourself, the one thing you couldn't do. You ran that saber through your chest like a moron. What the hell were you thinking?"

Saber?

The final moments came back to me with the crashing surf: Cathy's voice, Petty's blade, and the ancient Magician's mental sea.

"I died?"

The House sighed and pointed to the black ocean waves. "Just about. You can't hold up with a saber in your chest—nobody can."

A white shape swam against the crashing surf, his head coming up for air only to drop back down and vanish again.

"Is that him?"

"What remains of him. You can't crawl through so many bodies without losing a bit of yourself in the process. He's a chimera now, a soulless monster. He's become like me—he will be a perfect Void."

Cut out of the night sky like a perfect rectangle of inky black, a portal hovered above the crashing wave.

"It will all be over soon," the House said, his voice rough like the pounding surf. "I cannot stop him."

The ocean's cold waves washed over my tired feet. "That's it? You're just going to give up?"

"Yes."

"What happened to the infinite? What happened to being the source of all Magick?"

The House lay down on the wet sand, his body small and fragile. "I wasn't always this way. He'll see. Infinity exacts a heavy price. It eats at you, Gene. It starts slow, but like the ocean it keeps coming. Before long, the crushing power tears out your heart and erodes your humanity. He'll learn, just like I learned, but you and I won't be around to see it."

Another wave pushed the distant Magician back. His spirit flickered, distorted and without form, it popped in and out like pay-per-view channels on my television set.

"So this is it? You lay in the sand like a dead fish while he swims for infinity?"

"We are dead, Gene. What does it matter? You will never catch him. He's too strong. He will reach the Void, and then what will he do to you? You don't understand the power that resides beyond that door. Our monkey brains can't fathom it."

Another head surfaced in the distant waves, its sandy blond hair shining under the light of an alien moon.

Cathy!

That head was followed by another, and then another. All three shards of my daughter drifted together on the pounding surf. The sounds of a distant conversation washed over us on the chilling wind. I'd pulled the Calamity in with me, the broken shard of my daughter following me into the ocean of consciousness.

"What are they doing?"

The sisters vanished beneath the surge of a crashing wave, and my heart froze, only to start again with the kicking of their legs.

"It would appear your daughter is more than a little like you after all—St. Catherine of Lost Causes."

"No!"

I left the House on the wet sand and threw myself into the crashing waves. Bone cold and overflowing with the sounds of an uncountable number of voices, the mental ocean pushed back.

Come on, Gene!

My daughters weren't far ahead, but they might as well have been an ocean away for how slow I moved through the crashing surf. Confused and angry words tugged at my mind. Each one tried to pull me under and drag me down to sweet oblivion.

Another wave hit, and for a moment I lost my daughters against the black water.

Give up...

Join us...

The darkness beneath the waves hugged me with its chilling embrace. My muscles ached, and my soul faded with them. There was no point. Was I just flopping around like a dead fish? Were these the death throes of my final act?

I let my head drop beneath the surface, leaving nothing but the velvet grasp of the inky dark to carry me away.

Splash!

Tiny pink claws wrapped my shoulders. They pinched my skin and pulled me away from the unknowing depths. We broke the surface. A pair of undersized wings beat back against the smashing surf.

"Stewart?"

"Do you know any other Imps?" The dead Demon said, his wings driving us through the foamy white caps.

"But how? Demons don't have souls."

"Damned if I know, but I'm not going to look this gift Olganthi in the horns."

The saber...

"It trapped you, the blade trapped you too."

The tiny monster's wings pushed us beyond the powerful swells and into the deep water. "I guess so. Cathy and I have had such a nice conversation in here. You know, for a human, you really are a pretty good guy. She loves you, so try not to screw that up—having spent a decent bit of time with you I know that's a *big* ask."

Stewart released my shoulders and took to the air, while around me the three shards of my daughter swam for Ten Spins shifting body.

"Stop!" I shouted between great gulps of air. "Let him go."

The Calamity swung around, her eyes fierce in the moons light. "Dad? But I..."

"We can resolve who stabbed who and how later, but right now I need to keep the three of you together."

The newest shard stopped paddling. "You can't be here. You've missed your ride. There is no going back."

"I don't care. Don't you girls understand? You are what I care about. Let him go. I have all I need."

My musical daughter shook her beautiful head. "He has Tristan and we made a promise."

Ten Spins' shifting body flickered in the black water, in one moment it was the ancient Magician, and in the next it was Cathy's first and only boyfriend.

We made a promise.

The House was right, maybe they were a little too much like me.

"Damn it. Well, if we're going to do this, we're going to do it together."

"We are the Wild Reaving!" The Calamity drew an angry glare from her sisters. "Well, we are."

"Stewart." I pointed to the pale figure reaching for the black door. "Stop him!"

The tiny Demon frowned in the light of an alien moon. "Is this what it means to be the good guy?"

"Yes."

"Really?"

"Stewart!"

The monster's pink wings caught the wind, and he soared after the flickering Magician.

"He's going to reach the Void!" The Calamity cried, her voice rising above the splashing waves.

No, he's not.

Stewart's tiny claws grabbed Ten Spins' shoulders and pulled the Magician back. The Imp had given us a chance.

"Come on." I kicked hard in the crashing surf. "Let's drown this bastard and pull Tristan out in the process."

The shards swam with me and together we surrounded the Magician.

The flickering soul swung his arms, desperate to dislodge the tiny Imp, and in doing so completely missed the Calamity. The strongest of the shards slammed into him and dragged the ancient Magician under the rolling surf.

"Come on!"

Together we dove under the waves and into the mouth of madness. The voices of a thousand lost souls screamed out for justice beneath the cold sea of consciousness. Ten Spins and the Calamity twisted in a weightless battle for supremacy. She was strong, but he was crafty. A few well placed jabs, and the Calamity was forced to let go.

He shot for the surface, which took him right past me.

Not gonna happen.

My tired arms wrapped the flickering soul's neck. We broke the surface gasping for air, his hands reaching for the blackness of the Void.

"Let me go!" he screamed. "I promise I will restore you, and your daughter, once I am on the other side. I will give you the power to crush your enemies and remake your life. I will give you everything."

The foaming white caps splashed against my face. "I already have everything."

"You are dying. Your body will end, and with it any chance you had to be reunited with your precious family. Let me go and I will make you whole!"

"I am whole. For the first time in a very long time, I am whole."

"You are dying!"

I squeezed his neck tighter. "And so are you."

53

SACRIFICE

*L*ightning split the sky. It cut a hot line through angry clouds that rolled in to block the massive moon.

"It's happening," Ten Spins cried, slamming an elbow into my tired ribs.

"What?"

"This mortal coil can't survive much longer. Your heart is beating its last. Don't you understand? Someone has to enter the Void. Someone has to go or we all die."

"You're lying!" I kicked at the rocking surf.

"Am I? You feel it. The cold numbness in your limbs, the drifting sensation in the back of your skull. You are dying, Eugene Law, and you're going to take all of us with you."

Another flash of lightning arced between boiling clouds and the wind picked up. Salt spray stung my face, and the old Magician had his opening.

Crack!

An elbow to the cheek rocked my vision and sent me tumbling backward beneath the turbulent waves.

No!

I clawed for the surface, but the old Magician was right, my arms were numb and my vision blurred. The slowing pulse of a distant heart faded in my ears.

I'm dying.

Voices pressed in upon me. Frustrated, sad, and angry, the crushed hopes and withered dreams of Ten Spins victims pulled the air from my lungs.

If you die, we all go with you. Cathy!

Strong hands pulled me to the surface. The Calamity's face joined mine above the rocking surf. "Dad!"

The Calamity's eyes, Cathy's eyes, caught in the flashing burst of white-hot lightning. A world without those eyes would be robbed of what made life worth living.

Hope.

"Get me to the gate." I kicked off toward the ancient Magician and the Void that lay just beyond him.

"Dad, no!" My musical daughter joined her soul sister alongside me. "You can't do that."

"The rules are over, Catherine. The House is gone, there is only one way to stop him and save you all, and that is to reach the Void first."

The Calamity pulled at my arm. "It'll destroy your mind. You cannot fathom infinity, no one can. When you look into the abyss, the abyss looks back at you."

The waves crashed around us. Ten Spins reached for the Void then stopped, something holding him back.

"Tristan!" My quiet daughter cried, swimming ahead of her sisters.

"Cathy, stop!"

The young man's face appeared in the flickering light of Ten Spins' ruined soul. "I'm sorry. I'm so sorry for everything."

My daughter's hands reached for him, but a rising swell pulled them apart.

"Tristan!"

The boy's face faded away, lost to the constantly shifting light of the ancient Magician's fractured spirit.

The Calamity pulled at my arm. "We've got to do something."

"Just get me to the Void and I'll save him too."

The quiet shard's face surfaced above the next rising swell. "No, you can't. He's tied to Ten Spins. Tristan gave up his tenth turn. We have to pull them apart," she said, then dropped below the rolling surf.

"Cathy!"

More lightning exploded across the angry clouds, while all around us the wind picked up speed. A distant storm swirled across the white-capped tops of pounding waves. Another swell tossed me back, and away from the yawning gate.

My arms swung in tired agony and my legs cramped.

The Void...

Ten Spin broke the surface again, his face a contorted mask of frustration. Tristan was holding him back, the young man I'd spent so many days and nights hating for everything he'd done to my family was holding Ten Spins back from infinity.

Forgiveness and redemption, the bowl maker's final gift.

I kicked with my legs and pushed through the cold water, my eyes focused on the Void. An inky blackness cut perfectly from the dying prison of my mind. It was there, all I had to do was reach it.

The Calamity and her musical sister pushed through the waves with me, my daughters swimming with a grace and power they certainly didn't get from me.

"Argh!" Ten Spins shouted against the crashing surf. Tristan's spirit ripped free of the body-snatching Magician's grasp.

Cathy!

The quiet shard surfaced holding tight to the drifting soul of her boyfriend.

She did it!

All I had to do was reach the Void and put an end to all of this. I shot past the flailing Magician and extended my hand toward infinity.

"Dad!"

A startled cry pulled me back. The Calamity was caught in Ten Spins' arms, he clamped down and pulled her under.

"Gene, what are you doing?" Stewart's pink wings fought against the whistling wind. "This place is coming apart. We can't stay here."

"He's got Cathy."

Stewart turned his tiny head. "Which one?!"

Ten Spins surfaced briefly, his hands solidly locked around the Calamity. He yanked her back under the water. Their pale shapes vanished beneath the tide.

Splash!

The tiny pink Demon hit the water like a badly aimed pelican, while together with the sisters, I followed him. Thousands of voices pressed on me like a suffocating blanket. Their frustrations and fears bit at my soul like stinging flies.

Cathy!

The Calamity struggled against Ten Spins' grasp, her hands and arms flailing, but the ancient Magician wrapped her like a jungle snake and dragged her into the abyss.

Stewart reached them first. The undersized Demon's claws caught the Calamity's arms. Memories of the Hellgate came flooding back, my daughter falling away wrapped in the Imp's gentle arms.

No!

I kicked harder and swam for Cathy, the numbness in my limbs fighting my every move. Her soul sisters joined me and together we pulled against the ancient Magician's grip. Lightning flashed above, filling the dark water with a brilliant burst of white, and giving a face to the voices. Twisted souls, angry and vengeful churned in the black depths of the malevolent sea. Their faces brought with them memories of the Calamity, her pain, and the mistakes I'd made. Mistakes that would have worse consequences if I became the Void.

I let go of the Calamity's hands and instead wrapped my arms around Ten Spins' neck. The ancient Magician's grip on my daughter wavered just enough for Stewart to spring her free.

The souls of his victims pulled on us with icy fingers. They dragged us toward the bottom, and to oblivion.

The Calamity spun out of Stewart's grasp, and along with her musical sister they dove for me, but Ten Spins enemies pulled us away from their reaching fingers.

I extended a hand toward them, then stopped. The quiet Cathy, the one who'd spent all this time trapped in the dark recesses of Ten Spins' evil mind, locked eyes with me. In that instant, I knew what she was going to do. I opened my mouth to scream, to shout, to tell her no, but it wouldn't matter. My daughter was stubborn, persistent, and most of all, just like me.

Catherine...

She kicked off toward the surface, Tristan by her side. The two of them pushed as fast as their narrow legs could carry them. It wasn't long before Stewart grabbed her arm and used his wings to drive her faster through the icy current.

My little girl and her tiny pink wingman reached the water's surface. Stewart shot up and into the open air, but not my daughter. She paused, her tiny face staring down at me. Even in the dark, the sadness in her eyes lanced my dying heart.

I love you, Dad.

I love you, Cathy. I always have and I always will.

The quiet shard of my only daughter vanished from sight.

Ten Spins scrambled, but I let him go, content in knowing he would never reach the Void in time—his victims would see to that.

I closed my eyes in the final chilling moments. The remaining soul sisters found my hands in the ocean's dark.

Magick demands sacrifice, and so does family.

54

STAY WITH ME

"Gene!" Porter's scream jolted me awake.

I'm alive! How?

I might have been still with the living, but thanks to the silvery blade wedged in my chest I wouldn't be for long.

All around us Hell burned.

Ed Lovely, Demon Hunter extraordinaire, appeared briefly behind my wife, Revelore's crown atop his balding head, and the rest of him straddling the Demon Steed Obelleron. "Magick's back, Adam. Do it!"

Magick, sweet Magick, washed over me, a power of purity and purpose.

Cathy, you did it.

Cosmic energy rocked the collapsing house.

My apprentice opened a portal to the Gloom. The shadowy gate ripped apart the seams of Hell, and brought with it waves of hungry Demons.

Ed swung his hand above his head like rodeo clown. "You turkey's want a piece of me? Well, come and get it!"

My ex-roommate pulled on the black horse's mane.

Obelleron bucked beneath the wiry old salt, but somehow he held on and directed the monster toward the ashen walls of the burnt oak prison. "Hi ho, Silver, away!"

"Gene," Porter cried, tears in her eyes, and her hands pulling me close. "You're alive."

"I'm sorry," I said, my broken voice was barely a whisper, and the taste of iron on my lips. "Cathy…"

"She's here, Gene, she's okay."

Kaylee!

Ed's ex-wife appeared next to Porter. A weaving of green branches held her side together.

But how?

"No, she died—"

My daughter's face filled the void between them—no longer the hardened Calamity, but not quite the same sweet child I'd lost to Hell. "Dad!"

How?

My chest tightened, and with it, the bloody beating of a tired heart slowed.

"Gene!" Porter's hands clutched at mine.

"Mom, he's not breathing!"

The edges of my vision faded. The fires and the dark vanished until all that remained was the faces of the two most important women in my life—my family.

"Gene! Stay with me," Porter cried, tears streaking her frightened face. "Bobbin, take us home!"

But Sweetheart, I'm already home.

* * *

"Stay with me, Gene!"

Bright lights stung my closed eyes.

Porter?

Many strong hands picked me up and deposited me on the thin padding of a hospital gurney. "What happened to him?"

He's been to Hell and back.

55

CALLIE

"Tell it again, Uncle Ed," Kris cried, a plastic saber shining in his hand, and basking in the light of a dozen Tiki lamps strategically placed throughout the yard.

"Oh, I don't know, kiddo. Are you sure you aren't tired of hearing it?"

Thin smoke drifted up from sizzling burgers and hotdogs slowly blackening on my grill.

"Tell it again!" Kris jumped up, keeping one hand on the cardboard crown on his head, and the other swinging that shiny saber like the happy-go-lucky kid he was.

"All right, all right." Uncle Ed fished a beer out of the cooler and popped the top. "I'll tell you the story of how a Demon Hunter became the King of Hell."

Kaylee groaned from her seat in one of the many Adirondack chairs Porter had bought for the occasion. "Can you try telling it *without* embellishments?"

"But, Aunt Kay, everything I speak is the God's honest truth." Ed pressed the cold beer to his chest. "Right, Gene?"

"Huh?" I'd drifted away, my eyes in the hazy grill smoke, and lost in the memory of a face I swore I'd never forget.

Adam cruised by with a bag of chips in one hand and a bowl of salsa in the other. "He wasn't even there, remember? Gene was dead for... how long were you dead for, Gene?"

"Too long." My wife set down a bag of hamburger buns and lingered long enough to run a soft hand down my arm. "Entirely and completely too long."

Yip!

Bobbin's nose peeked out between my legs, his tiny mouth salivating at the glorious smell of meat drippings.

Not a chance, short stuff.

"Tell it, Uncle Ed!" Kris danced around the short grass, his little body practically vibrating with excitement.

"So there I was, surrounded by the hordes of ashen Damned. It was me against the combined forces of darkness—"

"And me." Adam shoved a salsa-laden chip in his mouth.

"Right, Uncle Adam was there too, except he'd just finished firing your Mom's gun and narrowly avoiding blowing a hole the size of Montana in my head."

Porter frowned. "Ed, keep it 'G' rated."

My old roommate pursed his lips and took that moment to enjoy the cold beer in his hand. "Fine, it loses a bit of its luster, but I can clean it up. Hand me your crown, Kris."

My son popped the paper ring off his head and handed it to his favorite uncle.

Ed squeezed the gold-colored crown on as best he could. "Right, so. There I was, your father run through with Private Petty's Saber."

"The Soul Blade!" Kris cried, pressing his plastic sword into the air.

The Calamity has come!

The hellish cries of the ashen Damned rolled over me and I froze in the hazy grill smoke.

"Gene!" Porter cried, grabbing my arm. "She's going to burn!"

"What?"

"The burgers are going to burn."

I shook my head and grabbed the tongs. "Right, sorry. I drifted there." I turned the blackening meat.

"You okay?" My wife's soft hand paused.

"Yeah, yeah. Where's Cathy?"

"She's inside."

I frowned. "Is she still—"

"It's going to take a while, Gene. It just is. You can't rush these things."

"School starts in two weeks."

Porter shook her head and laid out split buns on a plate next to the grill. "She'll be fine. I'm sure of it."

"How can you be so sure?"

"Because you're here. You're the glue that keeps us together. I couldn't do this without you."

I twisted a plumping hotdog. "You say that, but you did just fine without me."

"Don't, just... don't."

"I won't." I pressed the tongs into her hands. "If you take over the grill for a minute."

Porter hesitated, then accepted the utensil's wooden handle. "Who wants a slightly over-cooked hotdog?"

"Was that when Adam fixed Auntie Kay?" Kris asked, hanging on his bald uncle's every word.

"I think so." Ed tilted his head as if playing back the final moments in his mind. "How did you do that, Adam?"

My apprentice shoveled a thick stack of chips in his mouth. "Magick," he said through stuffed cheeks, but his eyes clearly indicated even he wasn't entirely sure.

Ed brushed it off and went right back into this story. "Anyway, there I was, Aunt Kay barely breathing, and that's when Adam sent the vines of..."

"Little Ed's vines, right?" Kris beamed, while Kaylee shifted uncomfortably in her chair.

"Yeah, let's move on." Ed pulled the paper crown down on his head. "Did I tell you how bad Obelleron's gas was?"

I pulled the French door open, and left my old roommate to tell the story of the Demon Steed's toots to his favorite nephew for the hundredth time. It was quiet in the house, but I knew where she'd be. You could take the girl out of her tower, but it was hard to take the tower out of the girl.

"Hey, Gene." Angela was putting the finishing touches on a double-decker chocolate cake. "You sure you don't mind that I invited—"

"No." I wavered her off. "After what we've been through, we're family. Anyone you invited is welcome in my home."

"That's a little generous, but thank you." Adam's mother smiled and carried my son's favorite food group past me and into the backyard.

Knock! Knock!

"I'm coming."

It took longer to get to the door than it used to. While I was healing, it wasn't the same as it used to be—a lot of things hurt that hadn't hurt before.

I opened the door and my heart stopped. The Leprechaun from my ill-fated attempt to destroy the House, the same one that I'd tried to fake in Brooksville, stood on my front porch.

"Hey, Gene."

"What are—"

"Let's get something clear right from the get go. I'm not here for you, or your memories."

The deal...

It had been so long I'd almost forgot. I'd made a deal for a year's worth of memories of my love and my life with that intractable fairy.

"What do you want?"

The tiny ginger-haired man wiggled his sandal-covered toes uncomfortably on my front porch. "Beer, a burger, and some of that cake Angela invited me over for."

I tilted my head. "And nothing else? No funny stuff?"

The Leprechaun pressed out the wrinkles in his linen shirt. "None. I wouldn't dare say anything against the Father of Magick."

"Father of—"

The tiny man brushed me off. "It's just something that's catching on in the circles."

"Well, stop it," I said, directing the fairy into my living room.

"Certainly, Gene."

Yip! Yip!

Bobbin shot across the living room. He must have come in when Angela opened the door.

"Stop, Bobbin, this is—what the hell?" The tiny dog leapt into the fairy's hands, catching me entirely off guard.

That undersized man held the dog with a practiced grace that brought with it memories of a woman I'd spent a good bit of time with, a woman who'd had no business in Hell, nor navigating the pathways between the worlds.

"It was you."

The Leprechaun gently placed the orange Chinthe on the tile. "Yes, it was."

The memories... Fairies deal in memories and he'd just experienced the adventure of a lifetime.

"But how—"

"Oh, Gene, come on." The tiny man winked. "You can't cheat a cheater. Kaylee is no more your wife than I am, but I got the sense you were about to do something immensely crazy, something that would be worth the risk."

I closed the door behind me and leaned my tired head against it. "No way, she knew too much, that was Adam's mom."

"I never said it wasn't. She let me ride along—she didn't

know it of course—but I wasn't about to let the angel that tumbled into my life risk hers following you into Hell."

"That whole time? All of it?" I threw my hands in the air. "At any point you could have completely taken over and saved my ass."

The intractable Fairy only nodded. "It was fun joining you on your adventure, Eugene Law. You've given me memories for a lifetime."

"But you could have helped, you could have—"

The Leprechaun smiled and pat me on the arm. "And who's to say I didn't?"

Kaylee...

There were a hundred questions I wanted to ask, but the gut-churning sound of a wailing violin from my daughter's room made them all moot.

"Gene." Porter opened the back door. "Ed's finished the last of your beer. Why don't you and Cathy go pick up some more?"

The tiny man took the opening my wife had left him and slipped out to join the party.

Fairies...

"Sure."

I followed the painful sound of screeching strings to my daughter's room. "Hey, Cathy. Your uncle drank all our beer. Come on, you're coming with me to get more."

"No."

I gently pushed the door open to find my frustrated daughter surrounded by complex sheet music.

"Not a request. You need to work on your driving."

My daughter kicked papers aside. "I am the Wild Reaving. I rode the Demon Steed Obelleron—"

"So did your uncle."

Cathy fumed. "I ended Revelore."

"Yeah, but your uncle can drive stick. Can you drive stick?"

My daughter's face turned red. "No."

"Then come on. The new Dad Wagon awaits."

* * *

WE JERKED and sputtered out of the parking lot, my daughter doing her best to get it into second gear while the engine whined in protest.

"You got it," I said, trying to coax a smile out of her, and to get her to stop pressing the clutch.

"Why?" Cathy popped us into gear and slammed me into the seat back. "Why did you get a—" The engine rumbled to an almost stall before the transmission kicked in and set us in motion. "—stick shift?"

"More fun." I placed Ed's beer in the back seat, and hoped I was there when he opened the first one.

It wasn't the Dad Wagon, but it was a Mazda, and cheap enough to not worry about when breaking in a new driver.

Cathy got the car in gear and I pointed to a side street. "Let's take a longer route. It'll be good for you."

"Whatever." My daughter sighed, and I caught a tear in her eye.

"I know it's hard, sweetheart."

"It's not the stupid car, Dad. It's just... It's everything. I don't feel like me. I can't play my music, and I miss... I miss being her."

"The Calamity?"

My daughter took the next turn a little harder than I would have liked. "She was so strong, Dad. So strong. She did things I could never dream of."

"She's part of you."

Cathy wiped a tear from her eye. "She wouldn't be crying about it."

"Here's a secret—the strong ones cry too."

A large moving truck backed into the driveway in front of

us. Cathy popped the clutch and remembered to press the brake just late enough to narrowly avoid crashing into the rental vehicle.

A young woman jumped out of the passenger side and waved.

"Dad…" My daughter's jaw fell open.

The young woman could have been her older sister. Long, sandy blonde hair was tucked up under a ball cap, but it did nothing to hide the wide smile on her face. "Sorry! Tripp, pull it all the way up so these people can get by."

Tripp?

The young man waved from the driver side, he wasn't exactly Tristan, but wasn't exactly not Tristan either. "Got it."

The waving young woman jogged around the moving truck to Cathy's window and motioned for her to roll it down. "So sorry about that. We just got a little carried away—new house and all. My name's Callie." She shoved her hand through the open window.

My daughter only stared at it.

"Cathy…" I gently prodded the stunned teen.

"Oh, right? Hi."

Callie shook my daughter's hand, a broad smile on the older girl's face. "Nice to meet you. That's my husband, Tripp—it feels so weird to call him that—and that's Stewie."

Callie's husband held a pink ball of feline skin, with an oddly mischievous grin on its fur-free face.

"Uh, hey." Cathy waved to the spiting image of her old boyfriend.

"He's a hairless—the cat, not Tripp."

"Come on, Callie," Tripp said, motioning to his wife. "Let these guys go. We've got a ton of boxes to unpack."

"Okay. It was great meeting you, Cathy."

My daughter only stared.

"You too," I said, filling in for my spellbound child.

Callie raced up the driveway and disappeared behind the moving truck.

"Dad…"

"I saw it."

My daughter edged the car forward, fighting it into first gear, before grabbing my arm to point at the beautiful bungalow. White and baby blue, with a perfect picket fence and a wide porch, it was stunning, but as nice as it was, Cathy wasn't pointing at the house, she was pointing at the number. "Sixty-nine. Dad, what street are we on?"

"Mallory Lane."

Callie waved as we drove by, her smile infectious.

"What do we do with this stool?" Tripp asked, setting a broken piece of furniture on the driveway. "I think a leg snapped in the move."

A two-legged stool can not stand…

Callie didn't skip a beat. "It just needs something to lean on —it'll be fine."

We reached the corner and Cathy powered us through the wide turn.

"What does it mean, Dad?" My daughter asked, a little more bounce in her voice.

"I think it means we're going to be okay," I pulled down the shade to block the last rays of a setting sun. "Now, let's see if you can get us home in one piece."

Was she right? Could my two-legged stool stand?

Cathy popped the new Mazda's clutch and rolled us into second gear. A smile appeared briefly on her face when the car didn't slam either of our jaws into the dash.

She'll get there…

I knew this like I knew the sun would rise again tomorrow.

Thanks to my daughter, I finally had back what I'd lost on the steps of 69 Mallory Lane so long ago.

I had hope.

AFTERWORD

Thank you.

Never have I been more grateful to write those words.

It is my sincere hope that these stories have been as enjoyable to read as they have been to write. We've taken a journey together through the deep and dark recesses of my subconscious, and if you've made it this far you didn't get lost along the way. Good work, otherwise I'd have to send Marco for you.

What started as a losing short story for a contest a few years ago has become an epic tale of love and failure, hope and forgiveness. Every morning before the sun rose I sat down to write the next chapter, and most of those days I had no idea what would happen next, thankfully Gene and company did.

Together we endured two stints of broken air conditioning in the Florida Summer, a hurricane, tropical storms, flash flooding, and a global pandemic. Weird Florida threw some curve balls, but we made it through unscathed. I am so happy providence and good fortune have allowed me to share this story with you, but I would be lying if I said I wasn't tearing up just a bit here at the end.

Don't feel bad for Gene, Porter, or the rest of their family. I have it on pretty good authority that he has a long life with plenty of highs and lows still to come. My real question is where do we go from here?

Well, I don't know about you, but I think it's time give Gene a much deserved break and try on a few new pairs of shoes.

How about it? Are you ready to explore the other corners of this strange state with me?

Yes?

Great, then let's turn the page on Eugene Law for a little bit, but, before you do. Thank you from the absolute bottom of my heart.

You will never truly know how much your time has meant to me. To know that each of you carries a small piece of me is immortality in its truest form.

Eternally Gratefully Yours,

Martin
No longer lost under the cypress.
July 2020

MARTIN SHANNON'S WEIRD FLORIDA

Short Stories - Season 1

0 - Danderous Delivery (Newsletter Subscribers Only)

1 - Hook, Line, and Slinker

2 - Ballroom and Chain

3 - Bahama Blues

4 - Plasma Pistols

5 - Lights Out

6 - Mourning Paper

7 - Ignorance and Unleaded

8 - Black Valentine

9 - Soulless

10 - Ten Turns

Novels - Season 1

1 - Dead Set

2 - Gathering Gloom

3 - Beaten Path

4 - Bloody Deed

5 - No Fury

ACKNOWLEDGMENTS

This book and the first season of Weird Florida could not have happened without the help of the following people:

My wife—thank you for never letting me give up.

My daughter—thank you for sharing your love of stories and of life.

My grandmother—thank you for Sunday conversations, and for your unwavering support.

My parents—thank you for reading, and for letting your son's imagination run a little too free when there were hedges to be weeded.

Anja—thank you for being my greatest fan and supporting all that is Weird Florida.

The Flock—thank all of you for keeping me sane, and for believing in the story.

Last but not least, thank you, dear reader. To know you've made it this far warms my heart more than you can imagine.

ABOUT THE AUTHOR

Martin Shannon's been using his imagination to avoid weeding since he was in short pants. His first series, *Tales of Weird Florida*, is an homage to the Sunshine State he knows and loves, and spent countless hours riding his bike through as a kid. It's got mystery, mayhem, and more than a little Magick. He hopes you enjoy the supernatural side of the upside down state, but if not, he's got a banjo, and he knows how to use it. You can find out more at www.martin-shannon.com.

www.ingramcontent.com/pod-product-compliance
Lightning Source LLC
Chambersburg PA
CBHW020326180626
46812CB00001B/61